This book is dedicated to all readers who enjoy this mystery novel and also to my three companion cats, Spencer, Dewey, and Mika. A special thanks to my attorney friend, Bob Gould who perfected my legal commentary. My forever friend Sue helped to create the cover for Books, Bites, and Murder, and her support throughout the years will always be remembered.

BOOKS …BITES… AND MURDER

PROLOGUE

Mornings were usually agonizing to handle for this young woman. A third-stage Lyme disease victim, Zoey's body had experienced a great deal of chronic pain for many years now. At forty-three years old, she sometimes felt rather aged with difficulty kneeling and her stiff hands refusing to bend early in the day. Well known in her community, people hardly believed that Zoey was still chronically ill from Lyme disease. Always smiling and full of energy, her wavy brown hair was usually piled high atop her head during a work day. Most noticeable were her greenish hazel eyes, inherited from her Dad, who was no longer with them. A healthy diet and some exercise kept Zoey at an acceptable weight, unless she ate too many of her freshly baked muffins. Then the diet went into action for just a few days. Each day the first stop was to her medicine cabinet where she enjoyed a glass of cranberry juice as she swallowed the daily pills that kept her moving. Foremost was an anti-inflammatory, along with a low dose of Prednisone. A handful of nutritious daily vitamins and a healthy diet seem to help get her through a very hectic and demanding schedule. Around 1or 2 p.m. Zoey needed a strong cup of coffee and her aspirin. It seemed like just yesterday that this youthful mother and wife ran circles around her friends but it was eight years ago when the teeny-sized black dot appeared on her upper chest area. Who knows for sure how long it had been on her. It was just before Thanksgiving, and for days Zoey had been raking leaves prior to heading over to work at the town library. By the time the tick bite was discovered, the little bugger had left the scene, leaving a red itchy mark on her breast. Dr. Joe told her it was nothing to worry about, and she was given two weeks of Doxycycline, problem handled. No worries, at least for now…..

It was many months later at the end of April when Zoey awoke to nearly tumble from her bed. Feeling very flu-like and with a headache, her feet were a bit swollen and her entire body was so rigid, it was difficult to even bend over. Thinking she had a spring flu, the doctor visit accomplished little with a diagnosis of most likely a virus. If not better in two weeks, return for blood work. Working twenty hours a week as the town's library director left Zoey no choice but to suck down a ton of meds for the weeks to follow. With her husband Will on another golfing excursion abroad with some of his wealthier senior patrons, Zoey continued to feel isolated in this marriage as Will had been very distant lately and not very supportive during these weeks of what the hell is wrong with me? Will seemed preoccupied and had no time to listen to his wife and her mysterious ailment.

May slowly crept into summer with days in the 80s and no one was prepared. Zoey felt like she was wilting away. Exhausted and fever-like, she headed to her PCP, Joe Haviland, a friend for many years. He had delivered her daughter, Hannah fifteen years earlier when Zoey was only 21. Blood work was done and days later, Joe phoned her to come into the office ASAP. We need to talk. It was early on Thursday and Zoey was on an afternoon shift at the Tuckerman Library, so she headed over to the doctor right away, wondering what was happening to her.

The office was not crowded and Joe's assistant, Cindy Trasker, showed Zoey into the first exam room. After a blood pressure and pulse check, Cindy left her in the hands of Dr. Joe. When he came in, he looked concerned.

"Your BP was pretty low, Zoey." He smiled over at her.

Tears began to drip down onto her cheeks and Zoey felt like she was falling apart. "What is happening to me?"

"Zoey, I can't be certain." In a grave tone, he continued. "With the few tests I did, I can't believe you are walking on your own." He breathed a heavy sigh and told her what he found. "Your sedimentation rate is 75, and your rheumatoid factor is over 1100. I am really worried that you may have rheumatoid arthritis."

"RA?? How can that be, I am healthy, active and....you have to be wrong." Zoey raised her voice. "This can't be right, it can't be right."

Trying to calm her down, he had a bit of hope for her. "There is a chance what happened to you is related to the bite from the Lyme tick you got last fall."

"I took the Doxi that you prescribed for two weeks. It made my stomach want to vomit every day, but I finished most of it."

"Most of it?" Her PCP sighed. "That was a big mistake, Zoey, and sometimes two weeks' worth is not enough if the bite is a strong one. There is still so much more to learn on the tick borne infections."

Zoey questioned him again. "Did you do a blood test for Lyme disease?"

"We did." Dr. Joe was disappointed." It was negative, but the test is practically useless."

Zoey sounded so desperate. "What can we do to see if that damn tick is what is making me so sick?"

"I have one excellent contact at the Hartland University Medical Center in the city." Joe continued with the name of someone who could possibly help Zoey. "Dr. Emma Parker."

"And who is she?" Zoey needed to know.

"Dr. Parker is the head of the Rheumatology Department at the hospital, well respected and acclaimed in this field. She is British and quite a respected physician. Her degree was from McGill in Canada."

Confused, Zoey continued question her PCP. "Don't I need an Infectious Disease physician?"

"Zoey, you need to listen to me." His serious tone made her frightened. "It seems from your appearance, that you have some form of arthritis. It doesn't appear to be muscle related and the medical field does not have many accredited Lyme disease doctors. It is still a mystery disease." He added, "Emma Parker is the top rheumatologist at the Hartland Medical Center and treats the symptoms, and listens to her patients."

"So, what is next?" Zoey asked concerned.

Dr. Joe gave her an appointment card. "Dr. Parker has a 3 month wait list." Trying to gain her confidence he told Zoey, "I have a good relationship with Dr. Parker, and I was able to get you an appointment on Wednesday, in less than a week. Get your schedule prioritized."

"Do I need to do any more blood tests?"

"You are all set there. I have already e-mailed her your lab work that I did." He went on to finish what else could be done. "I have sent a new Doxycycline script to the drug store, and it is a bit stronger than the one I gave you last fall. Take the pills with food, crackers, some toast, etc. to protect your stomach. Understand?" He got up and placed his arm around her shoulder. "Let's see if it helps. This is serious and I am on your side. It will work out fine with Dr. Parker."

With the appointment on the following Wednesday, Zoey had to rearrange her entire schedule. The University Hospital was an hour's drive in heavy traffic. At the library, Monday and Tuesday would trigger a stress schedule for the staff at Tuckerman Library. On the Monday before the important Dr. Emma Parker consult, Zoey had to attend a periodic monthly meeting at the State Library in Seymour. The Doxi she had been taking seemed to be helping her arthritic joints. Fingers crossed, maybe it was just Lyme disease plaguing her exhausted body. On the way to the state library, Zoey began feeling very light headed. Her monthly period was exceptionally heavy and she felt very weak. As she began to perspire out in the busy parking lot, she got out of her car and her entire bottom was soaked with blood. Panicked, a colleague she was meeting saw what was happening and called 911.

Feeling empathy for this young woman, the paramedic was kind, capable and strong, easily lifting Zoey onto the stretcher, her pony tail flipping around her face. Her name tag said Aria.

Zoey was coherent as they headed to the hospital, Aria hammered her with questions regarding her health, and the meds she was currently taking.

"I have had some pre-menopausal issues with on/off heavy bleeding but my gynecologist, Maggie Braeburn, thought we had this under control."

Aria continued to monitor Zoey and assured her that her bleeding had significantly slowed down. "In a resting position, you are doing much better and we are almost at the Seymour Hospital."

It seemed like hours before Zoey was released by the ER doctor who felt that a D and C seemed like her next course of action. He made her promise that she would see her PCP soon after she went home. Dr. Joe would receive the medical report from Seymour Hospital by the time Zoey made it to her house. One of the security guards offered to drive her back to get her car with a promise that she would go directly home.

"I do promise that." Zoey was sincere as she shook the hand of the security guard and was soon on her was back to Highland Falls.

Eight years had passed since the nightmare began. Days seemed to pass very slowly, and the nights were worse especially with the chronic pain Zoey was forced to endure. Zoey's marriage suffered as intimacy nearly vanished and Will had very little patience or compassion for his wife. Zoey sighed remembering how she fell madly in love with Will so many years ago due to his handsome demeanor and caring personality. Wavy brownish hair streaked with blonde that was always a bit too long as the ringlets circled down his neck. He so loved animals and children, and Zoey knew they were a perfect match. With her illness, that all changed.

After the bleeding episode in May of that year, Dr. Braeburn performed a D and C and for two months the bleeding subsided. The original appointment with Emma Parker at the University Hospital was canceled due to the D and C. The new appointment was three weeks later in mid-July when Zoey finally made it to the bustling office of the Head Rheumatologist at University Hospital. The wait time was nearly an hour and Zoey was a bit tense. As soon as she met Dr. Parker, Zoey felt less tense and she was told to call her Emma. A light British accent seemed to add to the attractiveness of this middle-aged woman. Short dark blonde hair and light brown eyes seemed to smile at Zoey as she tried to assure her that they would figure out this health problem.

"Well, you are in quite a mess, from what Dr. Joe has told me." Emma grabbed her IPAD to take notes and asked Zoey to have a seat on the exam table. "We'll have a full exam in just a few minutes, but for now, tell me about this tick bite. "

Zoey explained, apologizing for not finishing the Doxi, "I woke up one April morning and could barely get out of bed. In three months, my feet were slightly arthritic, my right knee was achy, and two of the fingers on my right hand had started to swell from arthritis."

"Very frightening for a young, vibrant woman." Emma continued to type up the notes regarding Zoey's condition.

“Do you think I have RA?” Zoey was concerned and her serious tone was very clear.

Emma paused from typing and looked directly at Zoey. “There are some blood tests we need to do that will confirm what you have or do not have.” Calmly, Emma continued. “For now, in my opinion, in addition to the lab work by Dr. Joe, you do not have RA. Many doctors would not agree with me, as you are 36 years old, a woman, and have significant signs of this disease.”

“What else could I havc?” Zocy sounded frustrated and frightened. Emma’s smile was no longer helping Zoey feel good about what was happening.

“Let’s get undressed for a full exam and then we’ll talk.” Emma asked her, “Are you on any Doxycycline now?”

“No, it ended about 10 days ago.” she replied.

Emma said, “How do you feel today?”

Zoey looked a bit confused. “Strange, but a day or two ago, after weeks of feeling better, I began feeling exhausted, achy all over, especially my neck and head and my right knee is swollen.”

“So, the antibiotic is helping. That makes some sense to me.”

“Doxi has a small amount of an anti-inflammatory ingredient, but not enough to help rheumatoid arthritis. Get undressed and we will draw some blood and figure out how to help you get better.”

After a full exam and two hours later, Zoey was dressed and ready to finalize the visit with Dr. Emma Parker. In her office, Zoey asked her “So, what happens next?”

“I plan to start you on a different antibiotic for three weeks, and let’s see how you feel. Make sure to take all of the medicine, and take it with some food, crackers, ginger ale, anything that agrees with you.” She went on to say, “I want to see you in three weeks. A soon as we get the blood work back I will e-mail or call you about the results.” Emma looked directly at Zoey with her diagnosis. “My guess is you have second-stage Lyme disease.”

“Oh my God, what does second-stage mean?” Zoey’s eyes seem to pop out of her head. “But the Lyme test was negative!”

“Not to panic.” She calmed her down. “We’ll help you, one step at a time. And as far as the Lyme disease test, they are very inaccurate. But, the new meds may help you feel better. As we progress, you may need to consider a stronger I.V. antibiotic treatment. Let’s not get ahead of ourselves.” So, Zoey drove home with a lot to think about. And, as usual, Will was not there to help her through this. He was, as usual, on an exclusive golf tour in Scotland.

The next few months saw Zoey on intervals of antibiotics. When the meds stopped, Zoey worsened, with arthritic symptoms now in both hands and an obvious swollen knee. Added to that was her menstrual issues. A vaginal hysterectomy was planned for mid-November. Dr. Parker felt that an I.V. of Ceftriaxone was the only hope for Zoey but nothing could be done until the hysterectomy was completed. Zoey finally had a great deal of faith in her doctors. Maggie Braeburn felt that Zoey’s only option was this operation. Will was totally against the procedure, feeling that Zoey was far too young. He had always hoped for another child. Zoey was exhausted, arthritic, and desperate to feel normal. Her plans did not include contracting a mysterious disease that doctors still knew so little about. Strange that Will seemed to be away more than usual and Hannah, just turning 15 years old, saw the writing on wall.

It was almost a blur now, eight years ago, when December arrived cold and snowy in Highland Falls. Against the wishes of her husband, Zoey went through a fairly easy procedure for a vaginal hysterectomy which promised a quicker recovery than a normal procedure, eliminating stitches on her abdomen and time off from her job. The operation lasted less than two hours and when Zoey awakened in the recovery room, Will and Hannah were there to comfort her. The only negative factor was nausea from the anesthesia. One thing was vital in Zoey's recovery, but not from the hysterectomy. It was for her Lyme disease. Prior to the surgery, Zoey was running a low-grade fever. Perplexed by this, Dr. Braeburn made sure that a heavy dose of antibiotics, administered with an I.V. was given to Zoey. Within three days, Zoey was on her way home. No soreness from surgery was evident. Dr. Braeburn ordered her to lay low for a week with no reaching or stretching her lower body or the internal stitches would tear. Zoey was a good patient. To her amazement, Zoey had no signs of Lyme disease. There was no exhaustion, nor any muscle pain or arthritic stiffness. Even her swollen knee improved. No one could explain why. She called Dr. Parker at the University Hospital, thrilled about her symptoms, afraid the pain would return. Zoey made an appointment to see her the very next day.

Her sister, Kim, drove Zoey to the medical center to see Dr. Parker and walking carefully through the hospital and doctors' suites, Dr. Parker was walking into her office. "Zoey, come in, we've some good news."

"I believe we have finally got the proof we need." Dr. Parker sounded so hopeful.

Suspicious and doubtful, Zoey asked her, "So, what is it?"

"I spoke to your doctor and Maggie Braeburn is certain that the I.V. given to you during your surgery has indicated that the bacteria infecting your body has been disabled, at least for now." She continued on, "Her letter to your insurance company along with my notes on your case has given us approval to administer a month's dosage of Ceftriaxone to kill off your Lyme disease."

"My God, someone really believes all I have been saying for almost a year now." Starting to cry, Kim consoled her with a sister's warm hug.

"However," Dr. Parker explained some other issues to her. "You need to recuperate from your surgery, allowing your immune system to bounce back a bit." She added, "That means in fourteen days, the I.V. will begin."

"But, I am feeling good now, looks like the antibiotics from Dr. Braeburn fixed me." Zoey stood up, facing Dr. Parker. "Maybe I am already cured!"

"Zoey," Dr. Parker put her arms around her hopeful patient. "If this is Lyme, it will return and we have no time to waste." Continuing on with strict instructions, "So, you are to rest, eat a healthy diet, and no weight loss, okay?"

"Well, Dr. Braeburn took care of my anemia…no more bleeding." Zoey asked if she needed to do anything with her insurance provider.

"We took care of it all. The procedure will begin on the twenty-eighth of December, with a visiting nurse setting up the entire process."

Dr. Parker was right, again. The muscle and joint pain returned, crawling up toward Zoey's jawline, a new area that bug had invaded. By the end of December, she could barely open her mouth without wincing in pain. And the process began three days after Christmas, one holiday Zoey did not want to remember. After the first I.V. dosage, Zoey was told she would have to do the remaining fifty-nine on her own. Two doses a day for thirty days. Will was very tense the entire month, gone a lot with his golfing clients. Hannah also seemed stressed, worried for her Mom. Added to that was Moxie, a lively Cocker Spaniel and two inquisitive cats running around Zoey trying to emotionally add support to their caregiver. Zoey, to no surprise, adapted to this important medicine injected into her left arm. The first week of January saw her returning to the library in her director's position. Limited to just fifteen hours a week, her staff rallied around her with kind and professional manners and a ton of support.

Weeks after the successful I.V. ended, lab work proved what many in the medical community doubted, Zoey was another victim of chronic Lyme disease. Inflammation was drastically reduced, and her white/red blood counts returned to normal. Her OBGYN doctor blamed Lyme disease on her bleeding issues, with a plummeting immune system and no energy to fight this off. Thus, the hysterectomy. Zoey was able to handle the physical aspects of her lifestyle, but Will was unable to stay by her side. He filed for a divorce, almost a year after the Lyme disease episode, citing irreconcilable differences.

Suddenly, Zoey's daily life drastically changed. Her only support came from Hannah, Moxie, her devoted dog, and her Mom, who was always there for her.

CHAPTER 1

The alarm clock was annoyingly dependable and it was sounding bigly on this chilly fall morning. It was Tuesday, shortly after 5 a.m. with the darkness and morning chill providing no incentive to begin her day. Zoey Mitchell stretched, yawned, and began the routine. Petting her two felines, still half asleep, they continued to snuggle against her warm body. "Time to rise and shine, girls." Both rescue kittens now nearly a year old, Spencer was the Bengal look-alike with dark stripes and spots stretching along her long, lean and caramel covered body. Dewey resembled a British shorthair breed with thick grey fur and golden globes for eyes that were an instant appeal for cuddling. Very different in appearance, they really were sisters. Arriving by bus from a no-kill shelter in North Carolina, the girls found a loving home in Highland Falls, a small beach community on the New England coastline. Zoey hopped from bed heading for the shower. Her long, brownish hair, brushed with natural blonde highlights circled her almond shaped face, but her hazel-colored eyes were what people noticed when first meeting her. Almost sparkly, these eyes projected a friendly manner wherever they took her. Zoey's past few years had been difficult, but a loving family and caring doctors had saved her. The daily pills to keep her healthy were part of a routine now. Divorced for seven years, Zoey was on her own, and being dependent on others no longer existed. She believed that she could, so she did. And, raking leaves in the autumn was forever a thing of the past. Within an hour, they would be on their way to Sips and Swap, a book swap/breakfast eatery just a few minutes from home. Zoey would pick up her business partner Liz McCaffery, more commonly known as her Mom. They began their business venture almost a year ago, last September, after Zoey resigned as director of the town library in Highland Falls. Liz and Zoey agreed on the hours to be open, from 7 a.m. to 3 p.m. six days a week. CLOSED ON MONDAYS.

As Zoey toweled off from her shower, she gazed at herself in the mirror. Damn, another wrinkle. At 43 years old, Zoey kept her body well-toned by biking and swimming several times a week. Her brownish blond hair had lost some shine through the years, but remained thick and wavy as she wore it high atop her head in a girlish pony-tail. Always a popular Highland Falls girl, her marriage to Will Mitchell had ended in divorce 15 years after it began. Their daughter Hannah Ann was the highlight of those 15 years and at 22, Hannah was now in Veterinary School in Virginia. Zoey and Will remained friends but he was now living with a younger woman, not planning another marriage. However, both parents remained very close to Hannah.

Sips and Swap opened promptly at 7 a.m. 6 days a week with only Mondays as the day the girls took off to rejuvenate. Spencer and Dewey accompanied Zoey and stayed close by her for most of the day greeting a selection of customers who appealed to them. Keenly aware of anti-cat people, they made no moves toward them. The kitchen staff included Selena and Caitland with Liz supervising and Zoey attending to the swap area. Zoey lucked out as Selena and Caitland were part-time college students, only taking night classes. When busy, Zoey would call her sister Kim, who was married to Jonas Parsons, the town's Marshall.

Kim helped out at his office with various paperwork and filing that he preferred not to do.

Driving over to her mom's condo, Zoey noticed how dismal it looked outdoors. The local weather predicted rain later in the day but as the rain drops began splashing on her windshield, Zoey thought…wrong again…..Liz McCaffery began a sprint to the car and made it before the downpour started.

"Gads, Zoey, what the heck!" Liz McCaffery frowned. "How can they be so wrong with all that expensive Doplar radar?" She glanced back at the girls in the rear seat. "Hi babies….ready to go to work?" Liz smiled at them and thought how lucky these cats were…just to be alive.

As Zoey glanced over at her mom, she was so glad Liz cared about life and looking so youthful. Since Zoey's dad died 2 years ago Liz McCaffery went through many changes, mainly positive ones. And, the Sips and Swap Shop was the highlight of her life. It gave her something to look forward to along with earning some extra cash for herself. Liz was tall and fairly thin, and in excellent health. Her naturally dark brown hair took years off her sixty-six years and thanks to her hairdresser, no gray appeared.

"What are the girls making today for the muffins?" She asked her mom.

"I know carrot is on the list, pumpkin, and some new French vanilla ones. Yummy. The quiches are all prepared in the refrigerator and the two popular choices seem to stay on the menu including bacon, mushroom and Havarti cheese, and broccoli and smoked Gouda. We can't keep them stocked!" Liz told Zoey as she made some notes on her iPhone.

“We need to order some egg nog coffee and also the pumpkin spice. Before we know it, is holiday time.” Zoey reminded her mom, who did all of the ordering.

“Will do. Hey, are you swimming today at the club?”

“Yes, I am, about 11ish” Zoey replied. “It seems to be less crowded then, and I will be back by 12:15. Kim will come by for an hour to get a break from office filing. The cats love her and I am sure she’ll bring along those freeze dried tuna treats.”

As they headed toward Sips and Swap, Zoey saw some flashing red lights in front of the library. Zoey slowed down to see what was happening but the rain prevented her from getting a good look as she passed by. Two state trooper vehicles were there with lights flashing but that was all either of the ladies could see. “What is going on here?” Zoey looked at her mom.

“Can’t tell.” Liz said looking back as they passed the library. “Maybe someone broke in?”

“It’s early,” Zoey looked at her mom, “but, text Kim to see if Jonas knows what is happening here.”

Liz told her daughter “It is not quite 7 a.m. and Kim is getting Andi ready for school, so I will wait a bit longer.” Liz went on. “It is probably nothing, maybe a false alarm.”

“But, state troopers only come out when it is serious,” Zoey reminded her. Her brother-in-law Jonas Parsons was the Marshall for the district of Highland Falls and handled minor offenses including speeding, break-ins, drunk and disorderly charges. Occasionally there was a domestic dispute. Last year there was a bank robbery and the state troopers were called in ASAP.

"All right, all right, gossip girl" Liz replied and began to text Kim.

It took a few minutes but the text came back to Liz as the ladies were pulling into Sips and Swap. "Hmmmm," Liz looked over at Zoey. "Kim has no idea what is going on. Jonas just got a call from the trooper who is at the library now. She says she'll be at the shop before you leave for swimming and maybe by then she'll know what has happened."

As Zoey unloaded her car, she was careful with the leashed cats as they were not happy to be caught in all of this rain. "Run kitties." Zoey ran and gently dragged them into the back door of the shop. Both Spencer and Dewey would hide for at least an hour before deciding to get social.

As Liz and Zoey entered the kitchen, the aroma wafted through the air. "I smell pumpkin muffins." Zoey went over to the countertop and buttered one, grabbed a cup of coffee and headed to the swap area. Both cats were behind the chenille covered sofa, where Zoey plopped down to have a bite of muffin and her wake-up beverage. "Yummy, girls!" She yelled toward the kitchen.

Customers were just starting to come in, mainly for the coffee and treats of the day. The swappers usually came by after 10 a.m. After inhaling most of the muffin, Zoey went to work on sorting material as Tuesday was a busy first day of the work week for her. Some books were left in the huge drop-off area and there was a lot of sorting to do. Organization was Zoey's foremost issue. When customers come in looking for certain material Zoey liked to go right to the correct spot. Several non-fiction titles were in a huge box that needed a space on the store shelves. Books on tape were very popular, along with MP3 discs too, especially for the younger crowd. Older adults still listened to books on cassette so there was a section for these too, especially the Cat Who Mystery Books by Lilian Jackson Braun.

The eatery was especially busy this Tuesday with most of the orders to go. Liz popped her head into the swap room informing her daughter that the residents were all buzzing about the state police vehicles at the town library. No one had a clue as to why they were there. Zoey checked the time on her phone and it was almost eleven o'clock. Where was Kim? Jonas would know the whole story.

Zoey got some plates of wet and dry food ready for the cats before she left to do her laps at the Swim Club, just a few minutes away from the shop. It was open year-round for indoor swimming for club members. Kim drove up to the back entrance and ran through to the swap room, apologizing for being a few minutes late. Zoey was a bit OCD about her schedule and felt that organization was the key to success. Being late was not on her acceptable list.

"Sorry, Zoey, but things are busy at the station with three state troopers here. You will not believe what has happened." Excited, Kim continued, "Boy, you are lucky you are no longer at the library."

Zoey pictured her sister, always on the go, full of energy. No time for unnecessary cosmetics, Kim had short, straight spiked hair, a pretty darkish brown, and big brown eyes, always smiling. Zoey replied to her sister, "You got that right." Her tone was more than firm. "It was the best move of my life."

"What about your divorce? Where does that land on your ladder of best to worst?"

"Will is happy with someone younger, I am okay, and Hannah is in Vet School paid for by Daddy. Can't get much better." Zoey stared out at the rain spattering against the window panes.

Kim knew enough not to pursue this worn out conversation regarding Will Mitchell. "Well, before you do your laps, you had better sit down for a shocker."

Zoey wasn't sure what could have happened at the library that would shock her, but there were two state troopers there after all. "Okay, Kim, let's have it."

"Well, the library is closed on Monday," Kim began. "Workers began excavating for the new handicap entrance ramp toward the back of the building, you know where the wooded area starts?"

"Right, go on." Zoey told her sipping cold coffee. She was eager to hear about what had occurred.

"This morning, as they dug deeper and closer to the woods, the digger thing hit something, like a large tarp with a huge something in it."

"Really??" Zoey was really paying attention now.

"Oh God, Zoey, it was a body."

"Are you kidding me??" Zoey looked a bit dismayed. "Are you sure it is not some kind of animal, like a hunted, dead deer?"

"Not unless a deer has two legs, two arms and a head…" Kim sounded serious unloading this piece of information.

"How old is the body, do they know?" Zoey was concerned.

"You know, Zoey, I am not with CSI and I only got bits and pieces as the troopers called this info into the station." Now, Kim had on her professional cap. "When you drive by to swim at the club, you'll see the crime scene investigation unit vehicle there at the library. It is a huge black van, you can't miss it." Zoey grabbed her swim bag as she patted her cats goodbye. "Kim, who could this be, dead in the back lot at the library?"

"I don't know, but those pros will find out and Jonas is part of this investigation!"

"Gads," Zoey looked frightened. "What if it happened when I was the librarian?"

Kim never thought about that aspect. "You had better think long and hard about this, Zoey. You may very well be questioned about this, so get ready."

CHAPTER 2

Zoey headed out the door to swim laps but her mind was filled with thoughts of dead bodies and possibly a murder. She was eager for a quick twenty laps. This scheduled routine energized and refreshed her body that she vowed to always keep healthy and thin. Driving toward the club she would be able to take a peek at the library and watch for the big black van. And there it was. A chill ran up and down her spine.

There were more parked cars at the library than she could count. Zoey smiled to herself thinking of how many people would be affected by what had been discovered. The twelve person library board had been working on this handicap ramp for years now and finally the money came through from various state grants and agencies. Because the library was privately endowed, funding was always limited for a number of renovations. However, the ADA (Americans with Disabilities Act) and the legality for this much-needed ramp left the Tuckerman Memorial Library with no choice but to install an acceptable ramp for handicapped patrons. While Zoey was the director there, she fought for wage increases, proper water and ventilation, among other needed modernizations. She was shot down on nearly every suggestion. Frustrated and after eight years of trying, Zoey left her position at the library for a better future. Her staff, including many good friends, were surprised and disappointed when she gave her notice. It had been a little more than one year since she left the library to open her eatery.

As she changed into her swimsuit, Zoey's morning smile turned into a frown as she thought about the head honcho at the Tuckerman Library. Samuel J. Watson, husband of Marjorie Tuckerman Watson, was the Chairperson and definite leader of the pack. Marjorie's family was a key to this privately funded establishment and the reason Sam Watson ran the Board. In the late 1800s, the Tuckerman family was responsible for the construction of this lovely stone building. Originally from South Carolina, some of these wealthy aristocrats migrated north to finally settle in Highland Falls. This family was well bred and overflowing with culture, and the library was built for residents to enjoy. However, throughout the years, lots of baggage erupted among several family members. Within the last several months, Marjorie became estranged with her mother, Victoria Tuckerman. For several years Victoria lived with Sam and Marjorie here in Highland Falls. But a serious argument occurred months ago and Victoria returned to her home in South Carolina. Then she planned a lengthy trip abroad, with Victoria seeming to fade away as Marjorie gladly lost touch with her mother. Liz McCaffery heard all about this estrangement as she belonged to the historical society and garden club where the drinks flowed freely at the luncheons, along with all of the gossip.

As Zoey completed her laps and headed to the showers, her mind slowly crept backward to another time in her life where she had to deal with Sam Watson on a regular basis. Zoey sighed as this relationship was loaded with some pretty heavy baggage, and she was so glad to have resigned her position well over a year ago, as Sam was the main reason for leaving. Lots of skeletons in *that* closet. Well known by many residents and patrons at the library as arrogant, rigid, and for the most part, ill-tempered he was a typical ladies man. In his late fifties with short, cropped black hair peppered with grey, Sam stood tall at well over six feet and as an avid tennis player, his body was well-toned and youthful. Zoey dealt with Sam weekly at the library as he was the president of the privately appointed board. Semi-retired from a New York investment firm, Sam was able to spend much of his spare time overseeing all aspects at the library. Along with a sizable family fortune from Marjorie's mother, the Tuckermans were able to enjoy a comfortable life in Highland Falls. Their only son, Andrew James (A.J.), was now seventeen years old and away at private school soon headed for college. A quiet boy, and very close to Marjorie, residents saw very little of this young man.

Driving back to the eatery, Zoey felt refreshed and hungry as the laps used up whatever she had for breakfast and her empty stomach began to growl. She also could not help but think about A.J. Watson. While Zoey was the library director A.J. would tumble in on occasion when life got boring in Highland Falls. Summer at the Tuckerman Library meant weeding out the book stacks to make room for fall orders and Zoey always asked for volunteers to lift any heavy boxes or old, unused books. A.J. was always glad to help out. A.J. was also told to bring home these old books to their home so Sam Watson could decide just what to keep or recycle. Although retired, Sam ran a rare and antique book business. He traveled the US for best buys and sold many items on-line. Zoey worked for Sam for two years on a part-time basis, only when he was away, to keep his business on-track. When Zoey left her position at the library, she also gave notice to Sam that she would no longer have time to work for him and his rare book business. He did not take this well. Because Zoey left so abruptly, she asked her sister to fill-in until Sam could hire a permanent part-time replacement. While working for Sam, Kim got a feel for who the real Samuel J. Watson really was and quite honestly did not want to put up with his selfish attitude. So, after only a few weeks of work she told her sister she was planning to quit. It was at that time, Zoey came clean and confessed to Kim why she really left that position as office manager. Zoey had discovered some inappropriate private material involving Sam. It was so reprehensible that she thought of contacting the authorities. She told Kim she was right to resign. It took several days to bury the memory of the conversation Kim had with Zoey. A difficult decision, the girls chose to not tell their mother about this. It had been more than one year now and Liz McCaffery still questioned the real reason why both her daughters quit their jobs for Sam. There was much more to this story but Liz, after months of querying her daughters, finally let this fade away. Knee deep in the eatery and book store, the past seemed to be better off where it was.

When Zoey arrived at Sips and Swap, it was a little past 12:30 and she parked in the back lot, making room for all of her patrons. It was the busiest time of the day for the eatery. Heading to the back door, both cats ran over for their daily pats, and Zoey scooted in to grab a salad and croissant for her lunch. Liz was busy packing up several orders to go. Caitland was busy creating lattes in a variety of fancy flavors while Selena waited on customers who wanted to have a bite right there, listening for any gossip about the library chaos. Then it happened. Jonas arrived.

As Jonas came in, silence descended. All eyes focused on the Marshall as he looked around and wondered if he should have just gone into the back entrance as everyone began buzzing about the body discovered at the library.

"Okay folks," Jonas smiled as many of these people were his friends. "You all want to hear what happened and you know there is very little I can discuss about this." Sighs were heard among the whispering patrons.

Realtor Georgia Lamont was the brave one. "Do you know who this person is, dead in back of the town library?" She looked worried. "Do residents need to be concerned?"

"Really, Georgia?" Jonas was a friend to everyone in Highland Falls. His broad smile and boyish looks reminded folks of how Robert Redford looked as a younger man. People trusted and respected Jonas as he was easy to talk to and understand. He removed his hat and rested against the counter, giving a quick wink to his mother-in-law. "The body was just discovered early this morning and it is far too soon to discuss or mention any facts about what occurred here. And, let's not get ahead of ourselves with the worry aspect."

Caitland looked over at Jonas. "The usual?"

"That would be great, Caitland, and do a tuna on croissant too, okay?" Jonas headed back into the bookstore hoping to catch his wife and Zoey.

"I will send it back to you in just a minute." Caitland flashed him a big smile.

Jonas looked at both Zoey and Kim as he gave Spencer and Dewey some well appreciated strokes over their backsides. The purring began. "Now, girls," Jonas whispered, "You know I am not about to discuss this buried body in any way or form. I only came back to tell you, there is no need to worry about our town becoming murderous Chicago (recalling Trump's words)."

Kim just stared at her husband. "Nothing?"

"Nada." Jonas smiled and the dimples appeared. "When I get home tonight, I will have more info for you all. It will make the nightly news I am sure and by 5-7 p.m. we should know a little more."

Caitland buzzed through with the coffee and sandwich. "All yours, sir."

Looking over at his wife, Jonas told her, "No need for you to come by the office today, honey." Jonas reminded her that he had to be at a Selectman's Meeting at 5 p.m. and would be late for dinner. And he was gone.

Zoey bit into her salad as she shook her head wondering just who that body belonged to. "Who could it be, Kim?"

"How would I know?" Kim replied. "You are the Jessica Fletcher here, you figure it out."

"Maybe I will make a few calls today, to some board members that still talk to me. Perhaps Sam told them something."

"Good luck with that." Kim began to laugh. "Why don't you just call your friend Sam?"

Zoey did not reply to this, but chose to finish her salad and coffee before making some calls.

The first one on her list was an old friend and colleague, Claire Harris. Some residents considered Claire an aging senior citizen who should consider resigning her position as the library's treasurer. Although she was nearly eighty years young, she looked years younger with blondish hair, speckled with grey and was as smart as a green apple. Claire remained dedicated and steadfast as treasurer wasting no time mincing words. If there was any news about this body found at the library, Claire would know about it.

CHAPTER 3

Zoey asked Kim if she would handle the bookstore while she made a call to the Tuckerman Library Treasurer, Claire Harris. Lately, Claire wore her greyish blonde hair in an attractive braid, and as an active senior citizen, she was involved with many town activities. A retired CPA, Claire was an attentive and clear headed bookkeeper, sharp as a tack, always noticing discrepancies in the budget. Sam Watson was not as cautious with the money allocated at the library. Claire kept him in line. Disagreements occurred frequently between Sam and Claire.

The after-lunch time period was busy for people browsing the shelves for some interesting reading or listening material so Zoey took her cell phone to a back corner window area to join Spencer and Dewey. They were seriously focused on the birds picking off sunflower seed scattered on the copper feeder that had just been put out there this past week. The cats were lucky, as two squirrels appeared vacuuming up all of the seed that was slowly escaping from the bird tray. Zoey opened the window and threw our several peanuts for the grey-tailed creatures.

The first attempt to reach a board member was a success. Claire Harris answered on the second ring. "Claire, this is Zoey calling." She waited for a reaction.

"My dear, Zoey, how you doing?"

Zoey sighed. "Well, Claire what has happened here?"

At first a bit hesitant, Claire tried to answer Zoey with the little bit of information she had been given. "I did get a call from Sam earlier today, but he was very guarded when he spoke with me. He said that the construction crew was busy working on the new handicap entrance ramp when a body was discovered. It was quite a shock for the men who were digging up the earth, when out of the blue, a bunch of what appeared to be human remains, erupted from the soil."

"Oh my God, Claire, that's awful." Zoey was also dismayed by what occurred. "Do they know how long the body was buried there?"

A slight laugh, Claire continued with just what she knew. "I am about out of news, Zoey." Clearing her throat, she finished with just what little she knew. "Sam said he was limited with what he could tell Board Members regarding the investigation but the State Crime Squad was called in as this was a suspicious death."

"I guess I feel some relief as I am no longer the librarian."

Claire agreed. "My dear, you have done so well this past year. This was a good move for you. You deserved to be treated better than you were, especially by Sam." She finished with, "If I hear any more, I will give you a call." And the call ended.

So, that was that. Zoey knew the complete story would only come from Jonas, or from the daily morning newspaper, the Highland Falls Bulletin.

As Zoey headed back to the bookstore, her cell phone rang and it was Hannah. Zoey smiled answering on the second ring. "Hey sweetie, how are you?"

"Mom, what the hell is happening in our town? The body discovery has already appeared on-line. Gads, who died there???"

Zoey could not believe it was already in the news. "Are you serious....it's online?"

"Well, there is a brief description only and I hoped you'd have more to tell me."

"Sorry Hannah." Zoey tried to sound positive. "I know very little, but when Jonas gets home later we'll all know a little more. It will be some time before the authorities know who it was. I don't even know how long the body has been there." Hannah sounded concerned. "What if I was the librarian when this happened?"

"Well, I have a full class load today, so call me tonight, after 7, to fill me in, okay?" She asked her Mom one last thing. "Are you okay?"

Zoey did not want to appear upset by all of this so she calmly answered Hannah. "We will all feel better knowing why this body was buried there, because many residents are a bit chilled by what has happened." She finished with, "We do not need a serial killer starting up in Highland Falls. I will call you later on."

Back in the store, several patrons were borrowing books and CDs, and also gossiping about the body at the library. With Kim there, all she could do was shake her head and say she was sorry but she knew very little.

Town gossip Bunny Maris commented, "But, Kim, surely Jonas was here filling you in with some news."

Looking at all of the hushed customers waiting for an answer, Kim just replied with a smile, "Sorry folks, Jonas is the professional here as our Marshall and would never compromise an investigation." She went on to tell them, "The paper is out at 5 a.m. and I am certain that you will all be up early reading about the body discovered at the Tuckerman Library."

Zoey smiled to herself, proud of her sister handling a tricky situation. Both ladies knew most of the residents in their small town and as business owners, being polite and tactful was appropriate.

It was nearly 4 p.m. when Liz, Kim, and Zoey had the eatery all cleaned up and doors were checked and locked for the evening. Cats on their leashes, Zoey headed for the car, and happy to be going home. Zoey threw out an invitation. "You two are welcome to come by for a bite to eat, I have your favorite mac and cheese from this past weekend."

"Maybe I will stay, if Andi wants to come by with me. Jonas has that meeting with the Selectmen tonight anyway."

"I'll pass on your invite, Zoey." Liz gave her a smile. "I am just flat-out and look forward to a long hot bath and a glass of sweet red wine."

"I hear you, Mom." Zoey added.

They all left for home and when Zoey got the cats inside, she flipped on her gas fireplace. It was a chilly, damp night. She saw her phone blinking red clear across into the kitchen. Seven messages! Zoey knew what this meant. She just wanted to unwind, feed the cats, and wait for Kim to arrive with her niece, Andi. The teenager gave up her 'real' name, Andrea, about two years ago when she turned twelve. Andi was just a real cool name. Absolutely a Barbie doll image with blondish hair and deep blue eyes, this athletic girl was on more teams than Zoey could count.

Lacrosse, basketball, and summer softball were the highlights of her life. And Andi loved Zoey's homemade mac and cheese with a buttery brown topping that crunched with every bite.

With a headache just beginning, Zoey popped an aspirin in her mouth along with some cold orange juice and pressed the button on her phone to retrieve messages. #1. Sam Watson here. Please give me a call, Zoey, when you have a moment. #2. Hang-up. #3. Hey Mom, it's Hannah. I will try you at the Eatery. Love you. #4. Hey Zoey, it's Millie, next door. What is going on at the library, all of the police cars, my gosh. #5. Hang-up. #6. Hey Zoey, it is Sam Watson…..again. Call me please. #7. Zoey, it is Claire Harris, give me a call back, dear, would you?

Well, Zoey thought to herself. It was a little before five and she did have time to call Claire back. She would also have to call Sam too, but wanted to hear if Claire had any news about what had happened. So, Claire was first.

"Hello." Claire answered in a serious tone.

"Claire, it's Zoey…you called me?"

Relieved to hear it was Zoey and not Sam Watson, Claire welcomed the call. "What an afternoon. Sam called me and has summoned an emergency board meeting tomorrow at 10 a.m. at the town office building. He has closed the library until the Crime Squad authorizes him to open it to the public once again."

"I think that is protocol, Claire." Zoey explained this to her. "I am certain that the library will reopen on Thursday."

"I so wish you were still at the library, Zoey." Claire sighed, disappointment clearly felt in her voice."

“Well,” Zoey replied, “I can honestly say I am glad I left, especially with this mess. Sam must be a wreck.” She continued to say, “He likes to be all fluff and feathers, but when faced with a serious issue, he is of little help.”

“I called you because I did discover a little bit about what has occurred. Surprisingly, Sam was most upset that the excavators had to change the design for the handicap ramp, as the spot that was chosen was full of ledge. So, the manager, on his own, moved the site over just a few feet. If they did not do that, it would have been a serious delay as blasting might have been necessary.”

Claire was a nice and well-educated person, but gave too long of a description of anything being discussed. Zoey really did not want to hear all about the new handicap ramp. “Claire, any news about who this was, buried there?”

“Well, it was an older woman.”

“Oh my God, Claire.” Zoey felt a bit shocked. Chills went up and down here body. Zoey kept thinking, maybe this was someone who just wandered off…maybe it was not a murder…..

“Sam did tell me to refrain from discussing this with anyone, but Zoey, you are not just anyone.”

“I appreciate your call, Claire.” Zoey told her in a genuine tone. “Sam did leave two messages with me at home today. So, I will have to call him back.” She needed her friend’s input.

“I can’t imagine what he wants from you, as you have been gone a year now from your job at Tuckerman.”

“After your meeting tomorrow, why don’t you stop by at the eatery on your way home and we can have some tea. I will let you know what Sam wanted and you can keep me posted too from what happens with the board members.”

Claire had a favor to ask. “Zoey, please save my favorite quiche, would you, and I will have it for my dinner tomorrow. The bacon, mushroom, and Havarti cheese one is usually sold out when I get there.”

“Will do, Claire.” Zoey was happy to do this for her. “See you tomorrow.”

Zoey knew she had to call Sam back before Kim and Andi arrived. Looking at the clock, it was already after 5 p.m. Oh, Lord, she thought as she dialed Sam’s number.

“Hello.” A perky voice chirped at Zoey.

“Marjorie, it’s Zoey Mitchell, is Sam around?”

Then the voice became icy. “Zoey.” Marjorie gave a deep sigh. “What a day for Highland Falls, for us all. And Sam, well, Sam is just so upset.”

“I am sure.” Zoey continued, “Sam phoned me earlier today, is he there?”

“I will get him for you.” The phone fell with a clunk. Marjorie did not like Zoey and Zoey felt the same so no words were needed here. Soon, Sam arrived on the line.

“You know Zoey, if I had your cell phone number, I would have reached you already.” Sam told her in an abrupt tone.

“Sam, you know where I am nearly every day of the week. There is really no need to have my private number anymore.” Zoey was no longer intimidated by Sam Watson.

Sam's tone lightened a bit. "Well, you know what has occurred at the library. A body of an older woman was found and I felt you should know the facts, or the little I was told. Your gossip center should have only the facts."

"Seriously, Sam?" Zoey was a little ticked off now and realized that making this call was a mistake. "If I want facts about what has occurred, I am sure the Marshall will fill me in, when he's allowed. You do remember I have an in with him, right?"

"We believe it may have been a woman with mental problems, maybe dementia, who wandered off and somehow died where she was found." Sam went on, "So, no rumors are to start here. Are we clear?"

"So, you are guessing that this lost soul of a person happened to fall in a hole and just got buried there?"

Sam cleared his throat in a firm manner. "Let's not pull a Columbo here, Zoey."

"No problem there, Sam." She was firm with him. "Soon the whole town will discover exactly what happened and who this poor old woman was." She was ready to hang up. "Sad, Sam, for this person who may have had relatives, somewhere." Time to end this call. Zoey got the mac and cheese out of the refrigerator and began setting the table. A salad was also needed. But first, a big glass of sweet Riesling wine poured over lots of ice….. Zoey had to smile thinking of her mother, now thigh-deep in bubbles in her Jacuzzi tub.

CHAPTER 4

As Zoey whisked the oil, vinegar, and secret spices into a creamy vinaigrette she heard her sister and Andi pull into the driveway. Mac and cheese was heating up and the kitchen had an inviting aroma as Kim opened the door to the kitchen.

"It always smells so good in here, Zoey." Kim gave her sister a quick hug. "Andi can stay for a little bit as she has a study date at Matt's house tonight."

"I could not miss that mac and cheese," she laughed a little. "Can't you teach Mom how to make it like you?"

"Your Mom is a great cook, Andi." Zoey told her placing the hot casserole dish onto the table. "Dig in!"

They all began scooping the buttery crusted casserole from the pan and watched it melt onto their plates. Andi nearly burned her mouth with that first bite. "Yummmm!"

"So, Kim, did you talk to Jonas for more info?" Zoey was eager for a response.

Crunching on the crispy green salad, Kim stopped to get a few words in to her sister. "I only spoke to him for minute and he was not too happy with all of the state police there at the scene."

"His turf, huh?" Zoey laughed a little.

"You got that right, a little intimidated by the big boys."

"Anything we should know?"

"Well, the body is an older woman and it was covered and re-wrapped again."

“Really?” Andi’s eyes were as wide as saucers. “Why would someone do that?”

Zoey and Kim looked at each other not knowing what to say. Recalling some murder mystery books Zoey had read through the years, she told Andi, “From what I remember, when someone kills someone and cares about them, I mean knows them, they make sure the body is covered and pretty well protected from the weather.”

“Whoa, Jessica, such a meaningful explanation for what might have happened.” Kim told her sister. “I need confidential here Zoey” She stared seriously at her sister.

“And?” Zoey stared back.

“Aside from sagging greenish skin, and some insect interest, the body has not been there for too long, less than 3 months. Also, there was some bruising on the woman’s neck, which may have meant strangulation. At least that is what the medical examiner explained to Jonas. And, oddly, no jewelry at all on the corpse. Guessing the age at in her 70s, the woman had thick dark blondish hair, still intact. Maybe a robbery that went wrong, thus no jewelry. Older women always have something they wear, earrings, rings, etc.” Kim added, “The woman had pierced ears, too. Strange, with no earrings worn.”

“That is really weird.” Zoey shook her head looking doubtful. “Could it be a local person then?” Zoey shuddered thinking of all of the older ladies that frequented her Sips and Swap place. “Gads, maybe it was a tourist?”

“Jonas said they are now checking all retirement and assisted living complexes in the area, perhaps finding out who this was.” Kim added. “Because of the condition of the body, no picture would circulate. Police only have a description of the body to offer to anyone who may know something."

"We are all looking forward to the morning paper unless it's fake news." Kim told them all.

"OK, Trump." Kim burst out laughing.

When the dishes were cleared, Andi left to walk down to Matt LeSeur's house just a few blocks down the street. They were really good friends and both focused on studying when they were supposed to. Kim and Zoey, shoes kicked off, plopped by the warm fireplace, enjoyed the last cup of coffee for the day.

"Sam Watson called me, like three times today." Zoey told Kim.

"What the hell did he want?" Kim was a bit annoyed.

"He gave me specific instructions regarding the dead body."

"Are you kidding me????" Kim sighed, sipping at the hot Irish cream coffee.

"I kid you not." Zoey continued. "He wants to make sure, and I quote, that our gossip center has the correct version as to what happened to this poor old lady."

"May I spit in his latté the next time he stops in?"

"Not worth the effort, my dear, just let it go." Zoey told her.

"If people only knew what he was really like, Zoey, they would freak out." She added, "How can Marjorie stand him, he is always so arrogant, and soooo right about everything."

Zoey could not help but add her opinion, "Marjorie is a real gem too. Her cold attitude and better-than-anyone-else attitude gets tired after a while."

"I guess, you know her better than I do." Kim had to continue. "She is very generous with donations to the local police department for all of their social events and charities, though."

Zoey just sighed but told her very firmly, "Kim, you need to clam up about Sam. I mean it."

"He is a horrid person, and he acts like he is God's gift to the world." Kim's smile vanished.

Skeletons in the closet began to appear. "Will you ever be able to put this behind you?" Zoey looked straight into her sister's eyes waiting for a reply.

"I never should have taken that part-time job with him, when you quit." Kim said in a huffy tone.

"Well, I was in a bind leaving the library so suddenly last year. I had to cut all ties with him." She was worried about Kim and what had occurred with Sam Watson. "I should have told you the truth about what I found but I had to leave right away…Sam was okay with my resigning as long as someone took my place. That was you. I assumed Sam would be gone most of the time, traveling and searching for his rare books."

"Having Sam gone most of the time was not the issue, Zoey." Kim reminded her.

"I know that. I told you why I quit and what I found as soon as I could." Zoey sighed. "I am so sorry I used you as my replacement. It was wrong."

Kim stared seriously at her sister. "And I left, as soon as possible, when you told me what a freak Sam is. Using my busy family life worked as a good reason."

Zoey gave her sister a big hug and finished cleaning up the dishes as the phone rang.

"Still got that land line?" She looked over at Zoey.

"Yes, it is dependable, unlike the cell phone that has its good and bad days." Zoey answered to hear Hannah at the other end.

"Hey, Mom." Hannah sounded tired.

"Long day?" Zoey tried to picture her daughter, after listening to her tired voice. Hannah was a bit of a perfectionist, wavy dark hair, inherited from her dad, tied back with some clips and large round glasses circling her fatigued eyes. Always a neat girl, even when worn-out.

"You could say that." She had to ask, "Any more news on the body?"

Zoey told her about how the body was found and it appeared that whoever killed this poor woman may have known her. It might have been a planned murder.

"Who told you this, Mom?" Hannah seemed doubtful.

"It just makes sense, Hannah with the body covered so carefully."

"Look, *Murder She Wrote* expert. I would be careful with that piece of info in our small town. Everybody will be freaking out."

Zoey snapped, "Oh, Hannah, you sound like Sam Watson."

Hannah laughed. 'I don't think so."

"Gotta' go, Mom." Hannah yawned. "I need a really hot shower and then it is study time." Hannah needed reassurance. "I hope when I become a Vet, these creatures appreciate me."

"Bye, sweetie."

It was nearly 7:30 and Kim slipped on her light jacket, ready to head for home. "Zoey, do you think we should tell Mom about what happened with Sam and why you quit?"

"Are you kidding me?" Zoey could not believe her sister. "A year has gone by and if Mom knew what happened with Sam, I don't know what she would do."

"That is not the issue," Kim sounded frustrated. They had discussed this time and time again.

"Every time I see him, I remember those images you found—"

Zoey stopped her from continuing. "You need to forget what happened to me, Kim. Sam Watson is connected all the way to the Governor's office." She sighed. "He could seriously hurt us or our business."

"Well, we could really hurt his character with what you discovered hidden away in his storage shelves!" Kim said in a defiant tone.

“Enough.” Zoey wanted a hot shower and bed. “Good night, Kim.”

Lights out, fireplace shut off and doors locked, Zoey headed up the stairs calling to her favorites. “Spencer…Dewey upstairs, it is my bath time.” Two huge balls of fur scrambled up the stairway, each competing for the top landing. It was a tie. After her shower, each cat needed to be brushed and insisted on this daily grooming. It was a daily habit not to be ignored. And that was it for tonight.

CHAPTER 5

Zoey had a restless night, Around 1 a.m. she flipped over and out of the soft flannel duvet, dislodged both cats wrapped around her legs and stumbled onto the soft Flokati rug aside her bed. Neither feline was happy about this. Looking outdoors into the woods, Zoey searched for the flying squirrel family who often visited her copper fly-through feeder hanging outside the window sill. A nocturnal breed, these mini squirrels visited almost every night, at various seasons. But tonight was a no-show.

She headed down to the kitchen thinking about how Sam Watson was still managing to disrupt her life. Years of working with him was most difficult, but she loved the patrons and her staff so much, she put up with him for as long as she could. When Zoey took on the part-time position for Sam, she never anticipated what would occur while Sam was overseas on one of his rare book jaunts. Sam was gone a lot and Zoey did some bookkeeping, lots of mail and correspondence, in addition to keeping correct financial records for Sam. Zoey was paid well for just a few hours a week, until one event changed it all. There was not enough money that would equal what Zoey had discovered, to keep her there as Sam's personal assistant. On one rainy afternoon she had to go through some restricted paperwork when Sam called and requested her to do so. Zoey was able to complete the task at hand, which made Sam shout with glee as it involved a pricey rare book and a letter that accompanied it. Zoey saw a bonus for her, for sure. After Zoey was done scanning and sending a copy of this letter to Sam who was in the UK, she tried to lock up the cabinet and somehow the door was stuck, as something was caught near the hinged slot. As she struggled to free it, she pulled on it and discovered there was a hidden space in back of it. A page from a magazine was blocking it. The area was quite large, filling the complete inner back side of the cabinet. Zoey was shocked at first and could not believe what Sam Watson was hiding away from his fabricated perfect world. A collection of sorts, a unique and personal selection of magazines, along with images he had taken of himself with other friends over the years. All of these friends were young in age, all under eighteen and they were all male. Most of the images showed boys in various sexual positions with each other and the photos of Sam were well-planned, apparently by Sam. Sickened by what Zoey had discovered, she did her best to assemble the cabinet to the best of her ability so Sam would never know what she has seen. Weeks later, Zoey gave her notice at the Tuckerman Library and left the position working with Sam. She got Kim to take over this job, temporarily as Sam was traveling overseas. When Zoey told Kim the truth and what she had found, Kim gave her notice, saying her family life was just too busy to handle. Sam was disappointed about Zoey leaving the library and also as his assistant, but life continued on. A short while later, Zoey and her Mom opened Sips and Swap. Over a year had passed since this all became Crazy Town and Zoey was still afraid of what she had discovered. She had an eerie feeling that this was not over and one day the truth would come out exploding into all of their lives. Tossing and turning for the rest of the night, sleep was not going to happen.

Zoey glanced at the clock and was glad to see it was close to 5:30 am. She glanced out on her front lawn to see the morning paper thrown near her driveway. Still in her skimpy chenille robe, she dashed out to see if there was a story of the body found at the library. Inside, sipping her coffee, Zoey glanced through the few pages and saw the brief article. For sure, Kim went into more detail last night than the article that was written. It mentioned what was found and a request from any residents who may have any information regarding this elderly woman, buried in a shallow grave behind Tuckerman Library. Zoey knew it would be a day of gossip at Sips and Swap because of Jonas Parsons, who was the connection to both Zoey and Kim.

Weeks passed by since the body was discovered. Sundays were exceptionally busy at Sips and Swap and this was a holiday weekend in October so travelers usually stopped by. Coconut pineapple muffins were always on the weekend menu along with some tasty breakfast casseroles. Vegan recipes were becoming popular so there were always two creative choices along with a ham or bacon combo for the hearty meat eaters. When Zoey woke up around 4:30, the cats were sound asleep so she decided to leave them at home for the day, making sure to leave some crunchy dry kibble for Dewey and freshly made tuna for Spencer. Zoey would be home by 3 p.m. and spend some time with her girls. A little after 6 am, Zoey picked up her Mom and they headed for work.

After pouring fresh cups of hot coffee, both Liz and Zoey began filling shelves with baked goods. A little past 9 o'clock, Zoey headed over to the swap area of the shop to check the returns box from the days before. People who were regular swappers knew the rules but Zoey, along with her mom, checked the CDs and videos that were returned to make sure all discs were included with every book on tape or video. Occasionally, Zoey did a shopping spree or searched online for the new hot items her residents seemed to enjoy. Always after bargains, Zoey frequented tag or estate sales on weekends. Her business was doing well with more and more customers at the eatery as well as the swap shop. In the swap shop area, there was usually a section for books and videos that were no longer popular and just took up valuable space, so these items were for sale. The tourists took advantage of these inexpensive items.

As she was unloading the returns from the previous two nights, one of Zoey's good friends came into the Swap Shop area and looked terrible, like she had not slept for the entire night. "Carol, you look exhausted. Did you pull a night shift at the hospital?" Carol McAdams was a receptionist in the ER at the local hospital, just minutes from the eatery.

"No, Zoey, but I need your advice." Carol sat in the chair near Zoey's desk. "I do not remember the tick bite, but I think I may have Lyme disease." Carol held her head in the palm of her hands.

"Have you seen the doctor?" Zoey suggested Dr. Joe Haviland.

"No, I have little time, with the kids and my job." She let out a deep sigh. "The severe headache and flu like symptoms began with a vengeance last week. Aspirin helps but it keeps getting worse."

"Carol, get to the doctor, today." Zoey was very serious. She looked at her watch. "Come on, I will take you. Carol. You look awful."

Close to tears and very weak walking, Carol was helped to Zoey's car in the back lot. She ran into the eatery and told her mother to take over the Swap Shop area and why she was leaving. Zoey prayed that Dr. Haviland would be there.

And he was. He saw how concerned Zoey was and took one look at Carol and led her to the exam room. Dr. Haviland did his own blood work when necessary and he took three vials from Carol. He also started her on a heavy duty antibiotic that focused on tick borne diseases. It was only a few minutes before they left the exam room.

"Well, Zoey, your friend is sick, all right, but my guess is Ehrlichia."

"Really?" Zoey looked doubtful. "Not Lyme disease?"

"The severe headache and having it appear in such a rapid manner indicates Ehrlichia, definitely a tick borne disease." He sighed heavily. "We'll know in a day or two when the lab work returns. In any event, she is on a strong 10-day antibiotic. It should help and certainly by tomorrow morning we should see some improvement with the pain."

Driving back to the Eatery, Carol thanked Zoey for her guidance and Zoey was glad to help. Because of her chronic Lyme disease, Zoey helped a lot of friends and strangers sending them to good doctors who believed in tick-borne diseases.

Returning to her Swap Shop, people began to dribble in around a little after 11 and Zoey perked up at her check out desk as A.J. Watson came through from the eatery. "Hey, Mrs. Mitchell."

Zoey always thought A.J. was the cutest kid. Tall and tan from the summer sun, his brownish cropped hair still had blonde highlights from all those days on the golf course.

“Hey A.J.” Zoey flashed a genuine smile at him. “Not on the golf course today?”

“Not any longer since school started. I just do summers now.”

“How is school going?”

“This year is better than the last one, that’s for sure.” A shy laugh escaped as he told her, “Had to come home to find out about the murder.”

“Well, we still don’t know much.” Zoey went on to explain, “Your dad must have told you what he knew, which is pretty limited.”

“Yeah, he did, some old lady died, looks like a homicide.” He sighed, “Pretty scary for our small town.” He waited for her to respond.

She knew by the questioning expression on his face, he was fishing for answers. “Well, Jonas has not gone into any detail with us about this poor woman. We know she was elderly, and it appears she may have been strangled, at least from the very faded marks on her neck. She was covered up very carefully before being place in the ground.”

“Really?” A.J. looked suddenly like the cream in Zoey’s coffee. Pale was being kind. “How long has that lady been there?”

“Read the latest version that has been covered in all of the papers, even the Times.” She looked over at him. “Did you see the articles?

“No, I saw the earlier article when they first discovered the body a few weeks ago. That was online.” A.J. wanted to learn more.

‘Well,” Zoey explained, “The authorities can only release so much information, so even Jonas who is connected to us, is very tight-lipped about this investigation.”

“Right.” A.J. thought he might have found out a bit more about the murder, but it was a no-go. “Hey, Mrs. Mitchell, I have a whole bunch of DVDs I don’t watch anymore, actually collections of them.”

“Really, which ones?”

“Oh, lots of Star Trek, Game of Thrones, and stuff the teens would like.” His blue eyes smiled at her. “May I donate them to your store?”

Zoey was surprised and pleased but would not take advantage of his generous offer. “We could offer to buy the sets if I could take a look at them, A.J.”

“No.” He answered firmly. “I just want to get rid of them.” He was unwavering with this decision.

“Well, I can stop over and take a look at them?”

He looked over at her and hesitated before asking, “Your café is great, how about a deal on maybe free muffins when I am home from school instead of purchasing these DVDs?”

Zoey laughed, silently to herself. “A.J., we have been good friends for years, and I think free muffins is a real deal for us here at Sips and Swaps. Let’s throw in a quiche once in a while, okay?”

“Deal.” He told her. I go back to school later tonight, short weekend, so if you want to take a look at the collections I have, maybe later today?”

“Sure, I leave here around 2 p.m. Tomorrow is the holiday, why are you going back tonight?”

“My Dad gets home from a buying trip late tonight. I want to head back to school and be gone by the time he gets home.” He answered, sounding a bit upset.

“Okay.” Zoey tried to look at him, hoping he would open up the dialog. “Are things okay with you and you dad?”

He just stared at Zoey. “Best response is NO response, Mrs. Mitchell.”

And that comment is where Zoey left it. “I can come by around 3 if that works for you.”

As he headed for the door, he told her, “See you then.”

As Zoey worked through the day, her mom came by to help her sort some things out, and brought her favorite tuna salad plate for lunch. “If the cats were here they would be sharing this with me, you know that, right?”

“I know, but I get more things done while they are at home.” Zoey asked her mother, “Well, how is the gossip going?”

Her mom smiled and bit into her own sandwich, as she sipped a hot caramel latte. “A ton of questions and some wanted to come back here and see you but I shrugged them off, saying you were in the midst of cataloging several new items for swapping.” Liz added, “All were really disappointed in the brief description as to the body found.”

“That does not surprise me,” Zoey went on, “They all want details, as gory as they might be. People love murder mysteries, and they will turn this case into one in no time flat.”

"Did I see A.J. come by earlier today?" Liz asked her

"Yes, you did, and he has a real deal for us." Zoey told her.

"Really?" Liz looked surprised.

'He has several choice DVDs he wants to give us in exchange for muffins when he's home on school break."

Liz coughed slightly, flipping her hair back from her face. "Seriously?"

"I am going over to their house in a little while."

Liz thought for a moment about what she would ask her daughter. "Does A.J. seem okay to you?" She shrugged her shoulders. "When he was young, he was such a happy boy."

Not knowing how to reply, Zoey stayed silent.

"I remember well," Liz began, "when A.J. helped you out at the library. I realize it was years ago, but it seems like yesterday Zoey." She paused, reflecting. "He was such a happy young man, very close to his mom. And then something changed."

As usual, Zoey knew her mom was right. Very intuitive. "I know, mom, and I can't put my finger on it. He used to sail and golf with his Dad and for some time now, he seems so far apart from him."

"What about Grandma Tuckerman…" Liz snickered.

"I remember when A.J. went down to South Carolina to visit her in the summer. Aside from the southern mansion that it was, there were the stables and tennis lessons daily." Zoey told her.

“Where is the old bird, lately?” As Victoria Tuckerman got older, she usually spent late summers here with Marjorie away from all the southern heat and humidity.

“Really, Mom?” Zoey shook her head. “Aren’t you about the same age?”

Liz McCaffery’s dark brown eyes bulged at her daughter’s comments. “I am much younger than her and I look twice as good too. Exercise, and a good diet.”

“Calm down, Jane Fonda.” Zoey laughed with her mother. “You do look great for your age and I can only hope I have your genes.”

“Well, the Lyme disease put a dent in your life, that’s for sure.” Elizabeth gave her a hug. “How are you feeling lately?’

Not totally honest, Zoey did tell her the truth on one issue. “My left knee has been pretty bad lately. I saw my arthro doc last week. Looks like arthroscopic knee surgery soon.” She went on. “Dr. Baxter says I am much too young for a knee replacement and I do have some cartilage left. But, not for long.”

Liz looked at Zoey, truly concerned. “Zoey, you keep things to yourself. I had no idea your knee was so bad.” She asked her, “Can you still do your laps?”

“Yes, I can.” She smiled. “It is on the approved list.”

“You know I can fill in for you here full time, right?”

“I know Mom.” Zoey never wanted to worry her mother. “Andi has offered too. But I will pick the time for this procedure, Mom.” Zoey dug her heels in deep.

“Okay” Liz knew when to agree with her daughter. “Want some company at the Watsons today?”

“So you can snoop?” Zoey lightened up a bit.

Both laughed at this. “We’ll head there in about an hour, okay?”

“Let’s get at it!” Liz told Zoey.

CHAPTER 6

Zoey left Sips and Swap a little before 3 p.m. and then she headed to the Tuckerman mansion, a 10-minute ride on scenic River Road. It was one of Zoey's favorite areas in her town, with most of the affluent homes having enticing water views. She hoped Marjorie was off at one of her meetings or classes, as she was a cultural guru of Highland Falls. In no time Zoey pulled into the long stone-paved driveway and then the impressive Tudor-style home appeared. The autumn colors exploded throughout the many gardens surrounding the Tuckerman home, all professionally manicured. Zoey chuckled to herself, trying to picture Marjorie with a spade in hand, knee-deep in the weeds…never happening.

A.J. saw Zoey as she got out of her car and ran over to say hi. "Mrs. Mitchell, you remember Jesse James, don't you?" A.J. bent down to pet the yellow lab who was very excited to see Zoey.

"I do," Zoey smiled and gave the dog a big hug. "He got so very big in just one year."

"That he did." A.J. smiled telling Zoey, "My Mom got him before I went to college, to make sure I would want to come home."

Liz couldn't resist a long pat on the dog's belly as he rolled over for some loving. "You two do your swap stuff sorting and I will take a little walk with Jesse James, okay?"

As they walked off toward the pond, Zoey told A.J., "He must miss you." A.J. seemed to gaze off where Jesse was walking happily with Liz. "Does your Mom give him lot of attention?" She added, "He was a puppy when you left last year and they need lots of love."

A.J. shook his head looking down at the ground and just sighed. "She does, but she is gone a lot. The staff loves him, especially Millie, our cook. Jesse goes everywhere with her, even grocery shopping."

"Well, love is good from anyone who shares it." Zoey could not resist, "How about your Dad, is he a dog person?"

A.J. hesitated and just looked upset by the question. "Dad has his own meaning for what love means. Let's leave it at that."

Okay, Zoey thought, let's not go there. "So, where are all of these treasures that you'll swap for our tasty muffins?"

A.J. smiled again. "Let's head to our media room to see what your customers would like."

And Zoey was impressed with the home as she walked through a warm, comfortable, and inviting mansion. The media room was enormous and Zoey was astonished as she looked at a movie screen, a large Smart television, and a Bose listening section with comfortable chairs and sofas where you would have to enjoy whatever you chose for entertainment. As A.J. brought out scores of DVDs, audio books, MP3s, Zoey was in Heaven. "A.J., I feel guilty taking these off of your hands. Are you sure it is all right with your parents with this deal?"

A.J. was stern with his reply. "I make my own deals, I'm nineteen now and soon I will be twenty-one." He added, "You have always been a good friend, please take whatever you like."

A.J. sounded so mature. Zoey's Mom was right, where did that happy little boy go? Zoey chose carefully, and ended up with three dozen really good choices, mostly what young adults would like when they visited Sips and Swap. "Well, thank you for all of these, and make sure you come by any time for muffins, or just to visit, okay?"

A.J. began packing up the deal of a lifetime and helped Zoey out to her car. Jesse James ran alongside him and Zoey saw that little boy appear only for a short while. A.J asked her, "How about a cup of coffee before you go?"

"Sure." She hoped A.J. might open up a bit more about his family. As they headed inside, Millie welcomed them into the sunroom and asked what Zoey would like, tea or coffee. Zoey should have brought some muffins…darn it all.

Along with the coffee, some really good butter brickle cookie appeared on a plate for them both. They were so crispy, filled with toffee bits, very addictive. Hmmm, and Zoey thought she was a muffin girl. As they conversed, A.J. opened up in a lively conversation about school, his plans to study law, and some new friends he met. Outside, Liz and Jesse walked back to say goodbye to A.J. Then, Liz and Zoey headed home.

Zoey tried to make some sense about where that happy boy went. As a teenager, he was always very close to Marjorie, playing tennis with her and enjoying his grandmother with vacations down South. But, something changed and fairly recently. What was it? Sam Watson was not the most ideal role model as father of the year. And in the past few years, Sam did travel a lot with his own rare book and antique business. The whole family seemed to have lots of skeletons in the closets. It was only a matter of time before

Zoey would have to discuss a lot with Kim and what happened when her sister quit the job working for Sam Watson. They might have to bring their Mom in on the discussion. It would be a real eye awakening talk and repercussions, for sure. Zoey was glad tomorrow was Monday, a day off. She needed one.

But, Tuesday morning still managed to make its appearance. Day-off Monday was now just a blur. Arising around 4:30 am was not a picnic in the park. Most people think having a cute cozy eatery is sooooo much fun. For Zoey, it really did fulfill her life, especially after she and Will went their own ways. However, the process and work never ended. Crawling out of bed to head for a long hot shower, cats began their morning aerobics, bounding up and down the stairway until their empty dishes became full. Dewey was the whipped crème kitty, getting a tablespoon each morning, prior to their main meal. Spencer heard the aerosol can in use and raced down the stairs joining her sister each day. Zoey showered and around 6:30 she then decided to call Kim. After all, what were sisters for anyhow, especially this sister, married to the town Marshall.

Kim's phone rang over and over, seemed like forever, and where was she this early in the morning? Finally, Kim picked up.

"Why aren't you on your way to work, you'll be late picking up Mom." Kim sounded a bit snarky.

"Wrong side of the bed today?" Zoey gave a little chuckle in her tone.

"I was saying goodbye to Jonas, in the driveway. He got home late last night and we barely talked."

Zoey hesitated before asking, “And?”

“Zoey, he barely said anything, it is pretty hush-hush, and he knows I mention everything to you. He just can’t take a chance with this investigation.” She continued on, “Loose lips, you know.”

“Really, Kim?” Zoey let out a deep sigh. “Jonas knows me better than that. I would never repeat anything this serious.” Sounding as convincing as possible, she went on. “I was the librarian for years, that place was my second home.”

Kim told her sister she would see her later. “Jonas needs me for a few hours this morning and then I can stop by to see you.” She hesitated then told Zoey, “I have a few things I can mention about the case that Jonas told me, but, girl, you need to clam up after I tell you or a divorce might occur.”

“Okay, okay, I got it.” She told her laughing, “Now, get to work, assistant to the Marshall and I will see you later.”

Zoey left the cats home for the day, as they were sound asleep after whipped cream and two dishes of flaked tuna shreds. Out like a light. Liz was ready and waiting, peering out the front doorway for the taxi to arrive. “Hey, Mom,” she told her, window down with a big wave.

“Good morning, a bit chilly.” Liz let out a sigh. “Winter is on the way, gads I should have rented that condo when we last visited St. Maarten.”

“And, what about the hurricane that just landed there a few months ago?”

“No worries,” she answered in an island tone.” I would be like the three little pigs in my resilient stone house gazing at the blue-green water from my veranda…and a generator ready to go."

"Okay, Mom, I think we need to plan a trip to the Caribbean this winter."

"Really?" Liz asked in a serious tone.

"Why not?" Kim can watch the kitties for a few days and I may need my knee done, remember? I will need a week or two to rest and get some warm sun on my body." She breathed a long sigh. "I need to look forward to something after the holidays and the doctor says early January is when I can do my knee."

"Well," Liz grinned. "That is a plan." She got her phone out and penciled in a date on her calendar. "When is the arthroscopic knee to be done?"

"I think on January tenth." Zoey sounded a bit apprehensive. "One good part is it is now an out-patient procedure, no hospital stay."

Liz beamed. "Well, by end of January we will be able to hop on a plane and head to my favorite island." She added, "Does Sam still have a timeshare there?"

"I think they are on St. Barth's. When Marjorie wants to escape the cold weather here, spending a few weeks there is always her decision."

Zoey remembered how many pleasant memories her mom and dad had visiting St. Maarten several times over twenty-five years. After her dad died, Liz could not bring herself to go. "Okay, mom, get your planner out and work up some magic for us."

After they arrived at Sips and Swap, there wasn't a moment to spare. Her mom was as organized as ever and the girls were life-savers in the kitchen. Within an hour the place would be busy with the early birds, wanting a favorite muffin, a latte or a flavorful cup of tea. Liz ordered some special tea blends from the Bahamas, and one was a rum flavor that several people asked for. It had a bit of real rum in it and as the tea leaves brewed, the eatery hummed like heaven. Zoey had boxes of the unwanted items from A.J. and she would focus on cataloging and getting them ready for swapping. People would love the selection, especially the younger adults.

As Zoey went back and forth from her car to the shop, she thought she noticed Sam Watson driving down the street, in his fancy automobile. The large 850 BMW he drove was a special ordered vehicle, with all the bells and whistles anyone would hope for. A shiny, dark blue beauty was hard to miss in Highland Falls. His wife, poor Marjorie had to tool around in her older model Jaguar convertible. A.J. told Zoey his dad would return from his trip today and then A.J. would be off to school, hopefully missing his father at home? That is the impression Zoey got when speaking to Sam's son. Zoey's mom was onto something, A.J. was not the happy kid he used to be. But, Zoey had no time to get involved in that mystery. Right now, she needed to focus on what happened in back of the library.

As Zoey finished unloading her car, the shiny, dark blue beauty pulled into Sips and Swap, right next to the front door entrance. As Zoey worked her way to the back doorway to unload the donations from A.J. she thought, what is Sam doing here so early? Sighing, Zoey knew she had to face him. After all, it was her eatery and no one there liked Sam. The girls never liked serving him, as he always found something to complain about. What a way to start this day.

CHAPTER 7

Zoey managed to get all of the donations from A.J. neatly into her back storage area before heading out to the eatery area. There was no way to avoid Sam so she wanted to get it over with.

Just opening up, the girls were busy scurrying around ready for customers on this crisp fall day. Liz headed over to the table where Sam sat, watching him brushing away invisible crumbs from the clean tablecloth. "Sam, very early to see you today."

He looked over the menu card which listed the specials of the day and Liz waited for the critical appraisal. "May I have a French vanilla latte, skim milk and one of your special Crumble Peach muffins?"

Liz was taken aback by his easy request, usually a difficult choice for one reason or another…does it have any almonds in it…or any heavy cream in the latte…Liz was quick to serve this customer. "No problem, Sam, it will ready in no time."

"Is Zoey around today?"

Liz hesitated, looking towards the swap area room. "She is, and will be out soon."

"Please tell her I'd like a word with her." Sam flashed a friendly smile towards Liz.

"Will do."

Liz made it back to the kitchen with Sam's order. "Do this ASAP, it's for Sam Watson, and no mistakes, okay?" Then Liz called Zoey on her cell phone to warn her about Sam.

She saw Sam as soon as she came out from the swap area and went right over to say hello.

"Sam, you are up early today." Zoey sat down hoping this would be a quick meeting. "How are you handling this messy event?"

"You have that right," he went on. "It is a mess and we need to clear it up quickly with holidays on the way and so many tourists visiting here."

Zoey thought to herself, gads how cold is that, just get it over with. "Sam, do they have any idea who this person is?" Zoey wanted more info. "Is it true that is an older woman?

He just stared at Zoey. "Yes, and that is about all I can say because we have no idea who she is." He couldn't help but embellish a bit more. "It could be a person who wandered away from home, from anywhere north or south of Highland Halls. Police are busy contacting retirement facilities for any missing persons."

"That sounds very sad to me."

In no time, Sam's order arrived. "All set, Sam." Liz smiled hoping to keep this going smoothly.

"Liz, did you not hear me, I said To Go."

And here it started, as usual. "Sorry, Sam, I will get this muffin wrapped up for you."

Liz really had to bite her tongue, but it was no surprise. Sam was a real spoiler of sorts. It was best to let it go as he always wanted some type of minor altercation, almost an attention getter.

He looked over at Zoey. "I hear you had a nice visit with A.J. yesterday, taking away a lot of his used books." He added with a sarcastic tone, "I hope you did not take advantage of his kindness."

That was it for Zoey. "Really, Sam?"

"Well, the books, DVDs, are worth quite a bit, do you have plans for them?"

"I thought I would hit the black market sales racks and make a bundle." Zoey let out a deep sigh. "They will be used for swaps in our shop for all to enjoy. I have a very successful business here and residents love to come here."

Liz buzzed over with Sam's wrapped muffin and latte. "All set, Sam, it is on us, and have a nice day."

Zoey got up and said, "Sam, it is always a pleasure to see you, but I have a store to run."

And that was that.

As Zoey headed back to the swap area of her business, she could not put Sam Watson out of her head. Knowing him and his rigid demeanor for years now, she was not surprised to see a positive attitude on anything, including his son, A.J. There was something wrong in this nest, with A.J. Marjorie and Sam. A.J. had the closest relationship with his grandmother and spent most of his younger day summers down in South Carolina. In no time, he was able to work at the prestigious Highland Falls Golf Club, these past few years. Then, the close relationship with his grandmother faded. Maybe that is partly why Marjorie split with her Mom. The town gossip gals were keen on this, as it was quite a distraction one day in town where Marjorie had a screaming fit with her mother. Days after, in late August, Victoria Tuckerman flew back to her hot and humid southern home. Rumors flew around and it appeared that in September, Marjorie's mother was due to take a three month European cruise to get away from it all. Marjorie insisted that Sam take her to Bradley International for her early morning flight. Sam was not all right with that order, but Victoria did still control the purse strings in that entire family, including the budget for The Tuckerman Library.

Back in the swap area, there was a lot of cataloging to complete as the donations from A.J. were plentiful with an assortment of titles that everyone would enjoy. A.J. was such a nice boy, now growing into a young man. Zoey missed her cats, as they really were her family now, always dedicated and loving, no matter what, unless she forgot to buy "Redi-Whip" for their daily treat. As she finished up listing several titles on her laptop computer, Carol McAdams came in the swap area to say hello.

"Carol, how is that Lyme bite doing?" Zoey asked her with a smile.

"Finally after weeks on the proper meds, I am doing fine, thanks to your help." Carol went on, "However, someone is not doing so well." She placed a tall wicker basket on the floor and uncovered the item in need.

Zoey looked totally puzzled as she peered into the basket and then heard a meek cry. "Oh my gosh, where did she come from?" It was a very tiny and frightened black and white spotted kitten.

"I found her early this morning in my back woods in this basket!" Carol sighed. "Can you imagine, someone doing this, and just knowing I would help her? She is a female and about 7-8 weeks old. I took her to Dr. Barkley. I hoped he might recognize who she belonged to, but no luck."

Zoey could not resist, having rescued two needy kittens just a year ago. She reached in and scooped her up for a warm hug. The purring began immediately. "Oh, boy, aren't you precious?" Not expecting a reply, Zoey continued to pet her.

"She needs a home, Zoey. Between the hospital's crazy schedule and my two big dogs it wouldn't work." Carol looked at Zoey with pleading eyes. "Would your mother consider taking her, as she has no animals now?" Carol sighed. "Or…how about you?"

Zoey just could not comment, not with this very loving creature in her arms. "I just don't know if I could do another cat…or if Spencer and Dewey would accept her. They are all females, so that is a plus." She shook her head, thinking. "I could check with Mom, she is right outside…"

Out they went with basket in hand and a mewing creature trying to crawl up and out of her crate. Liz was in the kitchen area and smiled a hello when she saw Carol. "Hey there, how are you feeling?" Liz could not help but peek into the wicker basket, after she heard some meek cries.

"I am fine, Liz, but I have a kitten who needs a home."

Carol reached in to scoop her up and into the arms of Liz McCaffery.

"Oh, my, what a darling and she has double paws." A small black and white spotted and striped creature with soft rabbit like fur was hard to resist. Zoey and Liz stared at each other.

Liz told Zoey, "If you want to try her out with your girls, see what happens. They could use a friend." Liz gently smiled at her daughter. "If it doesn't work, I can take her. Would that work?"

Zoey just couldn't say no. "Well, she will need to be spayed."

Carol told Zoey, "No problem. I did her check-up and all of her shots. Her weight needs to increase a bit before she can be spayed. Kevin Barkley said probably in just two weeks."

Zoey looked at the clock and in just two hours they would head for home. It was Sunday and tomorrow a day off. The best day to try out the kitten.

"Look, Zoey, I sprung this on you. Why don't you let me drop off this baby girl after you get home and get settled?"

Zoey smiled and was a bit anxious, thinking of her two other girls. "Let's give it a try-bring her by about 5 today." She looked over at Carol. "Will that work?" Zoey added, "By then, I may have a name for her."

The next two hours flew by. On her way home, Zoey stopped at the store for kitten food, and another can of whipped cream for her girls to make sure they were still on her favorite list. She knew their feelings would be hurt, there was no doubt about it. She would add some fresh tuna for Spencer before the new arrival at 5 p.m.

Once at home, Zoey's knee began to throb, after unloading some groceries, cleaning litter pans, and preparing for the new addition. Zoey decided to keep the kitten solo for the first few days, especially when they all retired for bed that night. That would decrease hurt feelings, with no third cat on Zoey's bed. As Zoey watched the news on MSNBC, a big Senate race in Florida was happening, a replacement for someone who had passed earlier this fall. Her favorite journalist was Mika Brzezinski, and she always liked her name. And, that was that. The kitten would be "Mika."

CHAPTER 8

It was almost 5:30 when Carol arrived with Mika. Dewey and Spencer were prancing around, peering out the front window to see who was coming to visit. They would be in for a surprise. As Zoey opened the front door, Carol came in, smiling. "Thank you so much, I would not ever sleep tonight unless I knew this little one was taken care of."

Basket on the carpeted front hallway, the curious feline, teeny as she was, prompted a very brave demeanor as she edged up and out of the basket. Zoey commented, "I guess she, or newly named Mika is tired of being in jail."

Both ladies laughed, but Dewey and Spencer were frozen, both on the bottom stairs peering at the new arrival. "Quite a strong name for this little girl," Carol told Zoey.

It only took a few minutes for Zoey's felines to edge over to investigate. Then the hissing started and Spencer ran upstairs, to the top of the landing. Dewey remained, continued to investigate, and soon the kitten crawled slowly over to Dewey, only to be sniffed. No hissing though. Just curiosity as Dewey's saucer-like eyes peered over at the squirming kitten.

"Well, I will be on my way." Carol told her. "Keep me posted where Mika will finally end up, and I have a feeling it will be here."

Zoey scooped up Mika and with Dewey following, they headed for the kitchen. A small bowl of warm milk for Mika and a tablespoon of whipped cream for Dewey. Both girls approved of the treats. The next important issue was an additional small litter pan, slowly coaching this kitten just what to do. It only took one time and Mika found her pan, later that night before bed. Smart little girl.

Zoey felt exhausted, and a bit overwhelmed, taking on this new feline. A comfy basket with soft fleece lining found the new girl fast asleep in the living room, near the gas fireplace. Dewey was asleep on the couch, resting on her warming pillow. It did not take long before Spencer appeared to oversee what had occurred. Zoey gave Spencer a small dish of tuna and all went pretty well. She looked over at Mika but kept her distance, for that first night. Zoey placed the litter pan in a convenient spot and kept Mika separate from her girls that first night. They all fell fast asleep before 9 o'clock.

Thank God for day off Mondays. A good night's sleep helped them all. Zoey was very stiff climbing out of bed, and it was around 7 a.m. when the day began. All hungry, cats and birds began the start of Zoey's morning. Surprisingly, there was little hissing from any of the cats. Mika edged her way over to both of the big cats and then scooted away to her basket. Having raised many cats throughout the years, Zoey was in familiar territory.

In the weeks to come, there was some hissing, hiding, and then final acceptance of Mika. She was too small to take to Sips and Swap, so the two senior girls went off with Zoey to work during the weeks to follow. They felt special doing this. Mika had her spay surgery on a Monday a week later so Zoey could be home with her and she rested at home. With holidays soon to occur, there were three crazy cats running all around the house, playing. There honestly is nothing better than a new kitten. But there was no hope for the small artificial Christmas tree, brightly decorated, and lit in the huge floor-to-ceiling window in the living room. The experienced girls showed Mika just how to climb up on those many branches that withstood the rigorous attempts to collapse the tree. Never happened. But it tired out the kitten as she slept soundly in her new basket. Zoey wished this could be her entire life, but work, her bad knee, and the murder in her small town took over her peaceful at home life.

As fall turned into winter, there was no progress in finding out the identity of the woman buried behind the Tuckerman Library. There were several residents who contacted the state police hoping they could provide info about who this could be. It began to look like an out-of-town visitor. Highland Falls was a well-known destination for its fall leaves attraction, with abounding fairs throughout the region. November was fairly slow at Sips and Swap, and then Christmas season saw a rise in many visitors to Zoey's store. With three cats now, most days Zoey left the girls at home. They all played and slept together as a family should. The only problem was the bed. King size was on order, as queen was just too small.

With Sips and Swap decorated for the holiday season, Zoey was feeling more tired than usual, due to her right knee, swollen most days and eager for surgery only weeks away. Damn the Lyme disease. Patrons loved visiting her store at this time of year and then on the day after a busy lunch period, a stranger appeared and asked to speak with the owner. Liz brought the tall professionally dressed woman in the side room for swapping and headed back to the eatery to see Charles in Charge (Zoey).

"Zoey Mitchell?"

"I am, and you are....?" Zoey looked doubtful, having recognized who this was.

Her hand stretched out to Zoey, "I am Miranda Prescott, from CRP news in Hartford. We have seen some interest in what occurred behind the Tuckerman Library some months ago. Not resolved yet, is that correct?"

Zoey thought she sounded like an attorney and did not like her serious tone. "I do not think I am the one that you should be asking questions about concerning this crime. Perhaps you should see Jonas Parsons, our town law enforcement officer."

Prescott put on her happy face and gently asked, "You used to be the town librarian, right?"

"Used to be." Zoey answered. "It has been well over a year now."

"We are trying to investigate this as a cold case as no one seems to care about what happened here." She went on. "We have a segment on our station that handles forgotten cases like this. This poor old lady may have been robbed, was homeless…" Zoey interrupted her.

"I believe the police should handle this, not an investigative TV show. I am no longer connected with the Tuckerman Library. Perhaps you should contact the director, Samuel Watson."

"We just thought you might be able to add something to the segment we are planning."

Gads, Zoey thought, wait until Sam hears about this. "Sorry, I have no time nor the interest to be involved with this." Zoey got up from her chair and showed Ms. Prescott where the door was.

Liz came in after the lady left and asked Zoey what happened. Zoey explained, "Mom, what is going on here? This is not an exciting murder case. I can't believe our peaceful little town will have a segment on a news station."

"Maybe they know more than we do and someone wants to get to the bottom of it." Liz sounded concerned. "Or, maybe they have no good news and this is a human interest story, around the holidays, perhaps a missing loved one…buried and forgotten."

"Mom, really? You have been reading too many romance novels. Let Sam deal with this," Zoey said with a big sigh. "He loves attention."

Liz added, "From what I hear, he is getting very little from Marjorie. They seem to be having separate lives these days."

"Certainly apart from A.J and he really wants no part of Sam." Zoey was sure of one thing that saddened her. "I think he only comes home to see his dog. He really misses Jesse James."

After they closed up shop, Zoey called Kim and told her what had happened. It was during dinner that Jonas called Zoey when he got home from the station. "Zoey, what the hell happened with this news person?"

"I told Kim everything, it was a brief visit. They wanted my take as the ex-librarian as to who this may have been."

"She never stopped here, you know that?" Jonas began to complain using some nasty language. "I would like to know what her angle is, though. Gads we have investigated, and have no idea who this was. No clues on the body, no connections to any elder homes in the area. We are just stuck with this case."

"Well, Jonas, I am not getting involved with this. Much as I like to solve fictional murder cases, this is way beyond my expertise."

"Okay, Zoey, just e-mail me her name and contact info, okay?" He went on, """I will see if I can call the station and see exactly what they are after."

The next morning arrived, after another restless night of sleep. Looking at the three cats spread out on the bed, now king sized, brought a smile to Zoey's face. Off to work, to see what the crowd would be talking about today.

It was only a little after 7 a.m. when the door to Sips and Swap flew open, partially from the wind, but mainly from Sam Watson.

CHAPTER 9

All eyes stared at Sam as he entered Sips and Swap. It was suddenly quiet for such an early start to the day. Zoey took charge as her minions were busy getting the eatery ready for the morning rush and also a bit shell shocked from seeing Sam as the first person of the day. “Sam, you are here early. Why?” Zoey’s tone was a bit frosty.

“How could you send that news lady to my home yesterday? I am glad Marjorie was off exercising or she would have been very upset as she blustered into our home. She began by demanding answers as to why nothing had been resolved about the body found at our town library.”

Zoey was used to Sam’s rude manner but she really had nothing to lose by snapping back, showing her honesty and truths. “Sam, I am not involved in this and I am no longer at Tuckerman. You as the board director need to handle this.” Pausing to make sure her words were clear, “They want some answers as Prescott is a decent investigative reporter. They do cold cases and it has been several weeks with no knowledge as who this poor woman was or where she came from.”

“We must stop Prescott as we do not need any nonsense in the news exploiting our peaceful seaside town that attracts many tourists.” He waited for Zoey to respond. Nothing. “Your own business could suffer from this, do you want to visit a town where a murder has occurred?”

“Really, Sam?” Zoey sighed in frustration. “Maybe she was a tourist and who knows what happened, but murder?”

"That is what I mean!" Sam's voice was becoming loud and stern. "We need to clamp this down. Talk to your brother-in-law to close this file. It is his job."

"I will call Jonas, but Sam, I am done here." Zoey put on her apron to help the girls, as they had fallen behind. "I have a business to run."

Sam left, slamming the door and skidded from the parking lot in his BMW. Such a teenager in that automobile. Driving home his stress was worsening and not only from that Prescott woman. It was mainly due to that text he had received late last night, and it was totally unexpected. Another issue he had to deal with ASAP. How did Gil Andrews get his cell number?? Sam was very careful about contact information on his last trip abroad back in October. He would have to e-mail him today because no trips to London were planned until the middle of January. What was Gil up to? Sam thought of changing his cell phone number but that would be a real mess due to his many contacts.

Marjorie was still asleep when Sam arrived home and that was all right with him. Lately all there was, was nagging, nagging. Their finances were tightening up, with all the school expenses from A.J. and Victoria Tuckerman was seriously reviewing their budget. She was just an interfering bitch, but Marjorie loved her mother and their good life was actually due to her.

Yawning as she came down the front stairway, Marjorie was a very attractive woman. She worked tirelessly to keep her youthful looks. Keeping trim was a goal for her and exercise was a must. Her dark wavy hair was just above her shoulders and the shiny highlighted streaks erased ten years off her age, as she resembled an energetic college student. "What are you doing up, so early driving in and out of the yard at ninety miles an hour?" she asked her husband.

"We are having a problem with a news reporter who is meddling in the police investigation of that dead woman behind our library."

Shaking her head in disbelief, Marjorie responded, "No compassion on any level, is that it?"

Sighing, Sam told her, "We need to end this issue." He added, "I hoped Zoey could help us out here, but she is too busy with her gossip shop. We still have no idea who this woman was. The body was cremated after weeks of no clues as to who she was or belonged to."

"She wasn't a lost dog, Sam." Disgusted with his attitude she added, "Maybe this reporter will find out just what happened here."

Sam exploded. "We need to end it. I have no time for gossip-loving busy bodies." He headed over to his den, serving as his private office. "I have a lot of work to catch up on, so do not disturb me today. Your mother has cut back some of the library budget and I have to perform miracles to keep this library above board."

Marjorie smiled telling Sam, "Yesterday, I got a postcard from her, as she was heading for another day of working her way through Great Britain, via trains, boats, or tours."

Sam was careful replying to her. "Really?" He was not surprised about the postcard. "I thought you were not on speaking terms with her before she left on the 3 month voyage?" Sam could only imagine how much that would cost. He was sure that was the real reason behind his budget cuts at the library. Selfish witch, and more work for Sam.

Staring squarely at her husband, Marjorie replied, "She is my mother and in case you have a memory fog, she pays for most of our expenses."

"Well, I'm glad she is enjoying herself." And off Sam went, into the den, to work on budgets.

"I have indoor tennis and my exercise class this morning and lunch with Lydia." Marjorie added. We are completing the volunteer efforts for the Toys for Tots Program and I will be gone for most of the day." She added sarcastically, "You know…compassion, caring."

"I have a dinner meeting with some library board members so you are not the only busy person." The door shut loudly as he entered the den.

"I will see you tonight then." And off she went back upstairs with Jesse James following her. "Come on Jesse, Millie will be here soon to keep you company."

Sam was happy he had the day by himself to resolve many issues. It was a little before 8 a.m. in Highland Falls and London would be around 2 in the afternoon. Sam answered his text, hoping he could reach Gil Andrews about *that* matter. The text went through and Sam waited.

Sam kept busy working on various budgets, personal as well as business and library spending. He had no love for Zoey but he missed her expertise as she was the best librarian you could have, especially for Highland Falls. Patrons loved her, from toddlers to seniors. Jason Ramsey took over for her, and people liked him too. But, he was very dependent on Sam for everything, the opposite of Zoey Mitchell.

It was a little after 3 o'clock when the text arrived. Sam asked for a phone number for Gil as he really needed to speak to him. In minutes, Sam unlocked a drawer, found a different cell phone and then he called Gil.

"And, how are you doing Sam, after our meeting back in October? On my end it went very well."

I'll bet it did, Sam thought. "How did you get my personal cell phone number?"

"Is that important?"

"Yes, it is." Sam was firm and a bit irritated. "You have this number to phone me, no texts, just leave a message. It keeps things very clear, stable, and private."

"Got it." Gil went on. "I just thought you might like to know the items you gave me to sell are a done deal and if you have any other items on the scale of those last ones, I have a buyer."

To help the budget constrictions, Sam was forced to grasp a desperate solution. No one needed to know about these details. He had, in his possession, a safe that he used for pricey items, personal as well as items in his rare books and antiquities business. In that safe were some of Victoria Tuckerman's valuable jewelry. Years ago, she chose to trust Sam to keep these separate treasures from her daughter. That was her wish and it was not up to Sam to question her motives. What a big mistake that was for her. It would appear that the old hag would probably forget she had done this. The first pieces Sam had given to Gil were worth close to a million dollars. Gil paid him a little more than half of this and off they went to the black market. Diamond rings, earrings and an emerald bracelet were high end products and now were relocated far away from Highland Falls. Sam smiled, knowing that doing the budgets today might be a bit easier than he thought.

“I will be in touch when I visit you after the holidays. I have your contact numbers, and please respect mine.”

“Sounds good to me Sam.” He added. ”Those jewels won’t be missed?”

Sam did not like that tone, a bit on edge, he was quick to reply. “Not your problem, Gil.” He told him in a firm tone. “I will see you in January of the new year.”

“I am trusting you, Sam.” Concerned, he added, “I do not need to go off to prison in my golden years should any of these jewels become questionable.”

“No worries.” And Sam hung up his phone, carefully locking it away in the third drawer down.

As the day turned into the dinner hour, Marjorie was still away. Sam finished polishing up the financial issues and all would work out well for a while. In January, Sam would do some business with his antiques in the U.K. where he always had interested and affluent buyers. He would also meet with Gil as there were a few more items he would be thrilled in seeing and he could relocate them for a sizable price. Before he showered, dressed for his dinner, to attend the board meeting at 7 p.m., Sam had to take another look into his private safe. Best to do this with Marjorie gone.

Opening the safe, there was more than pricey items in there. The collection of photos that Sam had made years ago were still there. He must destroy them soon. If there were ever found by anyone, there would be hell to pay personally and professionally. Years ago, Sam was in a difficult stage of his life. He began experimenting sexually with other interested persons. What he had done was now forgotten but it had to be erased, burned, or better off buried, like the body at the library. For now, he shoved them all to the back of the safe.

Opening a variety of small pouches and boxes, Sam's grin expanded. More emeralds and sapphires than Sam had remembered, along with a sparkling diamond tennis bracelet. Placing the jewels carefully back in their containers, he realized now just how much his mother-in-law was worth. She owed Sam a lot more than jewels as he had put up with her for far too many years. Her interference began on the day they were married. Sam realized that he would have little say in many issues during their twenty-five years of marital bliss. When A.J. was born, Victoria Tuckerman even controlled her grandson. A.J. was very close to his grandmother and as a youngster, he spent many happy summers in South Carolina, riding any horse he desired. There was also a bright spot in that summer scenario as for several weeks, Marjorie accompanied her son when he chose to stay with his grandmother. They say money can't buy happiness but that wasn't working out with this family. With Marjorie gone for a few weeks, Sam had unlimited freedom and he enjoyed this space. Marjorie would discuss finances with her mother, and end of summer, there was always a new piece of jewelry that Victoria bought for her daughter. That saved Sam the expense of an expensive bauble for his wife. One plus for Victoria Tuckerman and also the payments to private school for A.J.

So many jewels, too many to count or remember. Would Victoria ever figure out what he had done with these jewels? Never. He was very, very certain about that. However, Marjorie might someday discover something was wrong here. And, Gil's apprehension about the relocation of these jewels forced Sam to consider another option. Before Sam's next trip abroad in January, perhaps he should make some fine copies, as he had many contacts who could send him to a trustworthy dealer. He smiled to himself, thinking, enjoy your 3-month voyage Victoria. I am so relishing your being gone.

CHAPTER 10

With Christmas just weeks away, Zoey had far too much to handle. And her knee has been more than bothersome. On her feet daily for 10 or more hours was not helping. Whoever thought Zoey would look forward to outpatient knee surgery? She was really ready, not thrilled with surgery but she knew the trip to St. Maarten would happen weeks later as part of her recovery. So many years ago, she and Will spent their honeymoon on the Dutch side of St Maarten. It was magical, with friendly islanders, warm, clean sandy beaches with lots of privacy. Nude beaches were widely accepted on both the Dutch and French sides of this island. It was not part of Zoey's agenda but they did have their eyes full as both men and women strolled the beaches with little or no clothing. St. Maarten was a familiar destination for Zoey and that's why her mother chose this spot. Who wanted to learn about a new island destination when both Liz and Zoey just needed to rest and relax? Unfortunately, this rest period was weeks away, with Zoey was now immersed in the real world.

Sips and Swap was in a busy holiday mode with customers sampling all of the special winter flavors in hot beverages and pastries. Zoey always remembered to order the finest brand of egg nog coffee, rum flavored, that people loved. Puff pastries were now offered with an egg nog flavor, heavily spiced with vanilla. Some were plain, others had fruit fillings or were sprinkled with sugar-crusted pecans and almonds. However, none of these holiday treats could erase the memory of the body found behind the Tuckerman Library.

The latest news was that the Prescott reporter was planning a segment in early January on the body at Tuckerman Library. She had just been in contact with Jonas and Sam Watson, too. No one was stopping her. That was certain. Her rights and free speech had spoken. On Sunday, Zoey asked Kim and Jonas over for dinner. She hoped to be filled in with all that was happening for this programming event.

As tired as Zoey felt, she was eager to see Kim and hoped Jonas would finally give her some details about the dead woman. In no time, the story would air, so Zoey thought she was entitled to have some of this info to think about. So, she sipped down a large iced Coke and some cheese and crackers to snack on. Both gave her some energy so she could prepare a light meal for her sister and Jonas. Jonas loved a Cobb salad so that was on the menu. There was also some leftover ham and pea soup, so Zoey assembled the meal. She carved up some white chicken breast from a bought rotisserie version, added lots of crisp romaine lettuce, baby spinach, hard-boiled egg, crispy bacon, sweet sliced Vidalia onions, and chunks of pungent-flavored bleu cheese. Zoey always had her homemade creamy vinaigrette on hand so tossing on some croutons completed the meal.

Zoey had time to do the litter pans and feed her girls. Mika was already growing into a gorgeous young cat. Her black and white spots along with thick stripes on her rabbit-like fur saw her becoming the prettiest girl on the block. Spencer and Dewey accepted her into their home and thank God for the king size bed. Right before Kim and Jonas arrived, the phone rang and as Zoey checked her caller ID hoping to avoid Sam Watson, but she saw the number belonged to Will. She picked up the phone, wondering, a little worried why he was calling. It was a rare occurrence unless it involved Hannah.

"Will?" Zoey cautiously asked him. "Are you okay?"

"Well," Will faintly sighed. "Some changes in my life. I used to bounce things off you and I am hoping that you might find the time to talk to me."

Sounds pretty convenient, but the same old Will came through. Their marriage had worked out fairly well for the first few years, but then a selfish side erupted within Will's usually kind and friendly personality. He had a teacher's degree but chose to be a golf pro, the instructor for numerous classes and he was able to travel to many places in the United States and abroad for a good amount of money. Always financially generous and kind to both Zoey and Hannah, who he dearly loved, sometimes he was just out for himself on many other issues. Throughout the years, he just was not there for her. The Lyme disease bout did it and that is when Will filed for divorce. The once vibrant and healthy Zoey was no longer. When Zoey needed him the most he left. Always fairly independent, Zoey began to handle her life, alone.

"Bounce off me, did I hear that right?" She added, "Not using a golf ball, right?"

Will loved Zoey's humorous personality, among other traits. At this point in his mid-life, Will realized what a big mistake he had made. "I am thinking of moving back to Highland Falls, being a little closer to my Dad. Since Mom died, he is a lost soul. Still independent and golfing, but that is it for his social life." His dad, about 20 miles north of Highland Falls, had a small condo with a view of Long Island Sound that seemed to work for him.

Zoey was a bit shell-shocked with this news and the possibility that Will would soon be part of her life. Her dinner with Kim and Jonas would include a small disruption as part of the menu. "I am really busy right now, Will, dinner guests." However, she had no doubt in her mind that she would be there to listen, because that is who she was. "Can you phone me later, maybe around 8 o'clock?"

"Zoey, that means the world to me."

"And where is the Barbie doll?"

"Jamie and I have been apart for months now, it never developed, like we did."

That was probably good, because look how that ended. "Really?" Zoey had a hidden smile.

"Zoey, is there any small, even minute chance we could try again?"

Oh, my God, Zoey could not find the words. "8 o'clock, okay?" The tone was abrupt.

His quiet tone was almost like a silent cheer, "Will do, Zoey."

When Kim and Jonas arrived Zoey greeted them with a large glass of iced wine in her hand. "Come on in guys." The three hostess cats strolled over to greet them.

Kim looked a bit baffled at Zoey who was not an avid wine drinker. She looked really thirsty the way the wine disappeared.

"A beer for you, Jonas?" Zoey smiled warmly at him as he scooped up

Mika.

"This one is a winner, what a cute cat." Jonas snuggled against her soft fur." I think I will have some of that wine, looks like it has made you pretty jolly."

"Oh, this is not a jolly look." Zoey got their drinks and refilled her own. "Before you got here, I received a call from Will."

Kim was not sure how to respond. She always got along well with Will and for years Zoey and Will did really well, partly due to Hannah. She was close to both her Dad and Zoey and that was how it should be.

"And, what is going on?" Kim asked her sister eager to hear the entire story.

"I really don't know. A while back he broke it off with the Barbie doll and he is considering moving back here, to be close to his Dad."

"And close to you, maybe?"

Zoey drained her wine glass deciding she had had enough. "He says he'd like to bounce some ideas off me, I guess like to see what sticks?" Zoey shook her head a bit dismayed.

"And when is that going to happen?" Kim asked her. "He is not coming here to stay in the guest room, is he?"

"Oh, no, not going to happen." Zoey started to bring the salad out to the kitchen table. "I only promised a phone call, later tonight."

“Very generous of you to be his sounding board when life doesn’t go well.” Jonas would always be on Zoey’s side. He remembered what happened when Zoey was so ill with her Lyme disease. “Be careful, Zoey, your life, aside from that bum knee is going pretty well, these days. You have three lovely children still at home,” he told her laughing, “and pretty soon you’ll have your own Vet to take care of them.” He asked her, “Does Hannah know about this?”

“Not that I know of,” Zoey’s smile turned upside down. “I will get the details tonight.” Food was ready to eat, yummy pea soup and a crisp and tasty Cobb salad. “Let’s eat and then I want details about the body, okay?” She looked squarely at Jonas. He nodded a yes and everyone’s attitude lightened up.

After finishing dinner they were soon all relaxed with a fresh pot of Christmas tea and a warm crackling fire to enjoy. “Jonas, this news story is going to air and what Prescott says will be for all to hear.” She looked directly at her brother-in-law. “Spill it. I need details. Is the case officially closed?”

Jonas began.” Not officially, just not active. We had no other options. Please do not repeat this, Zoey.” He looked over at her with his official stare.

“Got it.” Zoey asked him, “What about dental records?”

“The woman had removed dentures.” Shaking his head, Jonas continued. “Searching that angle is always complicated. But, she had no teeth. We all found that strange. Who removes their teeth?” He added, “This confirmed that it was a suspicious death. Teeth were removed, we think, for identity reasons. That made us consider, maybe a local person. And, her neck area had marks that led us to believe that she could have been strangled. Her rings had been removed too, as the tone of her skin on two fingers was proof of that." Jonas concluded. "So, it appears that it may have been robbery, perhaps a relative sick of taking care of Mom?"

"That is just creepy." Zoey asked Jonas, "Why bury her in back of our library?"

"We have no idea. Someone stupid, as construction plans changed, moving plans further back on library property. I guess the killer wasn't paying attention to what was happening."

"And apparently, that poor old woman wasn't paying attention to her precious life either."

CHAPTER 11

Zoey cleaned up the messy kitchen, loaded the dishwasher, and turned off all downstairs lights. Door locked, cats fed, Zoey took a hot shower and noticed that the clock was very close to eight o'clock. Will would call on time, as that's what he did. Never late, never early, just precise.

Cats were snuggled all on the bed right near Zoey when Will called. "Hey Zoey."

"What is happening, Will, besides a mid-life crisis?" Zoey was quite frank with her ex-husband.

"I know this is a lot for you to take on, after what I put you through so many years ago." He let out a deep breath, hoping to make some sense out of this needy request. "Is there any room for forgiveness?"

Gads, what a really stupid way to win her back. Just say how really, really wrong he was to do what he did to her. Say the sorry part first thing and then beg for another chance. "Will, we are way beyond forgiveness. I have moved on with my life. We have Hannah. She is a major part of us but you and me is a really difficult stretch to accomplish."

"If I move back and stay with Dad, can we at least revive our friendship and see where it goes?"

"What will you do here, Mr. Golf Pro?"

"I have a coaching job all lined up at the college in Rockville, not far from where Dad lives." He waited for her approval.

"That's great, Will. We have been able to remain friends, but there are no benefits here. Hannah was our benefit."

"That is a start for me, after how I left you." He paused with another deep sigh. "I am really sorry, Zoey, and have been all these years." He added, "I just didn't know how to tell you."

And there it was, the I am really sorry. "I can't give you any answers regarding us. A lot to handle, Will. I have my business, and in just a few weeks, knee surgery, you do remember it is due to that Lyme tick nonsense."

Ouch. Will was really slapped hard with that remark. "Can I help you out?"

"Got it all covered, as I have lots of help. It is not major surgery, just a torn meniscus in my left knee."

"Okay then, but if you need me, just let me know, as I will be moving back in a week or so. Maybe we can do Christmas with Hannah?"

"That sounds okay, and I am sure Hannah will be very happy about your move." They had been successful around birthday or holiday times in recent years because of Hannah. These special times never included the Barbie doll.

"Zoey, you have not changed a bit, always giving to anyone who needs it. Thanks. I was really a big asshole, wasn't I?" He asked her permission about one thing. "May I call Hannah and tell her about my plans?"

"Well, our girl will be home day after tomorrow, so feel free to call her when you have some time." She added, "When you do come by, I have three special children, and they all have paws. Spencer, Dewey, and Mika. They are the major part of my life. And, I plan to keep it that way."

Not sure how to respond to that, he just said "See you all soon," adding, "I promise to bring some fresh catnip." And the call ended.

Zoey really did not want to call Kim. But, she knew if she put her head down on the pillow, warm and relaxed with the three cats nodding off to sleep, the phone would jingle and she would have to answer it. So she called her.

Phone rang once and Kim was already asking for details. "Well, tell me!"

"Are you doing marriage counseling, now?" She asked Kim, then gave her details. "He is moving back and has a coaching job at Rockville College."

"Wow, that was fast. He must have been really fed up with Jamie."

"Not sure what he is sick of. Maybe he is just growing up."

"So, what does that mean with you?"

Zoey was tired, her knee hurt, and she wanted no more drama tonight. "Kim, I need a good night's sleep. I am off tomorrow and we'll talk then, okay?"

Concerned with Jonas reminding her to make sure Zoey could handle this, Kim asked her sister, "Are you sure you are all right with this?"

Zoey smiled as she yawned into the phone, "Trust me, I have been through a lot. I can handle this. Will and I have always remained friends and he may not know it, but I never stopped loving him." She wanted her sister to know one thing. "Never repeat that, Kim. Got it?"

"Zoey, you know I will keep your confidence. I love you, and so does Will." She added, "Better keep an eye on that new Mika, she might be soon kidnapped." Kim laughed saying goodnight to Zoey. "Jonas thinks she is the cat's meow."

What a good way to fall asleep knowing how much Zoey was truly loved.

They all slept soundly through the night, awakening about 6:15, ready to roll out of bed. Good thing it was day off Monday. Zoey was excited about Hannah coming home for at least three weeks. She needed a rest from her demanding classes. Stumbling down the stairs, hanging onto the rail, as all the cats wriggled in and out of her legs, Zoey found the coffee machine hot and fragrant with an egg nog flavor ready to be poured. First was whipped cream for two girls, but Mika had no clue or incentive to try this white frothy stuff in a small cat dish. Some cats enjoyed a spoonful of cream, especially if they ate a lot of dry kibble which these girls did. Spencer and Dewey were already around thirteen pounds, and Mika was still a growing toddler.

Monday mornings were busy with Zoey going over finances and ordering for Sips and Swap. They were doing well, especially after only one year. She hired a cleaner to do it all at the shop each Monday, so it left the fun parts of creating, baking and serving patrons to Zoey and her staff. While Zoey completed her own household duties, laundry, vacuuming, etc., the phone rang. It was only a little after 7 a.m. Who was it?

The Prescott woman. Gads "Hello."

"Zoey, it's Miranda Prescott." She was trying to win her over. "You know about the show we are doing. Could I please get your perspective? I know you are not at Tuckerman Library, but we like to round off our segments with a little bit about the town and the library. You were, from what I hear, well liked and appreciated at the library. We would only need a few minutes and you'd have a brief part." She waited.

Zoey knew what she was to Prescott, a filler for this show to make sure it made thirty minutes of show time. "If it is brief and I have a say to approve this before it airs, I guess I can help you."

"Thank you so much." She added, "I am hoping that when we air this show, perhaps someone will come forward and we may be able to see who this woman was or who put her in that grave behind the town library."

Zoey was in agreement with that theory. That was for sure.

"When can you allow me some time?" Prescott asked her

"Monday is really the best day and today, I am swamped. Next Monday?"

"I will call you next Sunday evening to set up a convenient time for you." She thanked her again before hanging up.

What would Sam say about this? He seemed to want to erase it, but this woman belonged to someone and Zoey hoped this TV segment would help solve the mystery so the townspeople could feel more assured and safe.

As Monday passed way too quickly Zoey got another call from Caitland. She stopped by Sips and Swap as Caitland forgot her cell phone yesterday. As she checked the Sips and Swap messages, one was timely, as they had a huge order for pastries to help out the Toys for Tots program. Caitland called Zoey, "The message was from Marjorie Tuckerman and she voiced her usual professional, unfriendly request. Apparently, her caterer did not come through for the event later this week. She must think you work on Mondays."

"Gosh, we are full up with other requests, but I can't say no to this event, regardless of Marjorie." She asked Caitland, "Any chance you can come up with a list of just what and how many we need to do?" Zoey added, "Keep it simple as it is just a drop by event. We do need to feed the volunteers, though. I would not want to be critiqued by Marjorie and her minions. It is a very charitable event."

Caitland told her, "Happy to help, Zoey, and I volunteer. School is out for a while, so I will do the list, make sure we have enough supplies and drop it off later today. Okay?"

Zoey was so lucky to have Caitland as part of her staff. "See you later, Caitland."

Zoey could not forget what Jonas had told her the night before concerning the body found behind the library. Who did this woman belong to? For weeks, there were so many news articles asking the public for information and nothing came through, at least to Jonas and his office. She wondered if the news reporter had heard something from someone that may have inspired her to do this upcoming segment. Zoey had no time to play detective here, but the burial spot really made her shiver. She was glad she was no longer the town librarian.

Caitland delivered the list and the day came to an end, with some snow flurries in the air. No problems were seen with the Toys for Tots pastry order, planned for later this week. As Zoey got ready for bed that night the last phone call came from Sam Watson. What a way to end the night, she thought.

“Sam, how are you doing?” Zoey looked out on her driveway and the gently falling snow looked so calming. Look at the snow, she thought. Calm.

“Did you agree to be interviewed by Miranda Prescott?”

“I did, after several attempts at saying no.” She went on, “It is easier to get it over with, as I will only be a brief part on this segment.”

“Perhaps we should go over what you plan on saying.” Sam demanded in an unfriendly tone.

“Sam, I am capable of being interviewed and do not need an adult in the room.”

“Be very careful, Zoey.” He directed her. “This is our small town and wonderful library. I will not have it tainted with gossip.”

Zoey ended the call with no goodbye.

CHAPTER 12

As calming as the falling snow looked last night, Zoey was careful loading up her car as she headed to Sips and Swap on Tuesday morning. Three inches of snow did make it quite slippery. Cats remained at home, as there was so much to do, they were better off at home watching hungry birds on all the feeders. Zoey was eager to welcome home her daughter and she would be here for weeks, away from college and there was a lot of catching up to do. Will was certainly number #1 on the list. She was sure Will had already called Hannah before she packed her bags and headed for Highland Falls.

A bit rushed this morning, she hurried out the door on her way to pick up her mom, almost slipped and then decided to just slow down. Usually, Caitland and Selena arrived around 6 a.m. and started up. Zoey would tell Liz McCaffery about the call from Will. She asked Kim to keep it quiet until she talked to her mom.

"No cats today?" Liz looked surprised.

"No, too slippery to lug heavy critters back and forth and they have so many birds to watch today. Squirrels are nutso swirling around in the slippery snow."

"So, what will we end up doing for Marjorie and her Toys for Tots event?" Shaking her head she added, "Do we have time for this or for her after her caterer dumped her?"

"It's for the kids, mom." Zoey knew she had to tell her. "Will called me before Kim and Jonas came for dinner last night."

"Is he okay, you haven't heard from him for weeks now?" She looked a bit puzzled at her daughter.

"No, not all right, I guess he dumped Barbie and to save us all a long explanation, Will is moving back here to live with his dad."

A bit of a bombshell, Liz thought. "Doesn't Henry live in Rockville at those nice senior condos on the harbor?"

"Keeping track of him, mom?"

"Not really, but senior trips are for the entire county and he has been on some of the ones that I have gone on."

Funny that she never mentioned that to Zoey. "Well, Will has a coaching job lined up at the high school there and sounds like he has been planning this for a while."

"And why did he want your input?"

Zoey was pulling into Sips and Swap and told her, "He wants to renew our friendship. Let that sink in for a while mom." Out of the car, Zoey reminded her, "We've a lot to do today, let's not waste time discussing Will. Plenty of time for that."

Liz knew when to respect her daughter. Zoey went through a hellish period, so many years ago, remaining in love with that man. She was capable of landing back on her feet after many months of physical and emotional stress. However, they did remain friends and Hannah never faced a bad day due to them. When Zoey was ready she would unload her feelings upon her best friend, her mom.

"Well, girls," Zoey asked Caitland and Selena, "What is on the menu for Marjorie?"

A list of scrumptious treats was on this list. Mini puff pastries with various red jams always looked festive. Mini cupcakes with red and green sprinkles, along with a selection of crispy oatmeal cookies, decorated mini Christmas trees and one sugar free version, just in case. Caitland asked Zoey, “Sound all right?”

“Just super, Caitland.” Giving her a quick hug, Zoey told them both, “You and Selena are the best.”

Zoey was busy in the swap area as patrons flooded her store for weeks now. She had stocked up on many holiday books, DVDs and audio books weeks ago and that was smart of her. Around nine o’clock Zoey called Marjorie to confirm her order. Millie answered the phone.

“Hey Zoey, I hear you have come to rescue Marjorie, for her Tots program. Kind of you.”

“Happy to help out the kids in need of some happiness here.” She asked Mille, “Is Marjorie at home?”

“You just caught her, soon she is off to her exercise class.”

In just a moment, Marjorie picked up the extension. “Zoey, good to hear from you. Are we all right for this Friday?”

“I believe we are.” Zoey told her what the girls had come up with.

“Sounds marvelous. The kids will be excited and I would love to sample them myself.” She told her laughing, “That is why I exercise.” She told Zoey, “Please send me the bill and I will forward a check, is that all right?”

“We decided that the fee will be for food only, no labor involved, Marjorie. This is for the kids.”

“Thank you, Zoey.” Marjorie, hesitating, had to ask her, “How are you dealing with this Prescott woman?”

“The best I am able to as I am hoping when this segment airs, it may lead to the identity of this woman.”

“Well, Sam disagrees, as he is opposed to this segment. He wants it to go away.” Marjorie had to add, “Aren’t you worried this will hurt our lovely quiet town?”

“I think what happened had an effect on Highland Falls, and the segment is not the issue.” Zoey was very clear. “Let’s see what happens when the show airs.” And, the call ended.

The brightest spot this week was when Hannah stopped in at Sips and Swap to say hi to her mom before going home to unpack a bit, then collapse with the three cuddly cats. She had only seen Mika virtually, so Hannah would have lots of catching up to do.

Zoey hugged her daughter so tightly, Hannah had to slowly pull away. Then, Liz popped over to do the same. “You look so thin, Hannah, are you eating?” Liz asked her, a bit concerned.

“I am just fine, Gram,’” she smiled at her, “I have been in a non-stop mode and I need these few weeks to regenerate.” She went behind the counter to help herself to a peppermint latte and fresh croissant. Munching on the warm pastry, she told the group, “So glad I am home, mom.” She had to ask, “My bedroom is still there, right…..Dad didn’t talk you into staying with us, or did he?”

Well, I guess she knows, thought Zoey. “So, you heard. He is coming home, too, at least close by.” Zoey added.

"He called me last night and really excited he could spend some time with me at Christmas, and you as well, mom." Hannah waited to see just how long it would be to see how her mother felt. It wasn't long.

"I am so tired of being in the midst of drama." Zoey wanted to make some sense out of this issue. In a calm, genuine response she told her daughter, "Hannah, I was pretty surprised to see what has happened to your dad. I am sorry it has taken him so long to figure out his life. But, right now, I must focus on my life. That revolves around my business, my bad knee, and a murder in our small town." She finished with, "Your dad, my ex, is for now, last on the list. Understood?"

To everyone who was listening, the air in the room was now crystal clear. "Okay, Mom, I get it and totally understand. We'll see how it goes." Hannah finished with, "I have my fingers crossed." Smiling, coffee in hand, Hannah headed for the door to go home and finally meet the new Mika.

When Hannah left, it was a bit quiet as everyone was trying to take in all that was said about Will coming home. They all knew the history and everyone protected Zoey. As customers buzzed in and out of the eatery, Liz went into the swap area to see her daughter. "Hannah is handling this okay, Zoey." She confided in her, "It will all work out and it is Christmas. It may be a really nice time for you all to be together. Think about that." Zoey glanced over telling her mother, "We will see."

CHAPTER 13

It was a very misty day in London. Gil Andrews had been doing a lot of thinking about his business dealings with Sam Watson. What Gil did for a living was not the most prestigious of occupations. His buy and sell transactions were all legal and he was careful to always keep them on that scale. If any of Gil's associates failed to meet his standards, he ceased doing business with them. Financially, he and his wife, Carolyn, had a good life. Not fortunate enough to have any children, she traveled back to Connecticut to visit her family several times a year. Her mother now lived alone and was aging rapidly. Gil and Carolyn thought of moving to the US, but Gil said it just was not a good idea at this stage in their lives. His British heritage just couldn't adapt to an American way of life. Once, he owned a successful jewelry store in London. As he got older, he noticed just where more money could be made with easier methods. Thus, similar business dealings happened like those he did with Sam Watson. There was always a lucrative market for high end jewels in need of a new home.

While Carolyn was visiting her mother in November, she noticed a story about a suspicious murder in Highland Falls. Her mother's home was not there, but along the same coastline area. Her mom read a lot, especially the regional newspapers, and was always interested in the top stories. When Carolyn returned to London, she mentioned the story to Gil, as she thought one of his business associates was from that area. Quite a coincidence. Gil laughed and said New England was a big area and the media picked up on all kinds of juicy stories. He told her he would ask Sam

Watson what happened about that supposed murder. He knew that Sam was from a small coastline town, a very serene place to live. His only pleasure these days was his antique business where he traveled to various countries selling his merchandise. Sam was required to remain as the Director for Tuckerman Library because his wife's mother was the monarch there. She controlled all purse strings, personal and professional, at the library and inside their home. Gil knew that there was little love lost between Victoria Tuckerman and Sam Watson. But everyone makes choices when choosing a better life. Maybe he would give him a call about this instead of waiting to see him in London in a few weeks. Perhaps Gil should join Carolyn, the next trip to Connecticut. Highland Falls was only an hour away from where Caroline's mother lived. Wouldn't Sam be surprised to see him there?

A.J. was due to come home from school this week, Sam thought. He had better figure out just what was left in the jewel case for his trip abroad in January with everyone out of the house. Privacy was a must. He knew that the tennis bracelet was one of the items that Gil would be happy to sell for him. He would choose one other item, perhaps the diamond and sapphire necklace that had numerous oval shaped stones. Sam touched the numerous brilliant stones and he remembered Victoria wearing this at some important invite at the Governor's Inauguration some years ago. Then it vanished until she handed it over to him for safekeeping. That was a real laugh. Boy, did he have her fooled. Inside the locked safe, he uncovered the necklace, and placed it in a special holder, along with the tennis bracelet. That would be enough for this trip. He locked up the safe. After the holiday and before his trip abroad, Sam would also get rid of the images of himself with other young men. He shuddered thinking that was one big mistake in his younger life. And, it nearly ruined the relationship he had with his son, then just a young teenager. For years, Sam tried to make up for what A.J. thought he had seen, but A.J. never forgave him for what happened. And he never believed his father about what had occurred. Their relationship appeared to shatter, and Sam thought his son was a bit of a Mommy's boy and needed to grow up. A.J. led a quiet life after that, and stayed at school as much as he could. Marjorie missed him a lot and since Victoria Tuckerman was rarely here at her Highland Falls home, he could not confide in her either. Such is life for a teenage boy.

The Toys for Tots program was a huge success and the treats were a big hit. Hannah pitched in with the food delivery and Marjorie was very appreciative and friendly to her. With only a week left for Christmas, the rush was on. Will phoned Zoey and asked if they could all have dinner this week to discuss upcoming Christmas events. Hannah told Zoey that she had a lunch date with her father right after she arrived home.

"Really, already you two are putting your thoughts together?" Zoey was a bit dismayed and remembered how difficult it was seven years ago with this broken marriage. Will worked really hard to keep his daughter's love and after many months, all calmed down and life continued, without Will at home. He eventually moved to the Boston area and met Jamie, more commonly called the Barbie Doll, as she was almost ten years younger than Will and a fanciful young woman. In order to live stress-free and not vindictive, Zoey decided to try and make their divorce as calm as possible. Will was always there for Hannah financially and emotionally and they did spend holidays as a family minus Barbie.

"Mom, Dad hasn't been happy in a long time." She became very serious. "Let's just get through the holidays and see where it goes. It is totally in your court."

"Well, I will see if he'd like to come for dinner on Sunday and Gram can come too in case a fight breaks out." Zoey tried a lighter tone with Hannah.

"Sounds good, mom." She laughed as she told Zoey, "Wait until he meets the girls."

Actually, Will was a lover of all animals, and that may have played a role with Jamie. She wanted no pets so they could spend weekends traveling to various seaside inns or B and B's. Like a honeymoon, but no marriage, ever. Will would enjoy the cats and there was no option but to include them. By now they were all Zoey's family. Days were becoming just a blur and Sunday arrived after an exhausting week at the eatery. With a fragrant tender roast of beef for a pot roast dinner started in her slow cooker, Zoey left for Sips and Swap. Liz promised to prepare her honey glazed carrots and some crunchy coleslaw, so the mashed potatoes was the only thing left to do when Zoey arrived home around 3:30. Fresh croissants would suffice for the bread that would help to clean up all of any tasty gravy. Liz stopped over early to help her emotionally starved daughter before Will showed up. They planned to eat around 6 o'clock and all was going as planned.

Hannah did a simple appetizer of stuffed mushrooms, with some small pieces of crabmeat poking out of the crumb mixture. Will arrived right around 5:45, just ahead of the dinner hour. Zoey couldn't help but notice how young he looked. Still the blondish wavy hair, a bit too long and he now had grown a mustache. It looked okay, very trimmed and neat, and his dark blue globes for eyes had not changed. Liz was the first to offer a hug.

“Will,” Her friendly smile was so appreciated by her ex son-in-law. “Gosh, the years have made you younger, is it all that fresh air while you golf?” She added, “Maybe I should try it.”

“Liz, you look just fine.” Will told her. “Is Zoey keeping you busy at the Eatery?”

“She is, but it is so good for me. I love seeing all of the patrons. Lots of gossip.”

“Speaking of gossip, what is going on with that body behind Tuckerman?” He looked over at Zoey. “I bet you are glad you are no longer the librarian there, right?”

Something to agree on, thought Zoey. “Correct, but I am still getting pushed in, somehow. By Sam, of course.”

“He is still the same, then?” Will shook his head in a downward motion. “Is Marjorie still with him?”

“Well, they live in the same house,” Zoey continued. “There is definitely something off, though. A.J. only comes home when he has to and Sam travels a lot selling his stuff.”

“That is too bad, as A.J. was a really good kid.”

“He still is. But, he has become a bit reclusive and not close at all to Sam.”

Hannah offered her appetizer to Will. He asked if he should open the Riesling wine he bought for them. ”Crabmeat in these mushrooms, Dad." It must have been the odor of crab which prompted the three girls to appear, after sleeping away most of the day.

"Whoa, these are some big girls you have here. Who is the wee one?" Will scooped her up and Mika was happy to cuddle with him.

"That is the new rescue, found in the back of Carol's yard a few weeks ago." Zoey beamed a ray of love right at her. "We tried her out and she is now a part of our family."

So, that is why Hannah made this special appetizer, Zoey smiled to herself. "Very tasty, Hannah, with the crabmeat. I hope I get credit for teaching you how to properly prepare foods."

The wine was a nice touch and the food was delicious. Everyone was relaxed and cozy by the crackling, warm fire, with Mika becoming fast friends with Will. The phone rang, bringing all back to the real world and Zoey answered to hear Miranda Prescott on the line. Zoey totally forgot about the promised call.

"Miranda, how are you doing with the segment?"

Miranda was in her friendly mode. "Going well. We have had several calls about this woman, but so far nothing has developed." She asked Zoey, "What time is good for you tomorrow?"

Zoey thought, there is no good time, but she could not avoid her. Best to see her and forget her. "How about right after lunch, around 1:30 or 2?" She wanted to get one thing straight. "Will this be fairly quick, as I have a really busy day and rest of the week?"

“I promise one hour tops.”

“Sam Watson is very opposed to his being interviewed, but I will call him again tomorrow, while down at Highland Falls, to see if he’ll agree to a few moments of my time.” Miranda sighed. ”After all he runs the library.”

“I have dinner guests, so it’s goodbye for now.” She added, “Tomorrow at 1:30.” And the call ended.

Zoey apologized for the interruption but explained who it was.

“Mom, you are going to be on that show that Prescott does?” Hannah was unaware of this.

Zoey tried to squirm out of this but wasn’t able to. “I have a very small part in this-rounding off my position as the former librarian.”

Will told Zoey, “And Sam wants no part of this blemish on his perfect life, his tranquil town…”

Zoey sighed, “What is most offensive is he doesn’t care and wants this whole issue gone.” She told them all, “I hope this Prescott woman comes through and maybe someone, maybe just one person will tell us just what happened to that poor woman, buried behind our library.”

“My dad has been following this case.” He smiled, “He has no excitement in his life and he feels that there is more to this than meets the eye. Someone tried to really cover this up. No dentures and no jewelry?”

“How did you know that?” Zoey was amazed at this.

”My Dad knew a lot of people when he was the pharmacy director at the hospital. He called one of his friends, in confidence." He looked seriously at Zoey. "Maybe he will be the next Jessica Fletcher and help to solve this one."

And that is when everyone decided to say goodnight. Soon, the kitchen was cleaned up and doors locked, lights out. Zoey could not forget about this unsolved mystery. Her night was a restless one. She woke up around 4 a.m. and that was it. She wanted the Prescott interview over. Hours from now.

CHAPTER 14

Miranda Prescott arrived at almost 2 o'clock with recorder, camera, and an assistant to do the filming. The interview was very brief asking Zoey about her job as the library director and the many programs the library offered. Zoey focused on senior events, like their travel and book clubs. Prescott was interested in that age group and the senior housing in and around Highland Falls. The library offered a free delivery service for books and any material seniors requested to the few retirement homes in the area. Prescott planned to visit these homes hoping to narrow down the possibility of a missing older woman who may have vanished or simply walked away. Zoey thought that was a far reach or waste of time. Certainly if a woman with no relatives or friends disappeared from a senior home, the authorities would have been contacted. Unless, wrongdoing was involved. Maybe that was Miranda's angle.

"So, seniors were a large part of your patrons?" Miranda asked her.

"Definitely, but we have a very active senior community and for the most part, they come by on their own for different choices of books, DVDS, and they do a lot of online ordering from our interlibrary loan service. We can get just about anything you need."

With the interview done, camera off, Miranda Prescott asked Zoey, "Sounds like you miss what you used to do."

"I do miss the people, but I have my Sips and Swap Shop, so many of the same people come by to see me there."

Zoey had to ask Miranda, "Do you think that this woman lived in Highland Falls?"

Miranda was honest, "We are putting all the pieces of this puzzle together and we hope we can shed some light on this murder. It is what I do."

After the Prescott woman left, both Kim and Liz McCaffery called for details.

Zoey told them it was very brief and she really was just a "filler" for this segment. "Prescott thinks this lady was living in one of the retirement homes in this area and suspiciously disappeared."

"Really?" Kim shuddered at the thought. "Like a poor lady with no relatives and maybe some money promised to someone when she died, killed by a caregiver?"

"Whoa, Kim." Her mother stepped in. "Let the Prescott woman do the digging." She added, "Sounds far-fetched to me. But, it would make for an interesting segment, especially if there is no definite conclusion." Liz reminded them, "Ratings are important, keep people interested."

Zoey told her sister, "You are watching too many Lifetime Mysteries, Kim."

Zoey called Jonas to tell him about her interview. Prescott had stopped at the Police Station to see the head honcho that morning. Strange, she never mentioned that to Zoey. Jonas filled Zoey in on his meeting. The State Police Crime Squad opted for Jonas to handle the interview which was due to air right after the holidays. "Good thing I got a haircut and bought a new dress shirt." He said laughing.

"Well, did Prescott get enough info?"

"I guess." He mentioned the upcoming retirement homes visit by her. "I guess she is out to solve this crime, thinking there was foul play in one of the local retirement homes here or along the coastline."

"That is so far out on a limb." Zoey added, "Does she think someone will confess to this murder as she does this segment?"

"Sounds like it." Disappointed, Jonas told Zoey, "I have the distinct feeling that she feels we are all inept."

"There was so little any of you could go on. Gads, the Crime Squad was there for two days. Nothing."

"Hey, we did contact all relevant senior homes in the area." He sighed, "If someone disappeared, we would have been contacted. If there is a lost cat more than three hours missing, I get a call."

"Last year, some lady, angry with her visiting nurse, went off to walk out in her woods, do you remember?"

"I do recall, it was early in June and after it got dark, we got a call from a relative when no one answered the phone." He added, "We found her with a pack of cigarettes, not happy to see us."

"It's hard as you age and lose your independence, your identity."

"And your ability to breathe." He finished the story, told by the visiting nurse. "Mrs. Higgins had a very low oxygen rate, due to the smoking, that was not allowed. So, she got a scolding."

"We'll have to watch the segment together. Maybe I will be resting after my knee surgery."

"Hey, Zoey, you'll do fine. It is outpatient and you have help. Maybe more than you need."

"You mean Will?"

"I do." He reassured her. "Everything will soon settle in and work out just fine."

"Speaking of that, I see my surgeon this week with what to do pre-surgery. No anti-inflammatory meds for at least a week, No aspirin. Not a fun week before."

The rest of Monday seemed to zoom by and for once, Zoey and her cats slept right through the night. A ton of visitors popped in to Sips and Swap all week long. Zoey saw her surgeon on Wednesday, for a brief exam and orders as what to expect pre-and post-surgery.

Dr. Robbins knew Zoey's history better than anyone. Dealing mainly with her primary care doctor and with her rheumatologist, Zoey also saw Dr. Robbins as she recovered from the main bout of Lyme disease. He was a believer in the Connecticut-based Lyme disease. Seven years later, they still knew little about the disease. Zoey was lucky as it basically affected her feet and knees. The original IV given to her eradicated most of her aches and pains. She was warned, however, that as she aged, the arthritis would never go away and she would be on various meds for the rest of her life.

After a brief exam, the surgeon reminded her, "We are on schedule for January 11." He went on, "Here is a list of do's and don'ts. "I assume you have help and do consider getting a cane. It will help for the first few days."

Zoey was feeling a bit anxious now, unlike her. The purchase of a cane made her feel really old. What Zoey wanted was a new Victoria Secret's push up bra that would encourage her to feel young again. "This procedure is fairly easy, right?"

"It is a relatively minor surgery, Zoey, but there are always rare events that occur. We handle them." He comforted her, "You are very positive and active individual. You can swim, bike, and your business alone sees you physically busy all of the time." He added, "You will fly through this and feel so much better with a repaired knee."

After Zoey got home, she took the time to read her list of things, the before and afters. It looked doable and acceptable. In three weeks, it would all be over. And weeks later off to St. Maarten with her mom.

Will phoned Zoey later in the week with an offer she could not refuse. "With your mom and Hannah running Sips and Swap while you get your knee fixed, how about if I step up?"

Zoey thought that was a loaded question. Was she ready for this? "Will, that is kind of you to offer, but I don't think I will need much help, as Hannah is home." She added details. "Dr. Robbins says it is a piece of cake. I will be a bit sore for a few days and the more I slowly move it after that it will help. I have two weeks of therapy and after that I should be well on the mend."

"I would be happy be your taxi to and from the hospital, if that would help." He waited for her reply.

It really would help, Zoey had to be honest. Her mother and Hannah would be a bit too concerned and they were really needed at Sips and Swap while Zoey was MIA. "I think that would be good, Will."

"So, next week is Christmas and have you made plans for dinner on the Eve or Day?"

She filled him in with details, accepting the fact that he would join the family for both days. "Christmas Eve is basically appetizers, drinks, fancy desserts, and a nice get together. Like we used to do if you remember."

Ouch, thought Will. He deserved that gentle slap. "I do, and I miss those days." He asked her a favor. "Can my dad come on Christmas Day?"

"Of course." Her response was genuine. "He is welcome on Christmas Eve, too. My mom will be there and I hear they are still friends."

Will thanked her but explained sometimes evenings are not the best times for going out. "Dad settles in early and most nights, he is asleep, Bingo at his side, by 8 or 8:30."

"He still has that adorable Bassett Hound?"

"He does, and Bingo is almost 14 years old now. Still pretty lively."

"Has he done any more investigating about the suspicious murder here?"

"He is still very intrigued about this incident. He feels strongly that the woman is from Highland Falls."

"I do too!" Zoey exclaimed. "Jonas and his entire crew are at wits end and Sam Watson just wants it gone. No interest, no compassion. Just his usual selfish attitude as he does not want this reflecting on himself or the library." Zoey added,

“Sam could have posted a reward for info leading to who this might be. I suggested, he refused. What would happen if Victoria Tuckerman disappeared? Would he do anything? Would he care?”

Will looked very somber. “You very well know the answer to that question.” He asked Zoey, “Where is the old bat these days, still wealthy as ever?”

“You never liked her,” Zoey laughed out loud. ”And she did not like your golf lessons, either.”

“There is a right and wrong way to all lessons given in life. When you are Victoria Tuckerman, it is only HER way or no way. I never got past lesson #1.”

Zoey continued with details. “Mrs. Tuckerman has had a falling out with her daughter and is now on an expansive, expensive, says Sam, three month voyage abroad.”

“Strange that she will be gone over the holidays.” Will asked Zoey, “Don’t you think so?”

“Will, there is a lot of strange happening with that family. I will fill you in one day soon.”

That sounded a bit ominous. “I will hold you to that, Zoey.”

CHAPTER 15

Sam Watson was in total stress mode today. Just days before Christmas, and his librarian gave his notice that he is resigning from his position at Tuckerman Memorial Library as of December 31st. That was just great. Sam had his sales trip abroad already planned after the first of the year and now this disruption. He needed to call Claire Harris who handled the finances. Sam was not sure if they owed Jason Ramsey any severance pay. He was with them a little more than a year now and he was such a wimp. His excuse for leaving was that he no longer felt safe in this type of environment, with the body that was found on library property. Sam was correct that this must go away. He would call Zoey and ask for her help, once again. If Victoria Tuckerman were to find out, there would be hell to pay. Sam would bear the brunt of this eruption that she would have, calling him incompetent.

The Christmas holiday was fast approaching and Zoey was immersed in everything. Then the phone call just topped it off. "Zoey, I need to stop by and see you today." Sam told her in a serious tone. "It can't be postponed."

"Sam, this is a terribly busy time for me. If you recall I have knee surgery planned in just two weeks. I have a ton a things to do ahead of time. And you do remember Christmas? What can't wait?" Zoey was really aggravated with him.

"Jason Ramsey has resigned as of the end of December."

Zoey tried to breathe slowly and not lose her temper. "Call Claire." She made this clear again, "I am no longer associated with the library."

"I told you that we need this to go away. Now, our librarian is gone, he has such a weak character." He was letting all of his anger out on Zoey. "Ramsey does not feel safe in our environment there. All I need is for Victoria to hear about this and my ass will be kicked."

Zoey snickered at that thought, one positive aspect in her favor. Handle this Sam for all the money Victoria Tuckerman has given you. "What do you want me to do, Sam?"

"Can you sit in on a selection process for a new librarian?"

"Maybe one meeting with the Board, if I have to, but before the first of the year."

"I understand that and I will make it work." He added, "I have a trip abroad the second week of January and all must be running smoothly by the time I am gone."

"Sam, one thought for you." She hoped he would listen to her. "You need to contact Victoria because if she hears of this, you are the one she'll tangle with." She asked Sam, "When is she due back in the states?"

"Right around when I leave for London." He explained. "It was not a pleasant send-off with Marjorie. Victoria refused to give us numbers where she could be reached." The saga continued. "She told Marjorie that it was time for Marjorie and me to be the adults in the room and stop relying on her. She needed a long vacation from us all."

Zoey knew it was a bad relationship, but never thought Victoria would totally abandon her family. Zoey wondered if Sam had privately squandered some of her money away. Perhaps the library budget needed more and Sam usually insisted that the family finances should override any additional money spent at Tuckerman Library. "I am sorry Sam. I know how difficult Marjorie's mother can be." She made a promise to him. "I will help you pick a new librarian, and then I am done." Phone call over.

Liz strayed into the Swap area where Zoey was cataloging her recent purchases that her patrons would love. "Long phone call, was it Will?"

"I wish. " She tried to sound calm. "Sam Watson in a dither. What else is new?" Zoey explained. "Jason Ramsey no longer feels safe at the library so he is resigning and Sam needs me in on the meeting to choose a new librarian."

"He needs to understand that you have an overflowing plate and, by the way, you are not connected any longer with the library." Liz was very protective of her daughter.

"I know, but I promised to sit in at one meeting." Zoey shook her head. "Right now, I would try to contact Victoria Tuckerman. She insists on being the boss at this library, maybe not physically but certainly behind the scenes."

"You are right on that," Liz added, "Victoria has no clue about this body found at Tuckerman, does she?"

"I think Sam wants it secret, at least until she gets back here in a few weeks. Strange though, that she left no contact info."

"I think Sam has something to do with this soured relationship. He is overspending again and Victoria doesn't like it. Purse strings tightened."

"Are you listening to gossip at the hair salon?"

Liz shrugged off the comment, slightly turning a bit pink in her cheeks. "Marjorie has been very unhappy for quite a while now. Sam is lucky she has not seen an attorney to see about a split in the marriage."

"That explains why A.J. stays away so much. Poor kid."

"Hey, I am off to do my laps." Zoey felt a bit discouraged. "I will not be doing them for at least 3 weeks in January as my knee heals. Have to keep it dry and germ-free."

"Off you go, girl, we are in control here and Hannah just loves helping."

"If anyone calls, just take the messages." She thought about who would phone her. For sure, Claire Harris will certainly be on the list for my advice.

On her way to the swim club, Zoey wanted to swim, shower, and go home to play with her cats. Not going to happen. Sips and Swap would not survive. When Zoey got back to the eatery, she had a visitor.

"Hey, A.J., Merry Christmas." Zoey gave him a brief hug. She assumed that hugs were rare as part of his family. "Do you miss your grandmother?"

"Yeah, I do." He seemed unusually quiet. "She'll be home in a few weeks, though."

A.J. had ordered a large coffee to go and on his way out he told them all to have a nice holiday. "Zoey, do you need any help with the Swaps area, as I am home for a while?"

What a really nice young man, Zoey felt lucky to know him. "Actually, some of the seniors from The Mockingbird Estates aren't able to drive much in the winter. Can you deliver some books over to them for the holiday? They have things to swap back to me too."

"Sure thing." He asked her when would be best.

"Wednesday is good, with Christmas on Saturday, we are closing at noon on Friday and will not return until Tuesday."

"Vacation, huh?" He kidded with her.

It was so good to see him happy. "Come by about 10 a.m. and I will have a load ready for you."

The residents at Mockingbird Estates were grateful to see A.J. deliver all the books and DVDs that they had selected. The Estates was an upper scale active senior community, with a tastefully decorated section offering assisted living for very wealthy individuals. A.J. returned with a huge box full of the swaps that had been selected a few weeks ago. There were also several donated items.

"Holy smoke, those people want to be kept up on all of the gossip." A.J. seemed amused.

"Let me guess," Zoey paused with a deep sigh. "The body behind the library?"

"Correct." A.J. gave her the scoop. "They seem to think I am glued to you and you to the library. One lady stalked me on the way out and whispered, “You must know the truth behind this mystery.”

Zoey just burst out laughing.” Okay, Columbo, did you spill the frightening details that we do not have?”

“I humored her, just a bit. I told her I just got home and have not even seen my parents yet. When they fill me in, I would be back to see them.”

“You must have been very persuasive.”

“I am counting on that they will never remember what I said, or who I was.” He finished by telling Zoey, “They do know Victoria Tuckerman, though, as she has a few friends that live there.”

As A.J. headed for home, Zoey told him to enjoy the holidays and please say hi to his mother.

Zoey managed to organize her next three days before Christmas with planning a menu for both Christmas Eve and Christmas Day. Will called every day and Zoey put him to work. She had ordered groceries from her favorite market and Will planned to take care of it on Thursday. His donation was to bring some liquor, Zoey’s favorite wine and beer for whoever wanted it. He also planned to buy some special treats for the three felines. Prime rib dinner was a tradition for the entire family as Zoey had followed her mother’s many successful holiday events. It saddened her that her father was no longer with them. Family was so meaningful and Zoey thought of A.J. now at home with his family.

Marjorie had a menu planned for Christmas Eve that Millie was in charge of. Filet of beef with some large stuffed shrimp that both of her men loved. With Sam’s parents now gone and Victoria on her voyage, it would be fairly quiet. Sam's older brother Thomas and his wife, Cynthia would join them. It was a yearly event, since they drove down from Maine each holiday. They had no children and both were involved with their successful careers. Thomas was an investment banker and Cynthia was an attorney. They really enjoyed A.J. with each holiday.

When Sam arrived home, Marjorie asked him, "Is there any way we can find out where Mother went?"

"Well, dear, she does not want us to know, that was made perfectly clear." He stared directly at her. "You do remember…?"

"I did some sleuthing, into her charge accounts and found nothing. No clues." Marjorie said.

Sam reacted. "What do you want me to do?" He became angry at her. "I have a dead body in the back of our library and can't solve that one. I am not a detective."

"But, you know people, can you find someone who can track her down? We only got one postcard from her and that was a month ago." Shaking her head, she was distraught. "I am worried that something is wrong."

That was about it for Sam. He slammed down his glass of scotch and loudly told her. "Let it go, Marjorie. She wants to be left alone. She made that very clear. Understood?"

As usual, Marjorie stiffened, frightened of her husband, and knowing he would not help her.

There were always loose ends. Sam had to handle it all. Sam had an old colleague in London that had nothing to do with jewelry resales. He handled other matters for Sam, business contracts, dealings, recommendations. He was known for being discreet and that cost a good deal of cash. Colin E. comes through for me, Sam usually thought, but doubtful now with this latest request. What snag had occurred this time? First Sam would phone him, then an e-mail. Why hadn't he completed the business dealing Sam had instructed him to do, as it was very timely. He was well paid. Sam realized it was after 10 p.m. in London, but he needed to resolve this.

A strange set of several rings before Colin answered his hone. "Colin here."

"It's Sam here in the states."

"Hey man, how are you?" Yawning he proclaimed, "Happy Holidays to you and Marjorie."

"Colin, wake up." Sam was losing patience. "What happened with the last parcel request?"

"Done, weeks ago- no contact back to you?"

"Nothing."

"Hey, I do what I am told, especially by you. Perhaps the delivery is late, as the mail is horrid here in London."

"This type of correspondence has a reflection on my finances and business. If it doesn't come together by Monday, I will settle this with you again." The phone call abruptly ended. Sam had enough on his mind with personal and family issues strained to the max. He felt like he was surrounded by intolerables. Such a negative spin he was immersed in. He must turn this into a positive aura and soon.

CHAPTER 16

Zoey thought 12 o'clock on Friday, Christmas Eve day, would never arrive. She had so much to do at home and Will promised to come early that evening to help her out. Hannah was busy preparing her crabmeat mushrooms and Zoey had to smile about that. She was looking forward to seeing Charlie Mitchell. She thought her mother was looking forward to seeing him too. Liz had a hair salon appointment and bought a new outfit to wear that night. Zoey wanted to look her best too. She felt herself getting weaker as each day passed and accepted the fact that her love for Will was still very much alive.

Liz arrived ahead of Will and she looked just gorgeous in a red and black checked outfit, with her garnet bracelet and earrings to finish off a very festive look. "What can I do to help, Zoey?"

"You look so dressed up, I don't want any food splashed on you as we get ready."

A genuine smile erupted. "I have been doing this a long, long, time my dear." Liz grabbed an apron and told her daughter, "Let's fill this table with tempting holiday treats."

Liz unpacked her appetizer, a creamy, tasteful hot artichoke dip. Served with home baked garlic parmesan pita chips, it was a bit addictive. Creamy, hot, and crunchy.

"I am so glad tonight is light food, drinks, and a few petite desserts." Zoey added, "I got some creamy Fontina cheese chunks from the Marketplace this week and I will also set out some cured black and green olives. Nice combo."

"Okay where is the wine?" Liz looked around at the counter. "Or, maybe a nice gin and tonic."

"I have either one, Will delivered it all yesterday." Zoey was a bit surprised at the gin choice. "When did the gin and tonic start?"

"Usually in summer months but I read up on which liquor has some good virtues and gin was listed. It is from the juniper berry family and in ancient times, it helped people boost their immune system."

Hard to believe that, Zoey thought and retrieved the bottle of gin from her cabinet. "Okay Mom, here's to your health."

"I am not kidding, gin is clear, no additives or fake color, like some wines."

"I will stick to my Riesling, which is pretty clear, sweet, and calming."

As both women prepared the appetizers, Hannah came downstairs from visiting with the cats and joined them. Not interested in the gin though.

Everything was all set with Kim and Jonas arriving at the backdoor. Andi was with them and eager to see Hannah. Hugs all around.

Then, Will came in with a fragrant Jasmine plant for the hostess. It was Zoey's favorite. And he remembered. "Just so fragrant." Zoey told Will. "I have my plant in the bedroom window, but no blooms will appear for a while. It had a busy summer and needs to rest."

“Charlie, I am so glad to see you?” Zoey felt a bit sentimental but genuine. “How is Bingo?”

“Not happy to see me leave this late in the day.” He explained. "I rarely go out socializing in the dark nights of winter. But, this is a special day.” He looked over at Will. “I appreciate the invite, Zoey.” Then, Charlie went to sit down and visit with Liz McCaffery.

Everyone played catchup as Will filled them in with what he had planned for the near future. He was careful about including Zoey. Jonas and Will were busy discussing the body found. Charlie stepped in with his thoughts.

“When is this segment coming on so we can watch it?” Charlie asked Zoey. “Can’t wait to see the old librarian.”

“The first week of January, I believe on a Friday night at 8 p.m. Get the popcorn ready.” Zoey told them all.

Charlie was hopeful. “When I spoke to my friend in the pathology department, in confidence, she explained that it appeared to her that the woman was strangled. No jewelry yet there were marks on her fingers proving she had worn rings. The marks on her neck may have been due to a necklace worn. Perhaps ripped off during a struggle?” He looked over at Jonas. “I am right, aren’t I?”

“Indeed, but proof of intent is just not there.” Jonas added, “And if this was a jewel robbery, why bury the body, carefully, covered up with a new canvas tarp?”

Zoey stepped in, crunching on the pita chip and chunky dip. “Doesn’t that show you cared about the body, like a relative?”

“Yeah, right,” Kim shook her head, in disbelief. “A nephew in a bind, he lost at Foxwoods. In desperate need of some extra cash. So, auntie had some jewels. Take the valuables, get rid of her, and then think how carefully you’ll bury her.” Everyone had a laugh at that comment.

“I have to agree, Kim” Charlie added. “Someone wanted this lady gone. Let’s hope when this show airs, someone calls in to claim this cremated body.”

“Samples were kept of this body before cremation, just in case someone discovers who this is. That way DNA will come through for us.”

“What about the tarp, maybe who bought it?”

The group became quiet and doubtful. Staring directly at him, Will added his thoughts. “Dad, tarps are so common. Almost everyone has a tarp for something, it’s almost like duct tape.”

“I guess you are right, but finding the body only weeks later, at least it was not destroyed by the elements.”

Jonas reminded them, “We kept samples and DNA tells the truth. If someone comes forward and can supply a sample for the DNA match, if this known person went missing, we may have an answer and ending to this.”

“Enough of this solving a mystery,” Zoey picked up Dewey as Will offered some new catnip toys for the felines. In no time the cats were way past energetic, bouncing off the furniture. Mika thought it was finally her chance to climb that Christmas tree, but was unsuccessful. As she tumbled down through the branches, laughter erupted from everyone.

Appetizers gone, coffee and tea on the way, the desserts were laid out and all were dazzled by the assortment. Mini cream puffs, various cookies and a three layer Trifle cake that Liz made early that morning. This was a years-long holiday tradition. Cats were asleep by the fire, having had a bit too much catnip. It was nearly time to bid goodbye to everyone and Zoey made a small care package for Charlie to take home.

"I will not have to worry about breakfast tomorrow. I am like a kid on Christmas morning, having sweets with my coffee." He gave Zoey a final hug goodbye.

Will kissed Zoey goodbye and said he would be over tomorrow around noon as they planned to eat dinner around 2 o'clock. "Thanks for including my dad."

"Hey, he may be the one to help us solve this murder that has enveloped us all."

With everyone helping to clean up the kitchen, Zoey sat down really tired out. But, it was a good, deserved tired. So glad to be with Hannah and hopefully they would all work toward a new relationship with Will. Hannah really wanted this, as she had missed having a live-in father. Still unsure while on uneven ground, Zoey needed some time to turn all of this into a positive plan.

Surprisingly, everyone had a restful good night's sleep. Thank you for my calming Riesling wine. With no young kids wondering if Santa had arrived dropping off gifts, they all slept until almost 8 am. Coffee please. Hannah was at the kitchen table, munching on a cookie from the night before. "Mom, Merry Christmas." She engulfed her in a warm hug. Cats were busy enjoying their kibble, too.

“What a nice visit with everyone.” Zoey sipped at her coffee, taking a sliver of the leftover trifle. “I have my breakfast casserole to put in the oven, are you up for it?”

“Sure am.” She added, “I don’t get much of that at school, nor do I have time to enjoy it.” She asked her mom, “Is this your recipe or Gram’s?”

“It’s hers.” She couldn’t take credit for most of the recipes she made. The turkey sausage, cheese and veggie casserole was a favorite at Sips and Swap. It was on the daily menu, usually sold out well before 10 a.m.

“I have to feed the birds pronto.” Zoey looked out on the snow covered lawn as the small chickadees chirped, waiting for their seed, bread, and popcorn. They first ran off with the popcorn kernels as if they were gold. Zoey made a bag of corn every day for all of her critters. “I will quickly hop in the shower right after. By then the casserole will be ready.”

As they both enjoyed the creamy baked egg casserole, they talked about a lot of things. But, the prime rib must be prepared and a lot had to be done before everyone descended on the Mitchell home. Liz was doing the mashed potatoes, there would be fresh string beans with almonds. Zoey would do the Yorkshire pudding which was really a buttery, puffy popover. She had made these several times and everyone expected them with the prime rib. Hannah would do a crisp salad with baby lettuce greens, creamy vinaigrette, and croutons. They had desserts left from the night before, but Zoey did a crème brulee also, just in case anyone opted for the creamy dish gently spiced with nutmeg and vanilla.

As the morning seemed to fly by, all was going really well. The table was set, food prepared and with just an hour left before guests arrived, there was a knock on the door. It was A.J. Watson.

Surprised, and a bit concerned, she opened the door to invite him in. "A.J., Merry Christmas." Zoey paused and asked him, "Are you okay?" She could not imagine why he was there.

"Not really." He looked embarrassed. "I had a fight with my dad." He started to turn away.

"No, don't go." She pleaded with him. "Just come in and we can talk."

"I'm sorry to barge in here, but we need help." He went on, spilling out words. "My mom is worried about my grandmother. She only had one postcard from her. She is really worried. My Dad screamed at my mom and won't help us find out where Gram is. Zoey, Can you help us?"

Zoey sat down with A.J. and thought, what is happening here to this family? "I am not sure what I can do," and told A.J., "I do not have the best relationship with either your mom or dad now. Your grandmother left months ago, insisting to be by herself as she enjoyed her trip."

In a pleading tone he replied, "Something is really wrong, here Zoey. Please help me and my mom."

She stared back at this poor boy and had no positive feedback for him "All I can do is try."

"I'll stop by later this weekend." And A.J. was out the door.

CHAPTER 17

And Zoey thought this morning was going so well. What the hell was wrong with Sam? Poor A.J. worried about his grandmother. Gads, Sam was never going to change. So selfish. What a disruption erupting on this Christmas day.

Soon everyone would be here and it was clear as you looked at Zoey that she had something on her mind. Will was first to arrive and she thought she might bounce something off him for a change. She would go into details about A.J. stopping by with her mom and sister on another day. Today she needed to vent her feelings and Will was the one to listen. They both had a glass of wine before everyone arrived and Charlie was busy catching up with Hannah. He was so proud of his granddaughter and excited that she was going to attend Veterinary School.

"So, what time did A.J. come by?" Will sounded a bit puzzled. "Did he forget Christmas?"

"I can't imagine what he is going through. Christmas must be way down on his list." Continuing on she explained about his request. "I honestly do not have a clue as how to find Victoria Tuckerman. Clearly she wants a restful vacation, probably away from Sam."

"Do you think he is overspending her budget allowances?"

"That would be my guess." Zoey agreed with Will. "Maybe A.J. can bring me the postcard she sent to Marjorie. Perhaps there is a clue as to where she was during the first month of her voyage."

"What about the airlines, or do they even know when she left the U.S.?"

"I thought Sam drove her to Bradley. It was a week or two after Labor Day." Zoey remembered Victoria stopping by the eatery days before she left. Very excited about three months of peaceful traveling.

"Sound to me like Queen Victoria needed to step off her throne for a while. Maybe she wanted to see if Sam could run everything on his own."

"Without running it into the ground, you mean?" She looked over at Will for his opinion.

"That makes some sense." He asked Zoey, "How is the library doing?"

"Financially?"

"Yes, that is important." He sighed, "Maybe he needs more money and she said NO."

"Whoa!" Zoey frowned. "That would really set Sam on fire."

"Then throw in a dead body behind the library." Will had to laugh at that.

"But, Victoria was gone for weeks when that happened. She doesn't know about it."

"And, that is how Sam wants it." Will tried to make sense out of this. "If it can be resolved and forgotten when she arrives home in January, life will be sweet again."

"Will, you can't forgot or use a delete button to get rid of a dead body. Now, Tuckerman Library has a big red stain on it." Zoey sounded confident about this.

"Still better in January of the new year than weeks ago or even now should Victoria discover what happened. In one way, it is good for Sam if she doesn't contact her family. No news is good news."

"Well, A.J. will stop by in a few days to see if my crystal ball and I can help him find his grandmother."

"Zoey, you will not fit well in the middle of this one. Think carefully about how to handle this, okay?" He added, "Sam, Marjorie, or Victoria will not like you interfering."

She knew Will was right. Good to bounce things off him for a change. The rest of the guests were coming in the doorway taking in the fragrant aroma of pepper and rosemary crusted prime rib, ready to come out of the oven.

Everyone had a nice Christmas Day, at least at the Mitchell household. The menu was a success and other than everyone feeling too full and wanting to take a nap after, the day ended on a happy note. By 4 o'clock everyone had departed, including Will and his dad. Zoey and Hannah settled down watching a Christmas movie and soon Hannah nodded off on the couch long before 8 pm. Waking her up, Zoey, the cats, and her yawning daughter went up to bed.

It was so good to be off for two days, and Zoey couldn't recall having a Sunday off in like forever. Practically holding her breath, awaiting a visit from A.J. but he never came by. Tuesday rolled around and Zoey was back at Sips and Swap at her usual routine. Felt good. It was close to closing time and A.J. did show up, headed back to the Swap area. He drove up in a brand new Audi convertible.

"Zoey, sorry about Saturday. I was so upset." He explained what happened. "Dad settled down and we just got another postcard from Gram." Finally reassured, A.J. said, "Victoria promised to be home in three weeks." He was practically beaming. "Mom and Dad gave me a new car for Christmas. I will need one when I head off to college next fall."

Stunned by this news, Zoey could barely comment. "Another postcard. That is great, your mother must be relieved." Boy, a new Audi, how could you not love Dad, now? Wow.

"Thanks for listening to me and I am sorry to have bothered you."

Smiling and touching his upper arms, she told A.J. "You are never a bother."

Whew, thought Zoey. I escaped that one. But, the Audi felt like a bribe of sorts. When she arrived home she got a message on her answering machine from Sam.

She knew calling him back was going to be about the Board choosing the new librarian. It was unavoidable. "Sam, Zoey here."

"Zoey, I respected your request not to bother you at work." He added, "But leaving a message on your cell phone might get a message to you faster."

Not going to happen thought Zoey. "Have you decided on a time and day for this meeting?"

"Tomorrow evening, 6:30 at the library conference room. Can you make it?"

"Yes, Sam, I can be there."

"We only have two choices, as the new person needs to start right after the New Year. Both candidates are able to do this. Pay rate will be less than Jason. It will be raised after a three month appraisal." He continued on, "One final request, Zoey?"

"What Sam?" She was feeling a bit annoyed.

"Stay out of our personal lives, if you would." He sounded a bit distraught. "I understand A.J. stopped over to whimper to you on Christmas Day. I apologize for him."

"He wasn't whining, but he is worried and misses his grandmother."

"Resolved, another postcard arrived yesterday. We are taking care of this, Zoey. Stay out of it."

That was the end of that.

Zoey did her best to comprehend what had happened. She sat down with a strong cup of tea, hoping to figure out what had transpired with A.J. and Sam. A.J. and his Dad had such a poor relationship, for years now. Hard to believe that a new car would fix this. And, an Audi. Gads, Sam had the best model BMW, Marjorie a Jaguar convertible and now add another pricey vehicle. No wonder Victoria Tuckerman was concerned. From the gossip circulating around town, word was spreading that the Watsons were having financial issues. Victoria Tuckerman controlled the purse strings and they were getting tight. On Christmas Day, A.J. was concerned, almost falling apart and three days later, it was all fixed. This was definitely not passing the smell test.

HALF WAY THERE

CHAPTER 18

In less than two weeks, the knee surgery would occur. Zoey was always ahead of schedule and most times, this worked out pretty well. She double checked her stock to make sure all supplies were ordered. She had to take care of the books, resolve payroll issues, and after all was organized, she would be ready for her surgery. The doctors assured her that being positive and composed days before the procedure would prompt a healthy recovery.

Soon, she would halt all anti-inflammatory meds, aspirin, as this had an effect on bleeding issues. She was told to wear loose comfy clothing, like jogging pants. After surgery, she would ice the knee several times a day. Tight jeans were not a good option. Zoey wasn't looking forward to showers wearing a large plastic bag over her leg. Getting the incision wet was taboo. She had an older lady friend who had the knee surgery and did really well. Following instructions was mandatory. It was all becoming so real.

The Board meeting on Wednesday went according to plan. Zoey was glad to sit next to Claire Harris and before the meeting began, she got to know both candidates. Moritza Alvarez was new to the area, recently married and had an MLS, so that would please Sam. With a friendly personality, Zoey felt that was important at their small town library. The other girl also had a library degree but was a new Mom, her little boy just 4 months old. Promising the Board members that her mom was a reliable sitter, she was eager to start her librarian job here. Jennifer McCloskey was an acceptable candidate, but Zoey remembered how difficult raising a baby was, especially if you had a fulltime job. Zoey's choice was for the Alvarez girl.

When the meeting concluded and the candidates left, the group stayed to make their decision. Nearly all agreed that Moritza Alvarez was the best choice. Sam would phone her in the morning with the good news.

As they left the library, Zoey could not resist a comment to Sam "What a nice Christmas gift for A.J."

Sam looked very sure of himself. "It's no BMW, but he is still young and needs a reliable vehicle when he starts college next year." He looked at Zoey's Toyota Rav. "Like your dependable car."

What a condescending remark. "Well, It's no Jaguar but it's paid for. Good night, Sam"

On her drive home, her heated front seat was so soothing. Still Sam always managed to unnerve her. How could Marjorie stand this man? Is it worth a Jaguar to withstand his attitude on a daily basis? And now, he is trying to buy off his son. One thing was still bothering her. Another postcard had arrived from Victoria and by God, wasn't it perfectly timed. Zoey just shook her head in disbelief. Something was happening here and Zoey felt like she was in the middle of a jigsaw puzzle. There were so many missing pieces and they would just not fit.

The week after Christmas was always unusually slow at the eatery, but everyone needed a break after weeks of busy. Zoey had no plans for New Year's Eve, as these past few had been very quiet for her. Hannah was meeting up with some old friends and she included Andi. Her cousin admired her, wanted to be like her and soon Andi would also be off to a college life. She had no idea what she wanted to do though. Hannah as a young teen wanted to work with animals. Having a fun night out with Hannah was also pretty safe as alcohol or drugs were not on Hannah's top list. She was such a serious young woman. She had lots of fun, occasionally some wine or a Coors Light, but never drove after a few drinks. That made Kim smile with a sigh of relief.

Sips and Swap kept the same schedule over this weekend as for Christmas. They closed at noon on New Year's Eve and returned on Tuesday after a long restful weekend. Will did stop at the eatery a little before noon to see if she would like to spend the evening with him.

"Do you have fancy plans?" She kidded him along.

"Not really." Will threw out a suggestion. "How about lobster rolls to go with some seafood chowder?"

"Sounds fancy to me." She was up for this. "Are you getting the lobster from Ned's Seaside Bar in Waverly?"

"It is on my way from Dad's place and it is the best seafood around." He decided honesty was the best policy. "I did a pre-order yesterday before they sold out today."

"So you are fancy and smart." She sold him, "Sounds really nice. I have wine left from Christmas and I will think of a light dessert."

"See you around 6, then."

Closing up the eatery with closing for three days took a lot of hustle. At noon, Liz and the girls put the CLOSED sign on the door and by 2:30, they were all on their way home. Zoey was so glad to see all the cats through the large living room windows scurrying around excited that she was home. She told the cats company was coming again so they would have lots of time to play with Will. Zoey had time for a nice long bath and laughed when her mother told her and the girls that she plans too. They included a luxurious Jacuzzi bath, lots of wine and junk food before retiring early. Her new down featherbed and heated mattress pad were calling her.

Let's see: My plan or her plan? A definite tossup.

Hannah was off to meet friends around 5 and Zoey turned on her fireplace to settle in with the cats. She threw together ingredients for a chocolate mousse before she hopped in her tub. By 7 p.m. it would have firmed up and be ready to serve for dessert with a dollop of cream on top. Sighing, she realized that she was actually happy, the first time on New Year's Eve for many years now.

When Will arrived, both were starving so they settled in by the fireplace with food and iced glasses of wine. Absolutely the best when you had hot buttery lobster on a toasted roll with peachy flavored Riesling wine to wash it down. With sips of seafood bisque to finish off the meal, neither one would want anything to eat until midday tomorrow. Zoey was feeling almost normal and felt that she wanted to unload a lot on Will, who always remained a trusted friend. Their marriage went through a really rough period and Will was not mature enough to handle what they were experiencing. So many unpleasant things happened to Zoey in seven years, and she chose to keep these silenced and not burden Will. She assumed that he had no time for her and Zoey learned to handle difficult situations on her own. She had her mother and Kim for support, but even then, she kept some unusual happenings strictly to herself. These involved Sam Watson. It was why she chose to leave the library and also her position as his office assistant for his antiquities business. With the latest family issues at the Watsons, A.J. so unhappy, Zoey was trying to connect the dots. She did not like what she thought might be happening. Time to bounce it off of Will.

"Before we have a small dish of creamy chocolate mousse, I'd like to talk to you about what the hell is happening around here."

"You mean the body at the library?"

"No, that's only a small part of it." Truly concerned, she began to explain, "Everything seems to circle around Sam Watson. I am trying to figure it out but first you need to know something that I found, a while back, before I left my job at the library." She hoped he was paying attention, after two glasses of wine.

"I was so surprised you left, Zoey." He looked downward. "You loved that job." In a hurtful voice he told her, "I tried to help you through it but you wanted no part of me."

"Right you are." She added, "Sam is why I resigned both positions."

Sitting up straight, Mika slipping off of his lap, "What did he do to you?"

Quickly she responded, "No, it wasn't Sam that physically did something, at least not to me."

Zoey was sorry that she was about to put a real stink on this New Year's Eve. She told him exactly what happened almost two years ago now. It appeared that Sam Watson was involved with Ephebophilia, his interest in mid-late adolescent boys. Zoey had seen the proof of this in vivid photos of him with teenage boys.

CHAPTER 19

Will stared silently, with a total look of shock on his face. "Zoey, you should have told me."

"Will, you were never there for me when I really needed you." Not angry, but firm, she continued, "It was years that slowly passed by and I finally learned to become strong. I had no other choice, physically and emotionally. You and I managed to be friends, because of Hannah." She took both of his hands in hers. "I think we will get through this stage of mending because I still love you."

Will, by now, had tears in his eyes. Guilt, sadness, a whole bunch of emotions. He had made the biggest mistake of his life almost eight years ago. Carefully he engulfed Zoey within his entire body adding a kiss that was firm but gentle, and very meaningful.

Zoey just cradled within the warmth of his arms where she felt safe and secure, something she had not experienced for a long time. Returning the kiss she remembered how much she had enjoyed these embraces with her husband throughout their marriage. "Are you sure about this?"

Will held her warm body against his and told her "I don't want to let you go." He was certain that he never wanted to be apart from her, ever again. "I don't want to lose you, Zoey."

"I won't allow that to happen ever again." Getting up from the couch, she took him in her hands and headed toward the stairs that lead to her bedroom. "Tonight you will realize just how much I missed you." The night lovingly turned into morning.

The birds were chirping loudly for some seed, singing outside of the bedroom windows with all cats watching them. "I can't believe I overslept. Happy New Year." She uncovered Will's face that was still partially buried under the sheets. "I have to feed my birds, way overdue, don't you hear them?"

"I do, Happy New Year to you, too." Will reached over to give her a quick hug. "Hey, is Hannah going to be okay with this?"

"I think she saw this coming." Zoey smiled. "She is a big girl now and really loves her dad."

As Zoey got dressed, Will told her, "After breakfast, we need to have a long talk about what happened with Sam, okay?"

"Yes, we need to hash this over, it has bothered me for a long time."

"Do your Mom and Kim know about this disgraceful incident?" He shook his head in disbelief. "I need details so I can understand when this actually happened and why and how you managed to stay quiet and calm when handling it."

Losing patience she told Will, "I have to feed the birds." She promised, "Coffee downstairs and be on the quiet side as Hannah is still asleep, after a late night out." She headed down the stairs and whispered, "Kim knows but not my mother."

Will poured a cup of hot coffee gazing out the kitchen window watching Zoey feed her many bird friends. She loved all of her creatures, and lucky they all were. Will thought about last night and realized that there would be an explosive conversation when Liz found out what Sam had done, what his lifestyle was like some years ago. Not surprising though as imperfect people portrayed perfect lives. There is no way Marjorie know about this, his obsession for young teenage boys. The bar would have to be very low, probably underground for her to accept what Sam had done. Maybe it was a long time ago. Perhaps Zoey did not know the entire truth. That sounded a bit unlikely for Zoey, though. She was a very articulate individual, careful in her actions and words. Sometimes she was a bit too honest, but she spoke from her heart.

Coming in from the freezing cold air, Zoey threw off her coat and gloves and hustled over to the coffee pot. Sipping her creamed coffee, she looked over at Will with a smile. "What a really nice way to start my new year."

Will hugged her and said, “It will be a spectacular year.”

“Breakfast casserole?”

“Gads, I haven’t had that in what, eight years?”

“Jamie not much in the kitchen department?”

“Too busy in the mirror,” He added, “Unlike you who just washes her face and plops her hair high up into a floppy pony tail.”

“Takes a little more than that, these days. Age just creeps upon you.”

Will looked at her always so fresh and natural and Zoey never thought enough of herself. She worked hard at keeping healthy, despite setbacks from her forever Lyme disease. Zoey was one steadfast individual who always, after several tumbles, seemed to land back on her feet.

Surprisingly, both devoured their cheesy sausage breakfast casserole. Zoey cut off a chunk for Hannah and left it covered on the counter for when she finally woke up. All would need a power walk after breakfast. They made no plans for the day but Zoey hoped Liz would come by for a bite to eat at some point during the day. Jonas had to work so Kim and Andi would watch a lot of TV today. It was quite cold out with a stiff breeze from the ocean's water just blocks away. Will told Zoey that he would head for home later and spend the day with his dad, as he wanted to know just where his son's life was headed. Now, he could give him some positive news about Zoey and him. They would slowly move forward and in time be back together as one family. Will had his new coaching job and the golf excursions would not be the main focus in his life. Perhaps he would consider restarting this in the future, but for now he wanted to spend most of his time with Zoey.

"I am going to shower first and dress. Feel free to do the same." She added, "Then, we'll have a nice energetic walk, okay? We'll check out the waves."

"Isn't it really cold today?"

She headed up the stairway to take her shower and told him firmly, "Not getting out of this one."

He wasn't planning to. What he was planning was to be long gone, before Liz popped over. It was time for Zoey to tell her mother about Sam. She had held this inside herself for too long. On their power walk, Will would persuade Zoey to confide in Liz. She deserved to know what had happened. It had a huge impact on Zoey's life and now we figured out why she left the library and her assistant's position with Sam.

Both dressed for this brisk walk along the ocean, the wind had settled down and the sun was as bright as a new copper penny. Will needed to delve into the Sam issue. "So, when did all of this occur?" Intently, he listened to Zoey who was still bothered by this happening.

"It was late in April and Sam was on one of his buying trips to London. We were not very busy at the library as many people were off on vacation so I had more time to straighten out what a messy office Sam had, above his four car garage. He had been asking me to do this for a while. He was gone for more than a week so I had enough time to really straighten up. I was nearly done that week when he called me at home. He asked me to please stop at his office area and look for two contracts that he had made months ago. Now the deal was ready and he needed me to scan and send him these papers. They were in a special area where no one could access them without his permission. That sounded a little weird to me. It was just paperwork. I had learned at the beginning to never doubt or question him and all would work out fine. The paperwork was in a locked cabinet in the rear storage area. That area needed to be cleaned up also. He told me where the key was and I decided to just go and finish this up." She stopped walking and leaned against a small fence along the roadway. "I need to catch my second wind."

She continued on with her story, "At least the main office looked pretty neat. Heading to the back area, I saw the huge locked cabinet that seemed to have two parts, a front and a back. Never saw anything like it. The key stuck and I had to twist and turn it and finally it gave way and the cabinet opened. So much material there, overstuffed, for sure. I saw the paperwork that he wanted and as I took it out the wall holding the back looked loose. It was like it was being pushed outward, maybe over stuffed."

Will thought he was in the middle of a Nancy Drew mystery here. "Okay, so what did you see, in that loose wall?"

"Photos and a few images fell out from the loose wall that was holding them in. Sam was with some teenage boys." She stopped walking. "I can't talk about this. It took me a long time to forget it. And, I think I recognized one of the boys."

"Are you kidding me? Who was it?"

"I really can't be sure. But they were practically nude, so I know Sam's intentions were not good."

"Zoey, you should have pursued this, for the sake of the teenagers involved."

"Oh, right." Zoey was upset now. "Sam and the Tuckerman clan have connections right up to the governor's office. Would I have a chance if I accused Sam of what I believe I found?"

"I don't know Zoey, why are you always in the middle of things?"

"I got out of the middle. Weeks later I left my position with Sam using my being too busy excuse I had Kim take over to save my sanity. I didn't tell her what happened at Sam's office. When I finally told her, she quit too. In July I resigned at the library saying my mom and I were planning to start a new business. Health wise I was feeling okay, the Lyme disease was pretty dormant. Sam was not happy with either one of us. Kim and I decided that we would not burden my mother with what happened. It took her almost a year to get over the death of my dad. My mom did question me about leaving the library. For years, I loved my job. I told her I needed a positive change in my life. Always supportive, she believed me."

Now, almost at home they were sure that calories were successfully burned off. "Well, now you know." She gave Will a lasting, sober look.

He replied, "Be careful where you meddle." Adding, "You don't think Sam bothered A.J., do you?"

"I did think of that, but no. A. J. would have gone to Marjorie with it. He has always been very close to his mother." Zoey added, "Sam did not want to ruin his perfect life and I assume he thought by being careful he would not be caught at these actions."

"Tell your mom today." He shook his head side to side. "She will help you through this, but she is going to explode for being kept in the dark for what, well over a year now?"

Before Will left, hugs all around. Hannah was beaming when she discovered Will had spent the night with her mom. As he sped off, Hannah told her mother, "It is about time Dad grew up, you think?" Hannah would be off visiting friends when Liz came by for lunch. And what a lunch it would be.

"Lots to discuss, Will stayed over?"

"He did, and that's the happy news." Hesitating, Zoey was tense, then remembered Will supporting her. "We have another unpleasant matter to discuss. Saying unpleasant is being kind." Liz McCaffery forced an uncertain smile at her daughter.

CHAPTER 20

“Zoey, what is it?” Liz looked concerned. “Are you feeling okay?”

“I am fine, Mom, actually more than fine.” She rubbed her knee. “In a few days I will have a repaired knee that has no pain in it and weeks later, we’ll be in St. Maarten. This is long overdue.”

“So, let’s hear the unpleasant part so my heart stops thumping.”

“You always wanted to know why I left the library.”

“It was rather sudden.” She suspected something had occurred. “I know we spoke about starting the eatery business, so I assumed you just needed a fresh start at something new.”

“Sips and Swap is the best thing we ever did, and maybe one day I will thank Sam for this. But you need to know what happened when I resigned from Sam’s business and the library.” Zoey told her the entire story asking her not to interrupt until she was finished.

It was difficult, but Liz followed through, letting Zoey spill out the entire story. “I can’t believe that you never told me this.” She glowered at her daughter.

“Kim and I did not want you burdened.” She continued on, “You would have wanted me to pursue this with the authorities. We all know how well this family, along with Victoria Tuckerman, is connected to important people. Victoria knows the governor like a best friend.”

"I agree, Zoey, but we might have put our heads together and done something."

"Trust me, the less I deal with Sam Watson is the best solution."

"At least I understand why you want absolutely nothing to do with him. It all makes sense now." Suddenly, Liz stopped in mid thought, "A.J., he can't have been affected by this?"

"No, he would have gone to Marjorie, I am sure of that."

"Really?"

"What do you mean?" Zoey grilled her mother.

"He has changed over the years. He never wants to be at home with his dad. Maybe he was not one of Sam's victims but A.J. possibly discovered what his father was doing."

Repulsed, Zoey told Liz, "That would be awful."

"It certainly would explain the personality changes."

Zoey thought Will was right. Her mother was helping her work through this.

"What are we to do now," Zoey asked Liz. "Should we talk to Marjorie?"

"That would be a basket of snakes." She hugged her daughter. "For now, let's make some grilled cheese, tomato, and bacon sandwiches."

"I don't think comfort food is gonna' fix this one." Zoey sighed.

"I want to hear all about your night with Will. Let's hear happy, okay?"

They finished lunch and neither one was able to resolve the Sam issue. It was in the past but, Zoey felt there was so much more happening here and she was unable to zero in on it.

"Let me soak this in, Zoey." After a deep heavy breath, she thought, "It may be best to stay away from this. Sam could easily ruin our eatery. He knows a lot of people. You and Kim are both involved with this." Liz was talking too fast and couldn't seem to slow down. "He would be the victim and you two would be just liars. He could ruin Jonas in his career. These perfect people have power."

"Calm down, Mom." Zoey did have to agree with her mother and for now she and Liz would set this issue aside. Her life was overflowing and she needed to be calm and positive, prior to surgery.

The week to follow was busy at the eatery and soon Zoey would have some time off recuperating from knee surgery. She and Will agreed that he would be happy to stay over prior to the surgery and also be there for at least a week after. He would tend to the cats, feed the birds, help at the eatery and, in other words, he would be Zoey. By then, Hannah would be back at school and not have to worry about her mother. Liz would run both the Sips and Swap business.

The new librarian had taken over and she phoned Zoey about a few things to smooth her transition. She wasn't keen on talking to Jason, preferring Zoey. Zoey was happy to help her, as Sam was not involved. Moritza was already enjoying her new position at Tuckerman Library. She mentioned that Sam had a trip planned to London in the next week or so and he would not be easily contacted. He told her if a serious event happened, call Zoey.

Typical of Sam, Zoey thought. Moritza asked Zoey, "Do you know Mrs. Tuckerman?"

"I do. She supplies all financing for this library."

"When I told him I would enjoy meeting her, he said, we have no idea where she is or when she will return. I would not hold my breath. Moritza added, "I thought, how strange is that."

Zoey was also astounded by this comment. Moritza, you are right. Something is very peculiar here in Highland Falls.

The first week of January seemed to fly by and Zoey felt very organized with all she had accomplished. Enough supplies, paperwork done and finances looked good, as Zoey approached her date for arthroscopic knee surgery. Not allowed to take any aspirin or pain meds didn't help her through this pre surgical period but it would soon be over and her knee pain would be gone. It was a surprise visit from A.J. before he headed back to school that caught her off guard. He actually seemed happy. His father let him take the Audi back to his pretentious high-priced private school just an hour and a half from Highland Falls. He thanked Zoey again for taking the time to listen to him on Christmas Day.

"I told you, no problem A.J."

"Well, I will be back in a few weeks and promise to stop by to say hi. Good luck with your knee surgery."

"Is your grandmother back yet?"

"Not yet, but in about two weeks. My mom actually misses her."

"They have a lot to catch up on. I don't think she knows about the body."

"Dad says she has no clue, not seeing any local news where she is traveling." He hesitated then told Zoey, "Dad hopes she doesn't see the cold case show that will highlight this missing person case. When is it on?"

"In two days, Friday night at 8 p.m."

As he headed out the door, he told Zoey, "We'll all be watching at school about our now famous town."

"And good luck with that new car." She yelled out the door. And he was zooming off with what appeared to be a better outlook on life. Hard to believe the new Audi did the trick.

When Friday night finally arrived, Zoey's house was swarming with gossip and possible predictions that might lead to a resolution as to why a dead body ended up at Tuckerman Library. All guests were eager to view "Closing Case Files" with Miranda Prescott to see if she had the answers they were waiting for. All Zoey offered was lots of popcorn and soft drinks. Hannah called earlier and promised to watch at school. She also asked if Zoey was feeling okay with surgery just a few days off.

When the show came on, there was a hush of silence as all were glued to the show. Prescott summed up all that she was able to find out from various state and local police teams. She told her audience that she also interviewed the medical examiner and pathologist hoping to narrow down the reason for this woman's death in Highland Falls. Zoey was mentioned at the beginning too. Prescott told her viewers that this case was not officially closed, so she was unable to view medical reports or files. She hoped by airing this show, someone would come forward with positive clues as who this older woman was. Phone and e-mail contact numbers scrolled on the bottom of the screen during this thirty minute segment. Prescott told her viewers that she, after many weeks of trying, was unable to help close this homicide case.

A commercial appeared and Zoey pushed the pause button on her television. Prescott's summation was a major disappointment as everyone at Zoey's house just sighed in disbelief.

Jonas looked at Will, Zoey, and Liz. "Really, you thought she found out who this was, who murdered her?" He looked at them all, saying, "Thanks a lot. I was the one handling it and none of us could find anything useful. We do know what we are doing."

Kim gave him a quick hug. "No one is criticizing you. But, Prescott investigates. She has solved a lot of these similar cases, Jonas. People talk to her, she has a lot of contacts."

Jonas still looked offended. "And how did all that investigating work go for her?"

The room was silent. Zoey told them all, "Maybe the show will wake up someone who may know something. People watch this stuff."

Liz agreed then said, "Let's finish the show. Hit that play button, Zoey."

At least Zoey was professional during her interview, and although Sam was on the agenda, Miranda Prescott mentioned who he was but no interview occurred as he was away on business. She promised a follow-up segment should any more information appear. Hopefully someone from the viewing audience would contact the station or Miranda. She reminded her audience that over 70% of her cold cases were closed with the help of her viewing audience.

Everyone was disappointed. A follow-up segment was not high on the wanted list. Many people watched this show. Would someone come forward with clues or evidence? Perhaps this woman was not from this area. Or, maybe someone from afar, watching this show would help us solve this murder. There was always hope.

CHAPTER 21

It was a very raw weather day in London. Gil Andrews was headed to Heathrow to pick up his wife at the airport. Caroline traveled to see her mother right after Christmas as she looked forward to seeing her family each year around this time. Traffic was brutal and it was near dinner time, so the rush was on. Helping Caroline with her luggage, he could see that the flight had tired her out. Her husband gave her a hug as she got into their Jaguar asking her, "Was your visit a success?"

"Always a good time with my mother. My brother remains such a happy soul," she told Gil, fastening her seatbelt. "His wife's educational career is flourishing. Brian is enjoying the financial end of that one." Caroline added, "Mom is so interested in that murder case at Highland Falls. She watched the cold case show a few nights ago with me. You really have to ask Sam Watson about this. The dead body was discovered behind his library."

Gil Andrews was totally taken aback with this comment. "Indeed," He told Caroline, frowning. "I will see him within the week." He finished telling her, "Strange that he never mentioned this daunting event to me."

"I can't imagine it would be anything to be proud about. Listening to how you describe Sam, he would want this totally forgotten."

Arriving home from the airport, Gil and Caroline Andrews both needed a strong drink. They opted for vodka and tonic, mostly vodka. Caroline plopped down of the sofa saying, "I need a hot bath and a warm bed as soon as possible."

Gil was still fuming over what Caroline had told him about the murder in Sam Watson's town, in back of his library. Gil had a really bad feeling about this. He had dealings with Sam over the years and had made a good amount of clean cash because of him. At first, Sam dealt with antiquities, mainly fine artworks, rare trinkets, etc. However, Gil ran clean business transactions and was beginning to feel like he was dealing with a dishonest person. The latest items Sam offered were a fine quality of antique jewelry. There was a huge profit for both Sam and Gil with these pieces. Gil could not resist the profits to be made. After all, one had to pay for service on the Jaguar Caroline owned.

Sam was due to fly into London at the end of the week and Gil knew what he must do beforehand. Research. Amazing what you can find out on the internet. He would look into this case and see if anything strange wandered about. He needed to find out more about Sam's family. He never asked Sam details about the latest jewelry sale but assumed that the items were family owned. Not a good idea to ask too many questions. Gil assumed that Sam Watson did own these jewels and for whatever reason, it was his right to sell them. The items were exquisite, quite old, and appeared to have been handed down from generation to generation. That is what made them so valuable. He gazed at his watch. Too late to begin serious research tonight. He would make a light dinner for Caroline and himself before calling it a night.

Hoping for a good night's sleep was futile unlike Caroline who was out like a light. He was always glad to have her very close to him, especially after a trip abroad. Her mother's health was failing and soon she would be gone.

Sad to even think that no one, after months past, had as of yet, claimed that body mysteriously buried behind Sam Watson's library.

The weather in London greatly improved overnight with the sun shining brightly in Gil and Caroline's flat. Because of his business dealings, Gil was able to furnish their apartment with fine antiques and alluring décor. This charming appearance found its way into a number of regional magazines. In a much better mood upon awakening, Caroline told Gil, "I am so happy to be home."

"I'm glad you slept so well." Gil handed her a steaming cup of tea. "Egg sandwich on a croissant?"

"Yumm." She sat at their small wicker table that looked out at their small back yard, birds chirping. "Did you feed them all, every day?"

"Of course." He looked out at all of the seed he had just put out. "Lots of Woodcocks while you were away, and the waxwings are daily visitors."

"I missed them." She added with a frown, "Mom isn't able to feed birds in her retirement home now. Makes her sad."

As they had breakfast he asked what Caroline what she was up to today. "Off for some food shopping. Let's have lamb for dinner, okay?" She also had a request. "You google all the time. Do some searching to find that cold case show that was viewed in the states." She looked at him hopefully. "I am certain you can locate it. We can watch it tonight." Adding a sly smile, "At least you'll get to take a look at Highland Falls where one of your best business associates lives."

Gil was not about to tell her how anxious he was feeling regarding Sam Watson. He would arrive here in a few days and would have some very pricey jewels to unload. Right now, Gil wanted to know where these items came from. Who did they really belong to? On occasion, Sam did have clients that requested some rare objects or antiques to be sold. Sam was an expensive middleman, but he knew his antiques and rare jewels. He would not be under or oversold. That was why people hired him to be the middleman.

"I am off, dear, foodstuff, the salon, so I will be here later on today." She gave him a long hug, and a short kiss. The Jaguar purred softly as she drove out of the garage.

With Caroline gone for most of the day, Gil had a lot to look into. He had to find out more about Sam Watson before his arrival here later this week. He had to be sure what Sam had to offer Gil this time would not have repercussions in the near future.

Gil was careful with all of his business dealings. Impeccable records were kept of all of the bought and sold merchandise. Photos were taken, logged into his computer, dated, and then kept in a separate file, in case of loss. In the ten years he had been in the buy and sell enterprise, he had never had any legal issues occur. He was beginning to feel very unsure about Sam Watson. So, the investigation begins. First would be to search for info on Sam. Then, he would appease Caroline and look for the cold case show highlighting the murder in Highland Falls.

There were far too many articles about the infamous Samuel Watson. Once considering a run for the State Senate, he had backed out citing family obligations as he and his wife Marjorie had a young son. Gil narrowed down his search focusing on the Tuckerman Library in Highland Falls. That is when Gil became intrigued with many articles of Victoria Tuckerman. There were many articles on her and her dedicated financial service to the library. Her family had moved north back in the late 1800s from South Carolina. It was then that her great grandfather built the small Tuckerman Library. Additions through the years improved the services offered to this shoreline town. She put her son-in-law, Samuel Watson, in charge as the library's prestigious Director of the twelve-person Board. A small pittance from the town also kicked in when needed. However, it still remained a private library, under the control of Victoria Tuckerman. That is when Gil narrowed in on the Tuckerman queen bee.

Most of the media coverage on the Tuckermans focused on Victoria. Known well for her charities, she also had a voice during the Women's Movement. There were many photos of her at various political events, including several political figures. Gil guessed her age must be close to 80, but all of the images were strikingly attractive. Gil wanted to find some family photos of Marjorie or their son that Sam rarely mentioned. After hours of digging for dirt, Gil saw a rededication of the Tuckerman Library some years ago, after an addition was added. There was Sam, Victoria, Marjorie, and Andrew James Watson, their son. The perfect family, all smiling. Gil's eyes were really tired, starting to get foggy, it had been hours searching. Then, it appeared.

Victoria Tuckerman and the newly elected governor at the Inauguration Ball. The article mentioned the generous donation to the governor, a popular Democrat, who won with a landslide victory. He probably did not need all that money Victoria had given to him. Then, Gil spotted it. Enlarging the image as much as possible, there it was. Victoria beaming, arm around the governor, and the diamond and emerald necklace around her neck.

There was no mistake, Gil had the image of this necklace, sitting right on his lap.

CHAPTER 22

For days, Zoey, Kim, and Liz discussed the cold case show. Everyone was chirping about in when they came in to Sips and Swap. Claire stopped by to wish Zoey good luck with her surgery that was scheduled in just two days.

"What did you think of the episode, Zoey?" Claire was reaching for some clarity but was not going to get very much.

"I am hoping that someone from our area or out of the area will help to resolve this. This lady had a home somewhere." She sighed, head down. "Maybe she was all alone and had no one, and at least that would explain this mystery."

"Did that Prescott woman search all of the homeless refuge sites around here?"

"I don't know, but that is a thought. I will give her a call later."

"Did Moritza stop by to see you?" She had to be honest here. "I told her if she ran into any snags at Tuckerman, you would be most willing to help her."

"I did get a visit last week. She is doing well and enjoying her job. But, I don't think she is too fond of Sam."

"Well, he is really not a people person with most folks."

"You mean if you are not a member of the country club."

Claire snickered quietly. "Right. Moritza is a bit too far south of the border for Sam to chum up to." She asked Zoey for her meal to go. "Zoey, you should win a prize for this quiche, the Havarti cheese really makes it spectacular."

As Zoey finished straightening up the swap area at neatly as possible, she picked out a few of her favorite audiobooks. She might enjoy listening to them as her leg was resting up on a pillow after surgery. Audio books always seem to provide a calming effect, relaxing her while hearing an interesting story unfold with little effort. On her way home that day, Zoey knew Will would be there with a welcoming smile. With only one day left at the eatery, after today, as she left to head home, she already missed it.

Will had a pot of soup on when Zoey arrived home, greeted lovingly by Will and the three cats. It could not get much better than this. He told her, "Well, one day left at work and then you'll get fixed."

"Will, I don't plan to get spayed or neutered." They both burst into laughter.

"Poor choice of words, I guess." Proud of his cooking skills he told her, "Soup is almost ready, your favorite, lamb and barley stew."

"I do hope you know how long it takes to steam barley."

"Yes, I do. Google was my favorite companion today…aside from Mika."

Zoey made her way to the stove, grabbed a spoon and had to sample the broth. "You do know how to google."

They had a nice quiet dinner with buttery soft rolls that Will bought. He was not up to baking any yeast breads, as of yet. Before bed, Zoey had to pack a small bag for the hospital with a few necessities, just in case it turned into more than an outpatient visit. She felt exceptionally achy for days now as she had no aspirin to take, doctor's orders. However, it had been seven years now with all kinds of aches that would crop up with no warning. That was forever Lyme disease. Her immune system had been traumatized and as her rheumatologist at the university hospital told her, she had learned to live with recurrent pain and that made her a stronger individual. No blue ribbons on the agenda though, just a positive attitude to get her through trying times.

Hannah called before Zoey and Will headed off to bed to see how she was feeling. Hey, I watched the show and it was a bit of a dud, except for your interview. You did great, Mom."

"We were all disappointed, hoping Prescott would help resolve this issue and the identity of the buried body."

"You know, if it were a robbery, why would you bury the body, cover it up with a tarp. Just leave it on the side of the road." Hannah sounded a bit pissed off. "Covering a body with a tarp gives an impression that there was a connection somehow to that body." She sighed, "I'm just sayin', why didn't anyone notice this?"

Zoey had to agree with this oddity. "Don't have any answers."

"Promise to call me after surgery on Friday?"

"I do and maybe I will be on some happy pills for the pain." Zoey had a slight laugh with this.

"Surgery is minor. You will skirt right through this." Hannah hung up and Zoey headed off to bed with Will. To help her relax, the gentle massaging back rub she received was most welcome.

On her last day at work, things went smoothly until Sam Watson stopped by to see Zoey prior to leaving on his sales trip to London. "Our new librarian seems to be doing quite all right. Did she stop by to see you last week?"

"She is doing well and she knows I can assist her while you are gone. Why isn't Jason helping her out?"

"When he resigned, he made it clear that he was starting a new job and was unable to help."

"All right, then." Zoey added, "I have surgery tomorrow on my knee, if you recall, so I will be out of touch for several days."

"I had forgotten about that, sorry."

Wow, thought Zoey, a real apology. "It's all right. It's outpatient and I have help at home for a few days until I start walking like a normal person."

"I am off then, leaving day after tomorrow for a week or maybe a bit longer." Looking slightly disgruntled, he spat out, "I am glad the show is finally over. That Prescott woman never gives up. She calls and calls and has been quite an irritant."

Zoey had to poke the bear with a white lie. "I was told there would be a sequel." Adding, "Maybe you'll have an interview after all."

Sam just stared right through her. "For God's sake, it looks like this old woman had no one, was robbed and left there. There really is no mystery. Prescott just wants a television segment to earn her salary."

"It really doesn't concern you that we'll never have this resolved?"

"I have other things on my mind, like my trip to London." He told her as he left, "See you when I return."

At the end of the day, Liz came back into the Swap area encouraging Zoey that all would be fine at the eatery in the days to follow. "Go home, have a nice hot bath and a good night's sleep. Can you have a full meal tonight?'

"I can, but I am choosing to eat light. The anesthesia is not a strong one, but sometimes it causes nausea. I rarely, by choice ever vomit, Mom. You know that. Not on my agenda for tomorrow either." Zoey was showing a bit of anxiety with her nonstop rambling. "The hospital just called. I have to be there at 6:30 a.m." Sounding a bit gleeful, she sighed, "Yeah, I am first to be done. Home by 2 p.m. I think."

Liz tried to calm her down a bit prior to leaving. A warm hug and a wish for successful surgery was the best she could offer. "Good thoughts only. Forget about the body behind the library. Not your responsibility to resolve this. Got it?"

She returned the hug before leaving the eatery. "Thanks Mom. I love you. Will call you tomorrow."

CHAPTER 23

Gil Andrews was now thinking, gads why did I play detective and do all of that research on the Tuckerman clan? He was still stunned to say the least. He must not jump to conclusions. However, there was no doubt who owned this half a million dollar necklace. Who knows how long it had been in Victoria Tuckerman's possession, it was undoubtedly a family heirloom. Sam never told him it was owned by the Tuckermans. But, Gil had never asked, either. Gil was beginning to perspire, wiping his brow. Heading over to his liquor cabinet, he got a stiff portion of scotch swigging it down in two swallows. If Gil remembered correctly, Sam had mentioned that his mother-in-law was on an extended trip abroad. Oh my God, was he selling this stuff without her knowledge? What happened when she returned? Maybe she was already back in the states. Gads, what would Gil due if there was a backlash? It appeared that this woman, this queen bee who controlled all finances, was connected to some very important political people. She had clout. Gil felt like he was in a boat with no paddle and could not see any land.

Should he confide in Caroline? Looking at the time, it was after 3 o'clock. Gil promised his wife to find that article on the murder, and google the television show that aired it. Maybe watching this show might prove something as it did have a connection to Sam. Gil realized only days were left for him to decide if he would confront Sam Watson. Gil was counting on a nice profit from this next batch of jewels. If the sale did not go through, Caroline would have to scale down from the Jaguar to a Yugo.

Caroline got home really late that day but did have some fresh lamb chops to grill. A little garlic and rosemary for seasoning and the whole house was alive with an appetizing fragrance. While eating a scoop of buttery mashed potatoes, Caroline asked Gil, "Well, do we have entertainment tonight watching a murder mystery?"

A bit disturbed by her unfeeling comment, Gil had to voice his opinion. "Really, Caroline, your mom has nothing interesting in her life so this intrigue is just an attention outlet."

"And how is that so bad?" She snapped back at Gil.

"It isn't bad for your mother." He continued, "Caroline, this is a dreadful happening, especially in a small town that sounds ideal to me, from what Sam Watson has said." He added, "You are making it sound like entertainment."

Carrying her empty dish over to the dishwasher, she just shook her head in dismay. "There is a dead body in back of your buddy's town library, one where he is the big wheel in that town. I would call that entertainment."

She always had a quick reply. Caroline, a journalism major, worked as a copyeditor for a magazine in London for years, before she retired. She was quick witted and had an answer for everything. After many years, Gil just let her have the last word. "All right then, maybe we need to be entertained for a while."

"Doesn't it seem strange that Sam Watson never told you about this?"

"It does." Gil had no other honest answer. "I told you, he is flying in this week and I will grill him, if you like."

"Or, invite him over for a luncheon."

Oh, sure, Gil thought. "Why, so you can be the investigative reporter on this?"

"Really, Gil." She added, "I could certainly have some gossip for Mom if he stopped by. I could tell her I met Sam Watson, the person who runs Tuckerman Library where the body was found."

"And that would make your mother's existence better?"

"Don't be cruel. Mom has so little to do now. She enjoys her retirement village, but Gil she is well into her eighties and is fading away on me. This issue has brought her back to life, especially since you know this Sam Watson fellow."

"I am sorry. I do understand." He added, "Your mother never forced us to give up our home here in London to live in the states. I am thankful for that. I think we'll visit her together next time. How's that?"

"That would be wonderful, Gil." With a questionable glance, she asked, "Maybe we could drive down to Highland Falls?"

In a snickering voice he replied, "You really want to visit the crime scene, don't you?"

"Let's clean up the kitchen and get ready to watch your show, all right?" Caroline readied the dishwasher and made a large pot of steaming tea.

With some crisp butter cookies and a hot cup of tea, the taped cold case show was about to start. Gil felt a bit anxious, wondering if Sam Watson would appear trying to calm everyone down and make this look better than it was or hoping it would all go away. At least Caroline would have some gossip for her mother and

maybe Gil might have some answers he was also searching for. The show was only thirty minutes in length so Gil could not expect a lot of answers about this body and why no one knew who it was.
Miranda Prescott was a thorough and interesting reporter with all pertinent information discussed in chronological order. She first summarized the show and told her viewers that she was unable to help close this cold case for the Tuckerman Library in Highland Falls, Connecticut.

Prescott then showed the roundtable of people relevant to this unsolved case.

As Carolyn watched the interviews there were a number of people that prompted her interest. She was disappointed that Sam Watson was not included. Prescott mentioned that he was away and unable to do a personal dialog.

"Really, Gil, he is like the most important person here," she told her husband hitting the play button. "Yet, he avoided an important interview?"

"I am sorry you have never met Sam. He is actually a very charming man." Gil thought to himself, what the heck was that about, not being interviewed. Sam loves that attention. "Hit the play button, let's get on with it."

Several people examining the case were the State Police, local Marshall Jonas Parsons, and the medical examiner. The medical examiner was allowed to list some facts for anyone watching. The woman was between seventy and eighty years old, her dentures were removed, prior to burial. Marks on her neck area showed that jewelry had been worn for some time, along with certain faded coloration marks on her ring fingers. Rings were missing. It appeared that jewels were removed prior to her death. In addition, marks on her neck may have been from strangulation, perhaps when a thick necklace was forcibly removed. Caroline hit the pause button again. "Gads, Gil, this is awful, it really was a murder."

By now, Gil's stomach was stating to upheave. Why the interest in the jewelry? Who would strangle someone for a necklace? Even Sam wouldn't stoop to that level. "Hit the damn play button, let's get to the end."

Caroline unpaused the remote and different images appeared showing the Tuckerman Library. There were interior and exterior shots and of course Prescott zeroed in on the crime scene, a hole dug in back of the wooded area on library grounds. Prescott was able to contact the contractor doing the excavation work at the library for a new handicap ramp. He spoke for only a brief time, telling viewers how the body was discovered. Continuing on was the previous librarian, Zoey Mitchell, who appeared for a brief few minutes. She spoke highly of the library and the generosity of Victoria Tuckerman who supported the institution through decades. Sam Watson, her son-in-law, had been the director for many years. There were some images of Victoria Tuckerman on the grounds of the library, shovel in hand, planting a tree in her late husband's honor.

Gil was getting tired of this rambling library history. He gazed at the television when a new image appeared. Victoria on the steps with the state librarian for an important day at Tuckerman. A state grant for the handicap ramp was handed over to her. As she accepted this folder, smiling at the crowd, Gil saw the ring on her finger. The emeralds and diamonds could not be overlooked as Gil felt sickened by the sparkling gems. They looked way too familiar due to his intricate documentation of records and images. This was becoming a nightmare on wheels.

CHAPTER 24

What was most difficult on the morning of knee surgery was taking in the aroma of freshly brewed coffee and being unable to have any. Will tried an apology, "Sorry Zoey, pot was on automatic. I should not have tempted you and shut it off before bed last night. He drove Zoey to the surgical center arriving promptly at 6:30 a.m. A few hours later, the patient slowly came back to life.

It was a little past 11 that morning when Zoey began to come awake. She was greeted by her doctor and Will who never left the hospital after she was wheeled off for the procedure. Surgery was successful and the doctor had some news for her.

"We retrieved so much fluid behind that left knee. I am doing some lab tests to see if any Lyme particles appear. Getting rid of this fluid will truly help you improve."

In a very drowsy voice Zoey replied, "Great. And I did not throw up."

Everyone laughed at that comment. Dr. Robbins told her, "Well, you are a lucky patient, nausea is a common side effect with this type of surgery. So, how do you feel, maybe a little wobbly?"

"Better now than when I first came awake. When can I go home?"

"You did really well and your vitals are good. You will probably be ready to go around 4 p.m. By then we will have double checked everything."

"I brought my cane, just in case." Zoey looked cautiously at her doctor.

"And for a short while, you will need it. Best to stay on one floor for the first two days, then stairs are all right with caution."

"Got it." She looked over at Will, the person who would be constantly watch over her, preventing any harm that would happen.

"I assume Will is your guard keeper."

"He is." He took her hand in his, careful not to disturb the tubes still attached to her monitor.

"I will stop by before you get discharged. Have a little lunch, you'll need your strength for later."

As Zoey became fully awake, she sat up and said. "This was not so bad, at least so far, as I hardly feel any pain."

Will, snickering silently, commented on why she was pain free. "You do realize there is a pain blocker that will last about 12 hours. By 9 or 10 o'clock tonight, you'll need those pain meds he gave to you."

"Understood." When the hospital staff came to her room, they asked if she could tolerate some crackers and soup with a little ginger ale. She replied a grateful yes.

The day raced by and Zoey was discharged a little before 5 p.m., carefully placed in her wheelchair. Surprisingly, she did feel very tired and was careful when slipping into the front seat of her car, with Will as her driver. Heated seat on, she relaxed. "Will, thanks for your help."

“I would say it is long overdue.” He leaned over and gently kissed her, a deep meaningful embrace. “I got the downstairs guest room ready for you. Sorry it’s just your old queen sized bed, but the fluffy down duvet will be really comfy.”

“It will be fine, and you can sleep next to me, so I don’t fall on the floor.” She had to laugh at that. “The cats will just have to accept and make room for you. I may smell like hospital though, so they may abandon me for a day or two.”

“I promise not to do that.”

Zoey was very careful after she crawled carefully from her car that was parked inside the garage and close to her kitchen doorway. Slowly making her way to the living room couch, Will started the fireplace and the room was soon filled with warmth. One by one, the cats slowly crept near Zoey, but with much uncertainty. Spencer rubbed against her and then Dewey and Mika thought it would be okay to do the same. It was a quick visit as they followed Will into the kitchen eager for their dinner.

While Will made dinner, Zoey reached for her phone and needed to make three important calls to Kim, Liz and Hannah. They were short calls, but all were so glad she was home with a successful surgery. And no vomiting.

Zoey and Will had quiche and a salad. It was simple but one of Zoey’s best dishes. There was no need to shower tonight, but tomorrow she would need to learn how to protect her entire leg from getting any water near the incision. She was so going to miss those long hot Jacuzzi baths. For now, she would get comfy and take a pain med as she finally began to feel her leg, as the pain blocker was fading away. Will brought her the ice pack wrap that she was to keep on her knee hoping to prevent further swelling. Once settled in bed around 9 o'clock, Zoey was a bit stiff and uncomfortable. "Not as easy as I thought it would be."

"I am right here and you can take the meds every six hours. Don't be proud."

She lay back on her pillow, fluffy duvet covering her and sighed. "It's over and we'll look forward to happy days from now on."

"You are lucky that I don't start my coaching position for another two weeks. By then, I will be worn out from becoming Zoey. Gads, just feeding all those birds is enough for me."

"And, the possum who stops by around midnight for kibble and some bread."

Will reminded her, "I remembered, but he is one ugly friend."

Half asleep, Zoey managed a quick but touching kiss before calling it a night.

Waking up around 1 a.m., Zoey did take another pain pill. First she headed to the bathroom, using her cane. And she needed it. Zoey never thought how difficult it would be just going to the bathroom. However, the thick bandage she had wrapped around her knee felt like it weighed forty pounds. Exhausted, she made her way back to bed, glad she had those pain meds.

"You okay?" Will was concerned.

"As good as I can be. I just need to go back to sleep." She noticed just one of her girls on the bed, Spencer. As she reached over to pet her, the purring began. Spencer edged over to sleep right under Zoey's arms. In less than five minutes, Zoey was flat out. Truly a calming companion cat and better than using a sleeping aid.

It was bright and sunny when Zoey came awake, almost 7:30 a.m. Will was missing and she guessed feeding the birds or making breakfast. Stiff and a bit sore, the bathroom called. Again, the difficulty. Hobbling over, she was slowly learning how to do this as easy as possible. No other choice. The answer was slowly and carefully.

Zoey spent the morning watching all the various species of birds and squirrels who frequented her back yard on a daily basis. Most popular were the woodpeckers, who relied on the hanging screened in metal nut container. It was nearly empty every single day. Weather was warmer than usual and no snow in the forecast. She had a doctor's checkup a week later to see how her bandaged knee was progressing. Then a week of physical therapy and she would be good to go. She did pray for no snow as it would be almost impossible to carefully walk and not slip on icy surfaces. The long range forecast looked cold but no storms on the horizon. In between many telephone calls from her caring friends and relatives, Zoey managed to assemble all that she needed and decided to take a shower. She was ordered to keep the thick and uncomfortable bandage wrapped securely around her knee for two days. And, keep the area dry. Before heading for the bathroom, Zoey found a large plastic trash bag and some elastic strips to keep this huge bag in place while she showered.

As Zoey began to carefully get undressed before bathing, she felt very chilled, standing there in the nude and glad Will wasn't in there helping her. She was doing this job solo. Her body, unbending and not helpful, Zoey managed to secure the plastic bag, slipping it high onto her upper thigh. Shower on full speed, plastic cap protecting her long, clean hair, she edged her way into the stall. Standing there, water pelting off her plastic protection bag, she felt totally drained of energy. After five days, she would be able to shower and allow water on the incision. Thank God.

As several days passed by, Kim and Liz stopped by with goodies and Liz made a tempting beef casserole for their dinner one night. Claire came by for a quick hello offering Zoey a bouquet of fragrant carnations hinting that spring was not far away. "You are looking pretty good. Maybe it is due to your caregiver."

"He is certainly my main reason for fast recuperation. I could never feed all of my wildlife like this." She pointed to her bandage. "Tomorrow I unearth it and can take a normal shower."

"I had a call from Emma McAllister, one of Victoria Tuckerman's close friends here. I guess she promised Emma that she would help with a charity event next month and Emma has no idea where she is." Claire hoped Zoey would help Emma.

"She is not alone. Marjorie doesn't even know where she is. It appears that Victoria and Marjorie had a big family eruption. That is when Victoria decided she needed some time away from them all. Thus, the three-month trip. I spoke with A.J. though before he went back to school and he thinks she will be back in a week or two. He does miss her more than anyone else. Maybe pass that on to Emma."

"Will do." Heading out the door, she wished Zoey the best. "Catch up on your rest, girl. We need you at the eatery."

Contemplating how good this would be she told Claire, "I will be back in two weeks."

After the doctor's visit, Zoey was given an A+ on how well she was doing. Bandage was off and the incision was not pretty but healing slowly. She was now able to get it wet, keep it clean and protected. No cats jumping on her leg. Zoey wore thick loose jogging pants and it all worked out well. She and Will decided that before he started his new coaching job he could move back with her. They would talk about any future plans in the weeks to follow.

Will was really happy when she told him of these plans. "I wanted to ask you about that, but I wanted to wait until you were back to feeling like Zoey."

"I appreciate that, but I am so much better. The required therapy ends soon and I can go back to the eatery, but fewer hours. Then I should be able to leave on our trip to St. Maarten."

"Lucky you." He sighed. "Most beautiful beaches in the world."

"Good thing I can get my leg wet, right?"

As the next week passed, Zoey was determined to rebuild her strength and get back to normal. Finally, she found her way back at the eatery. Her rehab was a success but she tired easily and Dr. Robbins said that was due to happen, perfectly normal. Liz was getting excited, buying a few summer outfits for their trip and doing some safe tanning at the local sun salon. Zoey would need a few sessions too, as the St. Maarten sun was exceptionally strong and would wreck havoc unless she planned right.

Sam Watson was gone on his trip, but A.J. was spotted zooming by the eatery, headed for his house. Strange, as he was not due home for a while. But, Sam was not there, so maybe that was why. Zoey would soon learn that one of his classmates had taken his life, right at school. He came home to see Marjorie, but he really needed to see his grandmother. She would be the only one to understand why this young boy was traumatized enough to die at such a young age. Soon, skeletons would emerge from a very well kept and secret closet. It would not be pretty.

CHAPTER 25

It was a late afternoon arrival and another rainy day in London when Sam Watson flew into Heathrow for his latest business deal with Gil Andrews. This would have to be the last planned venture for a while. So many flames in the fire, Sam had to scale back and plan accordingly. With the sale of these extraordinary two pieces of jewelry he had chosen for this trip, the Watsons would do well for quite some time. All those years of putting up with Victoria had paid off. Selling these gems now was a necessity, especially while Victoria was out of the picture. Thousands of dollars were being sucked up on unnecessary travel ventures, especially this last trip. Who knows what all of those trips cost in relation to the finances of the Watson family? Only Sam could control this. It was way past due. He was now losing patience as the baggage claim area was a nightmare waiting an hour before his luggage finally came through. He spotted Gil Andrews across the way, amidst the crowd of other arriving travelers. He waved over to Gil hoping he would be seen.

"Sam, over this way, we are in the first floor garage."

Wheeling over his luggage, Sam frowned, "Gads how do you survive here with all this damp weather?"

He wanted to say, better than living in a lovely town with a murdered lady. But he did not. "We are accustomed to it. Most days are lovely, especially in the summer. You know that, having been here in June and July."

While driving Sam to the hotel that he used for all of his business dealings, he asked how his holidays went.

“As expected, everyone wants gifts.” In a smug tone he added, “Teenagers are never happy enough, so we got A.J. an Audi convertible.”

“And now he’s smiling again?” Gil thought there goes a chunk from the last jewel sale for that automobile purchase.

Finally arriving at The Savoy, Sam found his way to the check in counter and he told Gil, “I plan to have an early dinner and opt for a good night’s sleep. Do you want to come by here tomorrow about 11 and we can finish this jewelry sale?” He also asked, “Are we still on target with the sale price and your commission?”

“Right there.” Gil did add one thing, though. ”Let’s discuss some other things tomorrow. I am seriously considering going into full retirement mode.”

Taken aback, Sam could not think of how to reply. “Really?”

“Caroline and I need to spend more time enjoying our senior years.” Heading out of the hotel, he added, “I will talk to you tomorrow. Have a good night’s sleep, Sam.”

Sam ordered room service and sat down to think about Gil’s future plans. Retiring? Bummer on Sam’s end. Gil was a good contact, reasonable commission fees, and fast reliable sales. He would try and persuade him to stay with this resale business for a while longer. It was profitable and it did not demand a whole bunch of Gil’s time. Maybe he wanted a bigger commission. Sam would consider that. Noticing how late it was, Sam decided to text Marjorie to let her know that he had arrived. Otherwise she would be ringing him, long after he was asleep.

It felt rather damp and uncomfortable as Sam crawled into bed, exhausted from the flight and all that rain. Marjorie replied to his text with news that was very distressing. A.J. had come home from school and his classmate, Conner Holtzman, had committed suicide. A.J. was a wreck. They had been friends since grammar school, and Conner had been to the Watsons on many occasions through the years. She asked Sam if he remembered Conner.

Sam was speechless. He did know Conner as A.J.'s good friend. This was not a good scenario. He also realized how sensitive A.J. was and this would be a terrible ordeal for him. It was best not to respond and let Marjorie handle this. A.J. was always a mommy's boy, and for years now he had not confided in Sam. A good night's sleep was not about to happen.

Sam had a restless night for a number of reasons. Life was just not easy anymore. This business trip was supposed to be lucrative, enjoyable. Gil had thrown in a monkey wrench saying he wanted to retire, A.J.'s friend took his own life and he was not looking forward to going home to Highland Falls. He had to face Marjorie, who was not in a happy mood of late. She questioned Sam about everything, such a meddling bitch, sometimes. And there was always Victoria and how she persistently tried to ruin his personal life. That would not continue for much longer.

After a full breakfast delivered right on time and a long refreshing shower, Sam was ready to meet with Gil Andrews. Sam had other meetings this week including an affluent client interested in an antique clock Sam had owned for some time. They had agreed on a sale price and there was no middleman involved. This morning, he would deal with Gil.

Before Gill left his flat for his business meeting, Caroline demanded that Gil get to the bottom of this issue that seemed to have a connection to Sam Watson.

"I plan to do just that Caroline." Gil never discussed in detail what he had seen while viewing the cold case television show. He was able to hide how astonished he felt while viewing the image of Victoria Tuckerman and the ring on her finger. He also never told his wife about his lengthy research while she was out of the house, right after coming home from her trip to the states. He had discovered more than he wanted to know or see from those telling images. He was certain that those jewels he had recently sold belonged to Victoria Tuckerman. It was truth time and it was all on Sam Watson.

Arriving at The Savoy Hotel, Gil was more than anxious. Maybe Sam would provide some closure on this questionable issue.

When Gil got to Sam's suite he was invited to join him for lunch at Pera, Sam's favorite eating establishment in London. But, Gil decided no.

"Thanks for the invite, Sam, but I have plans later with Caroline and we have a special dinner out tonight. Too much fancy food in one day doesn't agree with me."

Disappointed, Sam would enjoy a top of the line lunch on his own. "So, what can I do to persuade you to not retire?'

"That will be decided by Caroline and me, but we have another thing to discuss." Sternly he asked Sam, "I need to know who officially owns these jewels that you have brought over to me for resale purposes."

Sam was taken aback by this question. How dare he question the ownership. “I own these jewels and where is this suspicion coming from?”

“Sam, Caroline and I watched the cold case show. She visited her mother over the holidays and this lonely old lady became completely obsessed with this murder that had occurred in Highland Falls.”

Sam felt rage deep within his senses. ”Jesus Gil, this case is over, no one needs to worry or gossip about this any longer. I knew this would happen and it would tarnish our town.”

Gil’s heart was racing, but he had to continue and face Sam with what appeared to be the truth. “Before Caroline and I watched the cold case segment, I did some research. Clearly I noticed, with no doubt, the jewels that appeared on Victoria Tuckerman. I saw the ring at some dedication event at Tuckerman Library and the emerald and diamond necklace was around her neck at the Inauguration Ball some years ago. Difficult to believe that she just gave them to you.”

Everything was beginning to unravel, so Sam had to be the smooth operator that had propelled him throughout his successful life. In other words a bullshit artist. “Gil, our finances have taken a slightly negative turn. Embarrassing, but fixable. It has involved personal, business, and library finance issues. I manage them all.”

Apparently, not too well Gil thought. “Are you certain, and will you promise me that I will not receive backlash from these sales?”

Sam had to appear calm and in total control. "Before Victoria left on her very pricey extended voyage, she told me to expedite some of the jewels. They belong to me."

"And Marjorie agreed to this?"

"Marjorie has no clue, as long as her debit and credit cards work."

Gil had to accept what he said. He greatly needed the cash from today's sale. So, they completed the jewelry deal as the sun decided to brightly appear on that chilly January day in London.

CHAPTER 26

By the middle of January, Zoey was feeling really good, her therapy was over and she was almost full time at the eatery. Normal was the way to be and so unappreciated. Now, making her way to the bathroom made her snicker as weeks ago she had to rely on a cane, and was so awkward. In one more week, she would do swim laps again, and in two weeks she and Liz would be flying to St. Maarten. It was strange how life flip flopped for her. Zoey had much to think about while she was away for a week enjoying sun, sand, and friendly islanders. Maybe a casino jaunt, as the Dutch side had several casinos to captivate their gambling senses. While away, her thoughts would focus on Will and their future. He had recently moved into her home, that was really their home. Surprisingly, all was working out well.

As January seemed to fly by, the eatery continued to thrive. Most of the rumors about the unidentified body found had calmed down and Zoey never heard there would be a second segment. Miranda Prescott hadn't been in touch and she was probably working on another segment with other cold cases that intrigued viewers. Maybe Sam was right, the show was all about the money and Miranda had to earn her salary. Obviously the dead body behind the library occurrence was a dud.

It was strange that for more than a week now, A.J. drove by the eatery and never stopped by. Why was he home? The Audi was hard to miss as he drove by, it was a gorgeous car. He was a lucky teenager. Zoey thought the death of his friend might have caused A.J. to need some comfort from his mother. That would be very hard to handle, if something similar happened to one of Hannah's friends. She asked her staff if they heard any gossip.

Liz had heard a few tidbits at the salon she visited weekly. "Marjorie has been really upset about the Holtzman boy. And Sam is away, and as usual, of little help anyway."

"It really is not up to me to call A.J. We are friends and he does confide in me, but I simply can't get involved with this issue." Zoey felt disappointed that she couldn't help A.J. "Marjorie has to step up here."

"Zoey, in a few weeks, we'll be away and catch up on some needed rest. Everything will work out with A.J. It takes some time. Maybe he needed a break from the sadness at school."

She discussed this all with Will when she arrived home and started dinner.

"Your mother is right, Zoey. Let it go. You can't save everybody. Concentrate on me."

Zoey had to laugh at that comment. "I plan to do just that while I am away."

Zoey was now permitted to take a long, hot bath and tomorrow she would resume swimming. Normal. She and Will got ready for bed and Zoey looked forward to their lovemaking that she had so missed for so many years. It was like it never stopped. Will was an attentive lover and cared about what aroused Zoey. He did the job with slow and enjoyable expertise.

Zoey was very drowsy, on the verge of falling asleep when the phone shrilled and she sat up in bed. As she gazed at the clock it was almost 10 o'clock.

"Hello?" Zoey answered a bit doubtful.

"Zoey, sorry it's so late," Miranda Prescott apologized, "I was away for a few days and when I returned, I had received an interesting e-mail."

Coming awake, Zoey was a bit irritated by the late hour call. She took the phone in the upper hallway so not to wake up Will. "And, how does this involve me?"

"I am not able to divulge any details yet, but someone may have a real lead on the body found behind your library."

"Oh my God, are you serious?"

"I am and I have a really good feeling this person is genuine."

"That is amazing. It has been almost three months."

"I just wanted you to know." Prescott added, "I have to check out the authenticity of this person and the connection to the body found. From what he mentioned, we could have a case closed sooner than anticipated."

"Keep me updated, okay?"

"Will do." And the call ended.

Zoey looked over at Will, sound asleep. They would have a very interesting talk at breakfast tomorrow.

Up very early, it was just past 5 a.m., and a busy day was on the schedule. Zoey made sure to pack her swim bag as today was the first one in weeks where she would do her laps.

Will woke up early too and headed downstairs eager for his first cup of coffee. Zoey was out filling the bird feeders and when she came in, she told Will, "You never heard the phone ring late last night?"

"I did not." He looked a bit surprised. "Who was it, not Hannah?"

"No, I would have shook you awake." She added, "It was Miranda Prescott."

"Again, the annoying newscaster?"

"Not this time, though. Do you want details?"

"Spill it, and please tell me there is not another segment that will tell us nothing."

"I guess Miranda received an e-mail from someone, a gentlemen I think, she kept repeating He." Continuing on she told Will all she knew. "She said this person had a clue to identify who this woman was. But, before she proceeded with a definitive story from him, she had to check out his authenticity."

"And when will this happen, how long will it take to see if this person is telling the truth? Is he from the local area?"

"Miranda was very vague. I'm sure it will only take a few days to verify if this information is useful or truthful."

"That will give you something to talk about today at the eatery."

"I think I will just tell Mom. If anything develops, we'll know in a few days."

At the Eatery, Jonas stopped by for his breakfast sandwich and she scooped him into the swap area before he left for the station." I had a call from Miranda Prescott last night."

"Really, what cold case is she on now?"

"It is still our body behind the library." Zoey added, "Please keep this to yourself, and Kim of course. It appears someone e-mailed her about possibly being able to identify the body of this poor older lady."

Upset by this news, he lashed out at Zoey. "She needs to see us about this. You know, the professional law enforcement officials." A bit irate, he asked her, "Why did she call you?"

Zoey was a bit offended. "Come on, Jonas. Tone it down. I didn't even have to tell you."

Jonas sighed, apologizing. "Sorry, Zoey. It is probably more gossip."

"No, I don't think so. If I was listening correctly, this person would only converse with Miranda, no authorities. He wanted to tell her all he knew as he wasn't totally sure if it would help."

"See, just gossip. Maybe he wants to be on the show."

"Well, this week when she verifies this person and speaks to him in person, we will know if he is going to help us solve this mystery, once and for all."

"I gotta' go. I am already late for work." He asked Zoey on the way out, "Keep me in the loop."

Zoey told her mom about the conversation she had with Jonas back in the swap area. Liz was not surprised. "I knew someone would come forward after watching this show. It just takes time. This poor woman had a home somewhere. If it was robbery, I find it hard to believe. This murder was planned." Liz McCaffery was usually very intuitive. Now,

Zoey felt uneasy and concerned for her picturesque Highland Falls. She would be on pins and needles this week until the call came from Miranda Prescott.

CHAPTER 27

Gil Andrews completed his jewelry resale with Sam Watson just days ago and had no further contact with him. Gil had to complete some banking business, moving funds around for protection purposes. Sam had at least a week's worth of additional business in London, but he was finished with Gil. Sam asked him to have dinner on a few nights, but Gil used various excuses. He wanted no more dealings, personal or professional with this man. It was very clear to Gil that Sam had lied to him about the jewel sales he handled these past few years. He felt strongly that the extraordinary gems belonged to Victoria Tuckerman. Images do not lie. And you just do not give away priceless stones worth millions of dollars. Sam tried to sound unconcerned that Victoria would say or do anything when she returned from her trip. Really? This was becoming a nightmare. Gil would discuss this matter with Caroline today and resolve what they would do next.

Caroline was on the phone with her mother when Gil got home later that day. After she hung up, she told Gil in a concerned voice, "Mother has a terrible chest cold."

"I'm sorry, dear." He reassured her, "She has fine doctors at her community."

"I know. But if she worsens, I have to fly over."

"Maybe I can go with you, how is that?"

"Yes, I need some support here." She was very teary eyed, afraid of what would happen next.

"Caroline, we need to have a serious talk about Sam Watson."

She seemed to just sag into her chair. "Now is not the best time, with my mother so sick."

"I know, but it can't wait. I am ending my dealings with him. They are actually done, now."

"Did the latest deal go through?" She asked Gil, "Will we be okay financially?"

"Yes, not to worry. You can keep the Jag, at least for now."

"What has happened here?" Caroline went over to get herself a strong gin and tonic. "Want one with me?"

"Double the gin, please."

Gil told his wife in length about the research he had done on the Watsons and the Tuckerman family the week before. He also showed her the images of the jewels in question. He had the cold case segment on hand and Caroline was aghast as she saw the enormous diamond and emerald ring on Victoria Tuckerman.

Caroline looked a bit pale. "You do keep precise records, don't you?"

"It's a good thing I do." He shook his head in dismay. "How could I have been so naive?"

"Sam Watson has gone through his life as a successful businessman. He's wealthy, important, and arrogant from how you have described him." Caroline tried to assure and comfort her husband that he was not naïve. "This is not your fault. Just get away from him, Gil."

"I plan to do just that. But, I don't know if that is enough."

"What do you
mean?"

"You and your mother planted this seed of doubt. The murder in Highland Falls. The dead woman in back of the Tuckerman Library."

"And how does that concern Sam Watson?"

Gil was not big on conspiracy theories, but he had a chilling feeling about these jewels. Where was Victoria Tuckerman? Sam said she did not want to be located and needed to get away from her needy family. "It appears that Victoria Tuckerman has disappeared from her family. I guess from what Sam said, they got two random postcards from her."

"Maybe she told them the truth, wanting to be away from them all. Do you doubt that? How could they get postcards from her if something had happened to her?"

"I have not figured that out. But, I do know that despite little interest in watching Prescott's cold case segment, I learned a few things. The dead body, or the murdered old lady, had jewelry removed before her death. If someone robbed her, just to take some jewels, why would you care about burying her? This woman was covered with a tarp. This was planned."

"Gads, you sound just like my mother. This is just what she thinks."

"And I poked fun after she became so interested in this happening."

"This sounds way too deep for me to ingest or understand." Feeling very uneasy, she asked Gil, "Just what are you implying?"

"I am not sure."

"What will you do to resolve this?"

"I am earnestly thinking of contacting Miranda Prescott about this case."

Caroline found this hard to swallow. "Are you serious?"

"I most certainly am. I need this current nightmare to end. The money we made from all these jewels is very dirty. I want no part in it."

Gil had made the decision. Contact information was clear and it would be very easy to reach Miranda Prescott. He thought very carefully while composing this e-mail to her. Asking for confidentiality, Gil told her about the dealings he had with Sam Watson, the head honcho at the Tuckerman Library. Of course Prescott knew this. He explained that he had, for a number of years, dealt with antiquity and jewel sales with Sam Watson. He held him to the highest level of trust and they worked well together. It was a lucrative business involving wealthy buyers.

It was mid-week when Gil composed the e-mail to Miranda Prescott. Then, he waited. Very overwrought as many days passed by, Gil wondered if he had made a mistake. Then the reply arrived. Prescott was very interested in what he had to say. She apologized for not sending a quicker reply as she was away working on another story. She asked for a few days to reconnect with Gil. They would either e-mail or do a Zoom call, if that was agreeable to him. It was. Gil sensed that Prescott would be checking him out, as that is what she did for a living. He was not worried as he had a fine reputation as a competent and successful businessman owning a prestigious London establishment for fifteen years. When the business was sold, he focused on resales of antiques and jewels.

Each day after the first e-mail was sent to Prescott, Caroline asked for an update. Finally six days later, Gil gave her the positive results. "Prescott is interested. She will be touch in a matter of days."

"Well, that is good news." She hesitated, concern in her voice. "My mother has developed pneumonia. The doctor just phoned me." Beginning to cry, she told Gil, "I have to fly out tomorrow and be with her. This is not good. Dr. Willard is worried, as she doesn't seem to have any will left."

"I will fly there with you." He wrapped his arms around a very troubled wife. "I'll call the airlines."

They were lucky enough to find timely flights from Heathrow directly to Bradley International in Windsor Locks, Connecticut. With the six hour difference in time, they would arrive around 3 p.m. US time. Add another two hours to the retirement home Caroline's mom was at. A very long, tiring day. Gil would have to put Miranda Prescott on hold until things improved with Caroline's mother. How did this happen to them? Gil was overwrought with anything that involved Sam Watson. Yet, Gil was in the middle of it all. Perhaps what happened in Highland Falls would reflect of Gil's connection to Sam Watson.

After baggage claim and the rental car, Gil and Caroline were on their way to Old Millbrook, an affluent seaside town on the New England coastline. Gil had to smile to himself as the day was raw and spitting rain on his windshield almost like being at home. He thought of Sam's comments of London's incessant rainy weather. There was a charming inn only a few miles from the retirement home. They arrived around 5:30, checked in and headed over to see Susan Rothens, in bed and looking poorly. After a short stay, Susan said she felt a bit rested and was on antibiotics. She told Caroline to come back in the morning, her eyes closing on the pillow.

They headed back to the inn in a very disheartened mood. There would be no rest tonight. Before he fell asleep, Gil saw the e-mail from Miranda Prescott. She wished to meet him as soon as possible. He needed to consider contacting the authorities. It was truth time.

CHAPTER 28

Back in Highland Falls, all was positive in Zoey Mitchell's life. It was about time. In less than two weeks, she would be on a sandy beach in St. Maarten sipping rum punch. Things were not going so well at the Watson residence. Sam was still away and A.J. remained at home, for almost two weeks now. Neither A.J. or Marjorie had visited the eatery and that was odd, as both were frequent visitors. Zoey thought of calling Marjorie to see if she could be of any help with A.J. especially after he lost a good friend to suicide. She was voted down by all of her helpers, telling her to just butt out.

A.J. was having a difficult time because of Conner Holtzman's suicide but that was not the main issue tearing A.J. apart. He needed to see his grandmother and she wasn't here. Where was she? She was due back a week ago. She never gave A.J. her contact information before she left. Victoria Tuckerman was very clear that she needed a long time away to do a lot of thinking. A.J. tried on several occasions to e-mail her, never receiving a reply. He thought that odd. However, he respected his grandmother and her wish to be left alone while she enjoyed time away. Always able to confide troubling issues to his grandmother, before she left in September, he unloaded a horrific issue on her. What A.J. told her, he had kept smothered away for almost three years now. It was about that time that he become estranged from his father. He no longer respected his dad because of what he saw one summer night, Sam Watson had actually sickened his son. Victoria Tuckerman listened intently to A.J.'s recollection of what happened and when finished, she hugged her grandson so tightly, he had to pull away. She became tense and angered by what A.J. had told her and promised him that she would remedy this as soon as she possibly could. She would speak to his father and straighten him out, once and for all.

A.J. had no idea what had transpired after he spoke to his grandmother. Within days, Victoria left on her extended trip and A.J. was left in limbo. Sam had driven his grandmother to the airport in Hartford and A.J. was soon back at school. This issue involved Conner Holtzman and may have had an effect on why he took his own life. He had no other choice but to speak to his mother. He was afraid of what her reaction would be or if she would even believe him. He had nowhere else to turn.

A.J. needed to get back to school but before that he would confront his mother and tell her what he had been silent about all of these years. He was fifteen years old when his life seemed to fall apart. Always popular with many friends, his teenage years were usually enjoyable. One weekend summer while his mother and father were away, A.J. was in Newport visiting friends. The family he was staying with had a family emergency back home, so A.J. was dropped off late one night at his home in Highland Falls, That's when he saw the outer pool area barely lit and someone was frolicking in the pool. That is when his life began falling apart.

Marjorie Watson was busy on her computer trying organize a list of volunteers for a fundraiser happening in early March. A.J. interrupted her. "Mom, I need to talk to you."

She looked up, saving her document and turned to see her son, unsmiling and looking very grim. "Do you want to see Dr. Avery? He has helped you handle things in the past." Marjorie assumed it was the death of Conner that had A.J.in such a funk.

"He can't fix this one Mom." A.J. added, "We had better sit down." He began with, "First of all, where is Grandma?"

"Let's not do this. She is due home any day now." She frowned at her son. "Why are you so concerned about your grandmother?"

"Before she left, we had a long talk. I have been struggling with something that happened to me three years ago. It involved Conner. And now he's dead." He added, "I told Grandma the whole story. She promised to fix what happened. And now she's gone."

Marjorie paled at this comment. "What is happening here?" Her voice shrill, she spat out, "Tell me what happened."

"I will try skipping details. I have tried to forget what I saw, but I couldn't." A.J. began, "That summer, I was fifteen and if you remember, I spent a weekend away in Newport with Rob Lowry and his family. Then they had some emergency back here arriving home late on Saturday night. It was about 11 o'clock and Dad was supposed to be on some business trip so when I saw the pool area lit up, I thought a burglar was here. I creeped up to look and there was Dad, with Conner, nude in the hot tub. I just ran back to the Lowry's saying I had no key to get in."

Marjorie felt total shock with what her son was saying. "Are you sure what you saw?"

"Really, Mom!" A.J. hoped she would not doubt her son's words. "I have no reason to lie."

"I can't comprehend this." Eyes growing wide, her heart was racing. "How is your grandmother involved in this?"

"I told her the whole story, right before she left on her trip. Dad and Conner never saw me." He grew very serious. "You need to find out where Gram is, now."

Startled by his tone, she asked him, "What do you mean?"

"Call the travel agency, or hire an investigator. We need to find her." He asked his mother, "Don't you care where she is, or if she is still alive?"

"We have had two postcards from her, A.J." She looked perplexed. "What do you mean, if she's alive?"

A.J. was insistent, "Let me see the postcards. I know her penmanship."

Marjorie scrambled through her desk drawers, searching for the postcards. She felt clumsy and lightheaded, trying to absorb all that she just heard from her son. It could not be true. But A.J. was her baby, her wonderful son who did not lie. "Here's one." She handed the card over so he could look at the penmanship.

"Do you ever pay attention to anything, Mom?" He lobbed the card back to his mother. "This is not grandma's writing. And it's not what she would say." He looked at what was written, “It says cheers to you all, having a grand time. She would never say that.”

“I was so angry at her for leaving the way she did, I barely looked at either card.” Marjorie found the second card just received two weeks earlier. “It says almost the same thing on the next card.” It was about time that Marjorie started to pay attention to her mother’s well being. “I believe you, A.J.” Tearing up, she continued, “I don’t want to, but now I know why you have been so far apart from your father these past few years.” Composing herself, she grasped her son into her small hands. “You should have come to me, and not gone to your grandmother.”

“We need to find her.” He asked his mother, “Call the travel agency and find out what happened. Get her itinerary.”

The rest of the afternoon, Marjorie began falling apart. It began when she called to check her mother’s travel schedule. When she called Sunscapes, her mother’s agency, she was told by the office manager that her mother no longer dealt with them. Now, what would they do?

In panic mode, Marjorie called her attorney who would hire an investigator to help her find Victoria. Martin Reed was a good friend and listened to the entire story. The truth needed to be told. She asked Martin to start filing divorce papers from Sam as soon as things calmed down regarding her missing mother.

She told A.J., “Dad is gone until next week. We need to get away.” She told A.J. in a hurried tone, “I will call the school and tell them that we have emergency travel plans for a few weeks. Let’s go to our timeshare unit and sort this out." She looked at her son who was totally worn out by this.

"Okay, Mom. I am sorry you know, for doing this to you." He added. "You have put up with so much bullshit from him over the years. He is horrible to you."

"I have tried to stay with him for us as a family. Now he is just a sick individual. I want him gone." Her wine glass shattered as she threw it into the sink. "We'll go away and keep track about your grandmother." Trying to sound positive, she told A.J., "My mother is a tough old bird, a true survivor. I will bet she'll be home soon, probably when we are in St. Barths."

A.J. did not believe his mother and was now unexpectedly frightened for Victoria Tuckerman.

CHAPTER 29

In just three days, Liz and Zoey would leave for their vacation. So much to do. Zoey had never left the cats before and she knew she would miss them. Added to that she would also miss Will, who was not in her life when these travel plans were originally created. Everything was good to go at the eatery with Kim in charge along with Caitland and Selena. Will was moved in and Zoey knew the three cats would have lots of attention from him. Looking ahead at the forecast, there was snow in the picture but not for several days. Their flight left Hartford a little before 7 a.m., connecting to Raleigh-Durham. With a two hour window, they would leave for St Maarten by 11:30 in the morning arriving by 3 p.m. They would have to go through customs, rent a car, and head for the hotel. An exhausting day, for sure.

Zoey still felt like something was wrong concerning A.J. She had not seen him drive past the eatery in the last few days and thought he may be back at school. She asked her mother if she heard any gossip at the salon. Liz did have some news. “I thought I mentioned what Marjorie was up to. She was there when I had my nails done and was having the entire staff work on her. Manicure, pedicure, and haircut and color too.”

“And why was that unusual?”

“It wasn’t that odd until I saw her at the tanning place where I go. Boy, if I could have her checkbook for just a day. She briefly mentioned she would be away for a few weeks and needed to go somewhere that was warm and sunny.”

"You do realize that if you had her checkbook for a day you would have to have Sam, too, right?"

"Let's delete that last thought." Liz snickered slightly. "I will keep my own checkbook, thank you."

"Have you heard anything from Miranda Prescott lately?" She sounded curious. "It has been over a week and you told me so little about that call."

"She made me promise to keep all that we discussed in confidence."

"I told you she would get to the bottom of this. Someone called her and knows who this is buried behind our library."

"I will call or e-mail her before we leave on Saturday, okay, Columbo?"

"Well, if there is a follow-up segment on this missing person and we are in St. Maarten, I won't be happy." Complaining, she added, "Who knows what TV stations you get down there."

"I will make sure and put in your request to stall the show until we get home."

"Zoey," Liz said earnestly, "This poor old lady needs to rest in peace, wherever she was from."

Miranda Prescott was one busy investigator. Now working on two other cold cases, the Highland Falls mystery was becoming the most interesting. The contact person who would help her resolve this crime checked out as a reputable businessman from London. Gil Andrews was married to his wife Caroline, a US citizen, their wedding well over thirty years ago in London. Apparently a happy but childless marriage, they lived an affluent life, Gil was a successful jewels and antiques dealer. That was his connection to Sam Watson of Highland Falls. And that was the one indicator that might help solve this murder case. Because his wife's mother was ill and lived near Highland Falls, Gil and his wife would be traveling here from London for at least a week. A meeting was planned in person, as soon as it was convenient for Gil. That was the best way to follow through, rather than a Zoom or Face Time call.

Miranda owed Zoey Mitchell a phone call to update her on the progress of this ordeal. At least this time, she had positive news and the possibility of a follow-up segment on this cold case murder in Highland Falls.

Zoey had actually forgotten, at her mother's request, to do a follow-up call before they left on their trip. So when Miranda Prescott called her around dinner time, she was caught a bit off guard. "Zoey, I promised an update a while ago and we have positive news."

"I appreciate that you remembered." Zoey was short on time, really busy with their flight leaving very early the next morning. "Have you been told where this missing body has come from, perhaps a local person?"

"We don't have that answer yet, but we are very close. Tomorrow, I am meeting my contact who will give us some useful information regarding this missing person. In confidence, and your promise not to allow this info to spread out anywhere, I will fill you in."

"May I ask why I am in the middle of this?" Zoey was confused. "You would be better off contacting my brother-in-law, Jonas Parsons. He is our head police officer and was in charge of this murder investigation."

"I am aware of that, but my contact, who is from the United Kingdom, London to be specific, will not divulge what he knows if I contact the authorities. He has promised to do that at a later date."

Zoey was out of patience. "Why me?" she asked, rather exasperated.

"Because the connection to you is Tuckerman Library's Sam Watson." She added, "It seems that Sam has been dealing with a London jeweler for several years now. His name is Gil Andrews and the latest business dealings he has had with Sam has caused him to be concerned about the validity of the transactions."

Zoey had just swallowed a cup of strong coffee and it began backing up into her throat. Pausing, she did not know how to reply to what had been thrown at her. "This is a lot to handle."

"You mentioned to me that for a while you handled Sam Watson's business office while he was away. Is that right?"

"Yes, I did, but it was years ago."

"Do you recall any dealings with Gil Andrews while Watson was in London?"

"Not to my knowledge," Zoey racked her brain for a minute. "Sam did not always tell me his entire agenda while he traveled abroad. And Gil Andrews does not sound familiar to me. Sorry."

"In any event, Gil Andrews, feeling apprehensive after the last jewel sale, did some research on Sam Watson and the

Tuckerman family." She offered more details to Zoey that Gil Andrews had told her. "He is afraid that the jewels he recently sold for Sam did not belong to him." Prescott added, "He said that Sam swears that he is the current owner of all the jewelry he plans to sell on his trips abroad. However, Gil has his own proof, from his business files that shows a good deal of doubt on just who these gems belong to. I have a meeting with him tomorrow at my office and we will know one way or another just what has happened here. Robbery and murder are two possibilities."

Zoey was sorry she had that cup of coffee as her stomach felt very nauseous. This could not be happening. What was Sam Watson involved in? And now Zoey was smack in the middle of this missing person, dead body scenario in back of the Tuckerman Library. "I appreciate the update, but I am at a loss for words. It is difficult for me to believe that Sam Watson seems to be the evil person here."

"We don't know that yet, but I will be close to resolving all of this after I meet with Gil Andrews in just a few days. He is here in the states as his mother-in-law is quite ill. I believe she is in a retirement home close to Highland Falls."

Zoey thought this mystery was becoming very complex. "That is quite a coincidence that he is now able to meet with you in person. Gads, he is from London and all of sudden he's here?"

"Some things are meant to be, like they fall into place. Or, call it a lucky break for me, as an investigator."

Zoey was now sipping some ginger ale to settle her stomach. "Please e-mail me after you confirm all that appears to be true from this Andrews person. I am away, out of the country for the next eight days. E-mail is the only way to reach me. Please, as soon as you hear what has happened."

After the upsetting phone call, Zoey made a decision. She would wait until they were on their plane to the islands before telling her mother what she was told by investigator Prescott. However she could not keep this secret from Will. She had promised confidentiality. First she would calm down and think carefully how much she would divulge to her almost husband. He would have to keep this whole ordeal to himself, and especially from Jonas Parsons. What had Sam done? And how involved was Victoria Tuckerman?

Will got home a little before 6 o'clock, eager for dinner. He would have more than a plate full of comfort food tonight as Zoey revealed all that she was told about the investigation. They did enjoy a nice dinner but right after the kitchen clean-up, Zoey told Will she had a rather telling phone call from Miranda Prescott. Not relating each and every detail, she did tell Will about the London businessman who seemed to be the missing piece to this mystery murder puzzle. After listening intently to all Zoey told him, Will was doubtful that this man would be able to help solve this cold case.

"Does Prescott think Sam was into a whole lot of illegal jewel sales?"

Zoey shook her head somewhat dismayed. "That is what it sounds like. I am not the head cheerleader for Sam Watson. But, it is difficult for me to believe he is involved with illegal stuff, like stolen jewels. It is just not Sam."

Will stared at her, not believing what was just said. "Your memory is pretty good. Have you forgotten why you quit your position as Sam's business manager?" He couldn't resist, "Sam was a pervert interested in teenage boys. That, I believe showed his true character."

Zoey could not deny what happened there. "Maybe Sam went through a difficult stage in his life." She went on, "I am not defending him, but felony accusations are serious."

"And what he did with that unknown teenager sounds felonious to me." Warning her he went on to say, "You certainly do not want this on your mind while you are away on a restful vacation. Maybe this Andrews guy isn't the answer." After a long dismal sigh, he finished. "Who knows where these jewels came from? If there is any illegal nonsense involved Sam will go away and wear stripes for a while." He laughed. "Marjorie might even like that."

THE END IS NEAR

CHAPTER 30

New England was well known for having nor'easters'', storms that produced heavy snow and brisk winds. Today the storm was winding down and Miranda Prescott had a scheduled meeting with Gil Andrews at 5 p.m. in Hartford. He phoned telling her the snow had stopped and he felt safe to drive to her office for the planned meeting focusing on Sam Watson and the missing body found behind the Tuckerman Library. Unfortunately, Caroline's mother was regressing, her pneumonia had affected her cardiovascular system and soon she would be so weakened it would be close to the end. Caroline was at her bedside, but she was heavily sedated, unknowing her daughter was there. Gil promised to make this a brief meeting and Caroline was agreeable, as no more could be done to help her mother.

The drive from Old Millbrook was slow, roads were slick and Gil was anxious with all of the information he would soon unload with Miranda Prescott. He was also concerned about his wife and what she was going through with her dying mother. When he arrived at the television station, he was impressed with Prescott's office and her accommodating staff, offering him some hot coffee, and perhaps something for dinner since it was almost 5 o'clock. He declined and wanted to move ahead with this meeting. His briefcase was full of images and documents. There was proof of the sales and who these were sold to, in case there was any backlash from these dealings. He told Miranda that, to his knowledge, Sam was still in London, working on some other transactions.

Miranda apologized but she had part of a thick roast beef sandwich on her desk, half eaten. “Sorry about my unprofessional area, but I had a very late lunch and I am just finishing it now.” She asked Gil, “Are you sure you won’t have anything as we have a great kitchen here?”

“Thank you, but no.” He continued on, “I would like to piece together all of the missing pieces and complete this mystery puzzle as quickly as possible. My mother-in-law is quite ill and I need to get back to Old Millbrook to be with my wife.”

“I am very sorry about that.” She cleared away her desk, the sandwich hit the trash can and the meeting started. “So, what can you show me?”

“For years now, I have dealt with Sam Watson and it has been beneficial for us both. However, the last year or so I noticed that the items he would offer me for resale were of a different quality than the others.” He added, “He deals in antiques, and rare prints too. He is very qualified and knows what each product is worth down to the penny.”

“When did you begin to suspect wrongdoing?” Prescott began typing her notes on to her laptop.

“I have no proof of this. That is the issue. Just my intuitive feelings.” Gil looked downward, head shaking. “I have asked him who owns these last set of jewels and he insisted that he owned them. Sam did say they originally belonged to Victoria Tuckerman but business was sliding a bit south and as the finance person in the family, a decision was made. This was Sam Watson’s version.”

“And, do you have images of these gems?”

"I do." Gil went into his briefcase and displayed the images of the latest pricey items he had sold for Sam during this past year.

He watched Miranda as her eyes opened widely, mesmerized by all of the sparkling jewels. "These must be worth close to a million dollars." Miranda studied all of the photos and also the still images that Gil downloaded from his computer which displayed Victoria Tuckerman wearing the priceless gems.

"More than a million, as some are very rare. Wealthy collectors yearn for such finds."

Having no knowledge of the worth of these items Miranda told Gil, "I guess I do not travel in the right circles."

"My fear is that Sam Watson has taken control over the assets of his mother-in-law, Victoria Tuckerman."

"You do mean while she is away and has no knowledge of this?"

"Yes, that's right, unless...." Gil hesitated, afraid to say what he thought had happened.

"Let's be honest, Gil, shall we?"

"Of course, but with no proof, what I think means very little."

"Are you thinking that Sam Watson took these pricey jewels from his mother-in-law's collection?"

As he told what he supposed was the truth, his anxiety slowly began decreasing and Gil told Miranda in a calm tone, "It appears so."

“In conclusion, do you think that Sam Watson murdered her, burying Victoria Tuckerman behind the library that her family had founded?” Miranda had to blurt it out.

“Yes.” Gil felt total relief overcome his very anxious soul.

“You do realize I have to bring all of this to the authorities. Jonas Parsons is the local Marshall in Highland Falls and he will bring in the State Police Crime Squad. You will be excessively grilled on this entire matter.”

“I feared that would happen.” He sounded somewhat reticent. “It must come out, whatever happened.” He asked Miranda, “Can they do any DNA testing?”

“Before cremation, samples were retained. I am not sure but I believe they are stored for a period of time, maybe a year. Not sure on that. But, they need to find something of Tuckerman’s for a match.” She looked over at Gil, who looked on the brink of exhaustion. “I will take it over from here. May I keep these copies that you brought?”

“Of course. I am sure the Marshall will want them.” In a hesitant voice, Gil asked her, “When will I have to meet with the authorities?”

“I will call them tomorrow, and I am certain it will happen fast.” She made one point very clear. “You’ll need to stay in the states until this is resolved. Will that possibly work for you and your wife?”

“We’ll make it work.”

“There is a chance for a follow-up segment now and you will be part of this. I’d appreciate it if you would consider an interview with me that would air on the show.”

“Yes, but it doesn’t look like my mother-in-law will be here to see it.” He added, “She was the key to the beginning of solving this mystery and I laughed at her for it.”

Miranda Prescott sincerely thanked Gil Andrews before he left for Old Millbrook and the sadness he was about to endure. She promised to call him about the meeting they would all have with Jonas Parsons. Leaving her office, she smiled to herself. Miranda knew that this murder mystery would be solved, but was disappointed that it took longer than usual.

The very next day, by 9 a.m. Miranda Prescott was on the phone with Jonas Parsons.

CHAPTER 31

Luggage was all packed, passports remembered, then Zoey fell fast asleep, still within Will's arms wrapped warmly around her. Alarm sounded loudly at 3 a.m. It was really hard saying goodbye to Will and the cats. Leaving soon after that, Zoey picked up her mother and they were eager to fly off to St Maarten at 7 a.m. Flight was right on time. Neither one enjoyed flying but with their goal of warm sun and sandy beaches they both encouraged a few smiles. Their connection was in Raleigh Durham, North Carolina and they had over an hour and a half before their next flight left. Plenty of time to tell her mother about Miranda Prescott's latest findings. She told her all she knew. Liz was not surprised at all.

"Mom, this is between you and me. We can't even tell Kim, or Jonas. I promised."

"How about Will?"

The look she gave her mother required no answer. "I wanted you to know the latest, but until she actually speaks to Gil Andrews, we can't even speculate."

"Remember just who and what Sam Watson is, always out for himself."

"I can't forget what Miranda said, two possibilities, robbery or murder."

"Also remember that she is a television newscaster. She sells her stories to viewers, like you and me." Adding, "It's all about ratings and the money."

"I know that but she can't fabricate or lie."

"True." Listening to the loudspeaker, Liz heard that their flight would be boarding soon. She told Zoey, "Let's get in line and put this issue in the pause pile."

Both ladies relaxed choosing to have a cocktail on this last connecting flight, and soon they were dozing, reclined in their seats. The intercom blared to prepare for landing and they did, eager to see the blueish green ocean and bright sunshine. Zoey was amazed at the beauty as the plane began the descent, landing on the narrowest strip of land with deep ocean water on both sides. After automatically holding their breath, they slowly coasted down to the Princess Julianna Airport, with seated passengers cheering aloud with a promised restful week ahead for all.

The busy airport was overflowing with loud and partially sloshed tourists. Both Zoey and Liz were eager to make it through the customs line so they could rent a car and head for the Pelican Resort Hotel. Checking in was done outside with the breezy ocean air welcoming them to the island. Their suite was superior with an ocean view and balcony that would be appreciated each and every day. All unpacked and settled in, Zoey texted Will that they had arrived safely. He told them that luck was on their side as several inches of snow would happen the next day all through New England. After they ordered room service for a light dinner, Liz could not resist visiting the casino, located right on the property. Zoey passed on the invite and wanted a long hot shower, a tropical drink on her balcony, and then bed.

Liz stumbled back into the suite after 9 o'clock and Zoey was fast asleep. She had won a few dollars on the slot machines and was offered free tropical drinks while she gambled. A nice welcome for her first night there. Before long, she fell asleep and both woke up refreshed and ready to hit the many beaches St. Maarten had to offer. Since it was the first day of vacation, both decided to stay at the hotel. Their beach offered a calm ocean, one they could wade into and calmly swim in without any crashing waves encircling them. The entire day was total relaxation, perhaps too many cocktails, but smiling and enjoying life was why they were there.

The local food was quite tasty, lot of seafood, spiced with island flavors. Their first dinner out included lobster, broiled to perfection. Local lobsters were very small, unlike the New England type that they were used to. The next day, Monday, they would do some shopping in town and looking at the mountainous road from their balcony, they hoped to survive the climb.

"We can do this, right?"

"Mom, piece of cake." Zoey laughed at her.

Indeed the road was very steep, and all of a sudden they had a rain shower, which believe it or not was a slippery ride up the mountain. It happens in St. Maarten a lot, just brief rain, then the sun comes out. The hotel guide told them that The Pelican Resort was on the Dutch side of the island and if it was rainy here, just drive 30 minutes to the French side and you'll see the sun. The parking in town was difficult, as tourists abounded, but they survived, buying some local items before heading back to the hotel. Zoey bought a charming solar wind chime of small baby pelicans hanging on tiny golden strings. They had already enjoyed two impressive days here. As soon as they arrived at the hotel, Zoey noticed she had an e-mail. It was from Miranda Prescott. She needed to speak to her soon, and preferred not to do this by e-mail. Could Zoey please make arrangements to call her back in Connecticut? Zoey wondered why.

"You had better contact her." Concerned, Liz assured Zoey, "Unless this was really important, she would not bother you on vacation. Something must have occurred. It sounds rather urgent."

It was too early for dinner. Zoey decided to call Miranda as it was nearly the same time back in Connecticut, minus one hour. Miranda was still in her office, just shy of the dinner hour.

Sounding official, she answered on the second ring. "Miranda Prescott here."

A bit on edge, Zoey put on her brave face. "It's Zoey Mitchell. You asked that I please return your call as soon as possible."

"I am so sorry you are not here for what has recently happened in the investigation." Prescott told Zoey, "Tomorrow, I will accompany Gil Andrews to see your brother-in-law because it has become a serious issue."

"What has happened?" Zoey was losing patience. "Is it Sam Watson, and is he involved?"

"Indeed." In a serious tone, and before Prescott told Zoey exactly what she was told and the conclusion they were considering, she had one question. "We need to locate Victoria Tuckerman. Her daughter is away with their son and unreachable. Do you know how we can locate her?"

Whoa, thought Zoey. She had put her phone on speaker mode so her mother could listen in. Liz looked stunned.

"She is out of the country, on vacation but I do not know where she has gone. Her son was going through a really difficult time and they needed to get away. This is all I know. I am really not friends with Marjorie Watson." She asked Prescott, "What about Sam Watson? He may know where Marjorie is."

"Sam Watson is still in London, home later this week." Prescott continued, "I tried to reach him and he refused to take my calls." Prescott then explained why it was not the best idea to involve Sam Watson at this point.

"I met with Gil Andrews yesterday. We had a lengthy discussion and he had several files and images he wanted me to see. He felt strongly that Sam Watson had lied to him on various business trips. After showing me the images of the jewelry sold there was proof positive that they belonged to Victoria Tuckerman. We need to reach her immediately. That is, if she is still alive."

Liz and Zoey just stared at one another almost in disbelief. Afraid to believe what they had just heard, they were finding it difficult to even reply to Miranda Prescott. Zoey forced herself to ask Prescott, "What are you and Gil Andrews trying to insinuate?"

"We will be closer to a conclusion once we confirm that Victoria Tuckerman is alive and well."

"Are you concerned that something has happened to her?"

"These priceless jewels that Sam Watson has been selling for quite some time now belong to Victoria Tuckerman. I saw images of these gems on Victoria Tuckerman. Either he has taken these priceless items from her without her knowledge or something occurred where she was hurt in the process, if she perhaps caught him taking these jewels from her."

In a confident, lawyer like tone Zoey told Prescott, "You have no proof of this."

"That is why we must find Victoria Tuckerman."

"Are you thinking that Sam could have harmed her?" Zoey exhaled loudly, "Marjorie's mother is their very affluent nest egg. Sam would not survive without her backyard money tree, nor would the library."

"Yet, if she were to die, the Watsons would retrieve it all, wouldn't they?

Zoey could not very well deny that theory. "What made Gil Andrews come forward?"

"His mother-in-law saw the program with his wife Caroline when she last visited her mother right here in Old Millbrook, Connecticut. Caroline became intrigued, only due to the Sam Watson correlation. That is when Gil decided to research the Tuckerman and Watson families. This unearthed too many coincidences in addition to photos of the jewels worn by Victoria. It was hard for Gil to believe that all of these fine gems were owned by Sam Watson. Worried that he was lied to or would receive backlash if wrongdoing was discovered, Gil decided to contact me with what he assumed happened."

"You are a top investigator. Surely you can backtrack to see where Victoria Tuckerman is. She went on a three month voyage. This type of trip is costly and well advertised."

“We did contact Sunscapes, Victoria’s usual agency. They said she did not do this latest trip. They did however mention another agency she may have tried.”

“And did you find out anything?”

Prescott sure of herself, replied, “We did. I just discovered that Magellan Travel did book her trip, months earlier. One day prior to departing, Victoria cancelled the trip.” She needed Zoey’s help. “I have tried to contact Marjorie Watson who is away with her son. No way to reach her. What is wrong with these people who travel and ask that they not be disturbed? Do you know where Marjorie and her son have gone? She needs to know her mother cancelled that vacation.”

“I am sorry but no, they took off suddenly just to get away.” Zoey was at a loss for words. So, was it possible that Victoria never left Highland Falls? “But, Sam took her to the airport.”

“Maybe Sam did take her…..somewhere.” Or, perhaps Victoria Tuckerman ended up as a missing person, covered with a tarp, and buried behind the Tuckerman Library.

CHAPTER 32

It was almost a week gone by in St. Barths and by then Marjorie and A.J. were finally beginning to relax. Their two bedroom beachfront condominium was small but comfortable and they had a six week rental each January into February. Marjorie had only heard from her attorney with one phone call. The investigator could not locate where her mother was. She kept this from A.J., for now. But, Marjorie was very concerned now. Her attorney had drawn up divorce papers and it would be a messy court issue. It involved the Tuckerman fortune and Sam would never consider giving any of it up due to a divorce. However, the latest discovery with what happened to the Holtzman boy would be leverage for Marjorie.

Marjorie and A.J. spent several days sailing around the island as they both were experts doing the sport. They had long discussions about what would happen in the near future. Financially they would most likely face a struggle. Divorce did that to couples, no matter how wealthy they were. Greed was the focusing item. "You will be able to stay at private school, but I think the Audi will most likely be sold." She looked downwards, "I am sorry about that."

"It's okay, Mom." He wanted to show support but he was so angry at his father for ruining their lives. "You and Gram should have booted him out a long time ago."

"I still have had no word from the private investigator searching for your grandmother."

"Something is wrong and I think we need to go home soon."

“Will you be all right with this mess?” Being honest, she explained, “It will be ugly. I will have a judge remove your father from our property.”

“I keep thinking that Conner killed himself because he was gay.”

“People accept homosexuals now, it isn’t what it was years ago.” She added, “Have you known he was gay all this time?”

“Yeah, I did.” Sadly he told his mother, “I didn’t care, and I never told him about what I saw years ago. I was afraid to embarrass him or lose his friendship. I think it was only once.”

“It sounds as if your father took advantage of a young teenager who was confused. His parents would never have accepted him in that way.” Marjorie was now angered by Sam. “He showed some caring, some compassion, and that’s why you saw what you did. It may have been a one-time thing. I can only hope so.”

“Well, Gram said she would speak to Dad before she left and now I don’t know what happened.”

“You don’t think they had an argument, do you?”

“All I know is, Gram was pissed, really mad at him and said, that was it for him. She also said not to worry. She was used to handling my father.”

A nice lunch place was planned for A.J. and Marjorie. It was a beautiful breezy day, full of sun and positive plans for their future. Strange how things occur in each and every life, some meant to be, others not so much.

As beautiful as St. Maarten was, Liz and Zoey decided to take a ride over to St. Barths for a day on a sleek catamaran. The crew was more than hospitable offering drinks and snacks as they headed to the small island only an hour from St. Maarten. They were given suggestions for restaurants and to check out a local beach that was filled with shells, not sand. A real tourist site, imagine a crunchy beach. After they had eaten, Zoey wanted to walk out on the long dock that reached way out into the ocean. It was then that she spotted them. A.J. and Marjorie. That is where they took off to for a rest away from Highland Falls. It was quite a twist of fate. Zoey had totally forgotten that their timeshare home was here in St. Barths.

A.J. spotted Zoey and began a slow gallop over to see Liz and her. "Oh, my God, what are you doing here?" He asked, with a broad smile.

"Did you forget that I was here to recuperate after my knee surgery, A.J.?"

"I did." Tanned and handsome, he was a bit shy, surprised at seeing them.

Marjorie joined them and asked, "So, you are in St. Maarten this week. Is it wonderful?"

Liz told her, "We are loving it. The Pelican Resort was a good choice."

Zoey felt like her vacation would soon be crashing like the waves against these rocks on the shore of St. Barths Island. "Marjorie, is there some place we can talk? You need to know what has happened in Highland Falls and the missing person buried behind the Tuckerman Library."

"I told you, Mom." A.J. stared at his mother, whose tanned face seemed to turn rapidly pale.

They all headed over to an open air bar to sit down and have this discussion. "What is going on Zoey, or is this more gossip from that Prescott woman?"

"It is not gossip, Marjorie, this is serious. Sam is involved." She asked Marjorie, "What has happened with Sam and A.J. that an Audi seemed to be the answer for repairing all that has happened?"

A.J. was livid. "Mom, we have to tell Zoey what happened right before Gram was going to leave. I told you something has happened to Gram!"

Zoey was afraid of all that she had foreseen and was now happening at warp speed. "The day before your mother left for her trip, planned by Magellan Travel, she cancelled her vacation." She continued on, "You can thank Miranda Prescott for that. She has been trying to reach you."

"That can't possibly be true. We received two postcards from her."

A.J. interrupted her, "They were not from Gram, it was not her that sent those cards."

Zoey thought, gads, who had planned this down to the last letter. Who had mailed these cards? Zoey went into details about Gil Andrews and how his input helped to solve this case. For several minutes, you could have heard a pin drop. Marjorie and A.J. listened intently to Zoey about all that had occurred between Prescott and Andrews. All of the recent findings were now being turned over to Jonas Parsons and the State Police.

"So, you are telling me that Sam has been selling my mother's priceless jewels without my knowledge?"

"It appears that is exactly what has happened." Zoey asked Marjorie, "Would your mother have given any of the items sold, to Sam?" The vile look she gave Liz and Zoey indicated a NO.

Marjorie Watson was facing a number of traumatic issues now and she believed that in order to retain her sanity, being honest and outright was the only route to take. Realizing she and A.J. could rely on Zoey, she told her, "You may as well know what we just discovered and that was why we decided to leave Highland Falls for a while." Marjorie, unsmiling became suddenly very somber. A bit embarrassed, she quietly explained what happened three years ago with Sam and the teenage boy, Conner Holtzman, enjoying the hot tub with him, in the nude.

Zoey a bit distraught, thought, what the hell has happened to my vacation? "Well, now we all know why A.J. despises his father. Did the Audi really help?" Zoey, hesitated. "Sorry for that comment."

"I never told anyone what I saw, just Gram right before she left on vacation. But, now I guess she never left. She said she would straighten out Dad before she left." A.J. started to scream, amid tears. "What did he do to my grandmother?"

Liz took control of this horrific scene. "Everyone, listen. Please. There is more that you need to know about Sam. It seems to me that you did not know him at all." She looked at Zoey who had to tell them about why she left as Sam's business assistant.

Zoey just kept shaking her head back and forth. After telling Marjorie and A.J. what she had discovered, some years ago, Marjorie's theory of a 'one-time thing' with a teenage boy seemed to explode before her eyes.

Marjorie was ready to erupt. "Bastard, just a piece of scum." She looked at Zoey, tears falling onto her island sundress, "Are you saying he killed my mother?"

"I am so sorry for you both, but it looks like that is just what happened." Zoey actually felt sorry for Marjorie, who was now just sobbing with her arms cradled around her son.

Liz took over again. "I think we all need to go back home soon. Marjorie, they will need a DNA sample from something that Victoria had at the house. Do you have something?" Marjorie had calmed down slightly and Liz continued on, "With Sam still in London, it would be a good time for the authorities to get a sample with your permission."

Zoey went over for a gentle hug, "We'll help you and A.J. get through this. Before anything else happens, we need proof that it is Victoria Tuckerman buried behind the library."

Each and every one was in shock mode on this calming sun-drenched Caribbean island. Usually this was a tourist's dream that promises tranquility and peace. What the hell was happening?

CHAPTER 33

What the hell was happening? That is what Gil Andrews was also thinking, back in the states. Very close by Highland Falls, Gil and Caroline Andrews were at their bed and breakfast in Old Millbrook. It was close by the retirement home where Caroline's mother spent her last few years. Now, the Andrews were making decisions about the burial of Caroline's late mother, Susan Rothens. Her wish was to be cremated and Caroline wanted to spread her ashes along the ocean as that is where this woman spent so much time enjoying her New England life. Caroline's brother was going to join them in saying goodbye to their mother. In the middle of all of this sadness was the meeting with Miranda Prescott and the local police officer of Highland Falls, Jonas Parsons. Gil was just beginning to understand what the hell was happening. His life was shredding apart like tissue paper in the rain.

Gil asked Caroline, "What time do you have in mind for the spreading of ashes?"

"Tomorrow, after my brother arrives. He can't stay very long due to business meetings. It will be brief."

"I am leaving in a few minutes to see Miranda Prescott and the Marshall at Highland Falls."

"I simply can't go with you, Gil. I am still a bit overwrought."

He cradled Caroline against him. "That is fine, I understand." He looked terribly stressed.

"I wish I could help, but your honesty will help solve this mystery murder case. Do you really think Sam Watson killed Victoria Tuckerman?"

"I do." With a sad smile he added, "He totally outfoxed me, all these years."

"I am sure you are not the only one he has done this to."

"I will be glad when this interview is over."

"When can we go back home to London?"

Not wanting to tell her, honesty prevailed. "We may have to stay another week until all the strings are tied to this crime. Miranda Prescott would like me to do an interview for her show. I will be well compensated."

"And you should be, you helped to solve this murder case." In a pensive tone she told Gil, "Without your proof, they never would have suspected Sam Watson. All would have been buried away for years to come."

"Not likely." Thinking clearly, he told Caroline, "What would have happened in the next few weeks when Victoria never came home? The truth would eventually come out, maybe not pinning the murder on Sam, but there would be more investigations for sure."

Gil was able to find the police station at Highland Falls and decided to stop for a cup of coffee on the way for some energy and a bit of courage. He saw Sips and Swap and it looked like an appealing breakfast place. After parking in a crowded almost-filled lot, he went inside, and noticed a police officer was having breakfast. Not wanting him to notice who he was, Gil sat in a booth by an outer window area. As Jonas Parsons left the eatery, Caitland was right there to take his order. "What would you like today?"

As he gazed at the menu, he told Caitland, "How about a large vanilla bean coffee with cream, please. No sugar."

"No sweets?"

"No thanks, but what is happening in your town? I heard that officer mention a local murder case being solved?"

"An old case with a buried body behind our library." Caitland noticed his British accent and the fancy floral tie he was wearing. "You are not from around here, are you?"

"No, just a tourist." A little anxious, he knew he had better leave now. "Please just bring over your vanilla bean coffee." He buttoned his suit jacket. "I am in a bit of a hurry."

"Right away, sir." Caitland told him. She thought, who is this stranger? And he was gone.

He sat in his car for a few minutes before he headed to the police station. It was just minutes away from the entire truth being told.

Gil saw Miranda Prescott getting out of her car and he hustled over so he wouldn't have to face the police firing squad all alone. He had no idea who would be at this meeting. He yelled over to her. "Miranda, it's me."

Checking the time on her cell phone, a broad smile emerged. She told him, "Thanks for being so punctual. Let's get this done."

The police station was a quaint, traditional building, grey shakes, white trim. It stood on its own, and not part of the local town hall, as he had seen in other small areas of New England. Jonas was there as they entered the office and introduced himself. “You must be Gil Andrews. I am Jonas Parsons.” He looked over at Brian DiLuso, a member of the local State Police who had been in charge of this cold case. “And this is Brian DiLuso of the Connecticut State Police.”

With a professional grin at Jonas, Miranda acknowledged the other person who would interested in interviewing Gil. “Lieutenant DiLuso.”

“Let’s sit down in my private office, down the hallway.” Jonas led the way.

After an hour of taped comments by Gil Andrews, both Jonas and Brian Diluso became very somber. “With the proof that you have regarding these jewels and all that has occurred, including the DNA match of Victoria that Marjorie Tuckerman allowed us to examine, we may have solved this cold case murder.”

“It has been extremely stressful for me, as I have been used by Sam Watson and am embarrassed by all of this. Am I in trouble, because of these jewel sales last year?”

Brian DiLuso was honest. “That is entirely a different matter. I will not handle that.” Reassuring Gil, he told him, “However, because you came forward, totally on your own, I will do my best to speak to anyone in charge on your behalf.”

A sigh of absolute relief escaped from Gil. “Thank you for that. If there are consequences, I will certainly be ready for any backlash regarding these jewels.”

All of the images and paperwork involved with these jewel sales were turned over to the State Police. Miranda Prescott had her copies and asked both Jonas and Brian DiLuso if they would be willing to appear on her show, as the second and final segment was ready to go into production. They both agreed. She said she would arrange a time for them to be interviewed sometime next week. Miranda planned to have other people appear also on this final segment.

Gil began explaining that he and Caroline really had to head back to London very soon. He told them about the death of his mother-in-law and said his wife, still grieving, needed to get back home, "What happens next?"

"We have a number of papers for you to sign, today. They are being notarized here and all that we have put together will be handed over to a prosecutor, then a judge. When Sam Watson arrives home from London, next week, he will be served with a warrant for his arrest on a murder charge."

Gil thought it sounded so simple and it was far from that in his mind. As he read over the massive paperwork with so many copies, he was relieved that it was nearly over. He was still apprehensive about Sam Watson. When he discovered what Gil had done, there would be more than hell to pay. As he finished signing his John Hancock on the forms, he had to ask Brian DiLuso, "Will Sam Watson be allowed out on bail?"

"That will be entirely up to the judge that he appears in front of. Bail will be at least one million dollars on a murder charge. And from what we have heard, Sam Watson has made many friends in high places throughout Connecticut, other nearby states and even in London. He has had a successful career and at one point in his younger life, Sam planned to run for a congressional seat here in our state." He added, "Something changed his mind."

"I did see that while researching Sam. Perhaps he should have pursued that career. From many of the images I saw while researching the Tuckermans and Watsons, it was quite obvious that Victoria engaged with a number of important political friends as well."

In a solemn tone, Brian DiLuso told them all, "Sam Watson should hope that the judge considering his bail was not a good friend of Victoria Tuckerman."

CHAPTER 34

After spending several hours together, Zoey and Liz raced to their dock area as their catamaran was due to leave for St. Maarten. Liz and Zoey gave earnest hugs to A.J. and said they were both there for him and his mother no matter what was to happen. They barely made it to the boat ride home. Zoey promised to keep in touch via e-mail and cell phones and they would discuss when they would all head home to Highland Falls. Liz did not want to cut their vacation short. Sam Watson was not going to ruin Zoey's life and well-being any longer.

Sitting on their balcony, with only three days gone on their long awaited vacation, Liz told her daughter, "Tomorrow is Wednesday and we have three days left before we leave for home. I am not budging on this matter. Zoey, this nightmare is almost over, thanks to Miranda Prescott. If what she believes is true, Sam is in a lot of hot water."

"It is still hard for me to breathe all of this in. Sam doing this. Difficult, and poor Victoria."

"It is starting to make sense, though, Zoey." Nodding her head from side to side, she told her what she had been thinking for all of these months. "It is no secret that Sam was not fond of his mother-in-law. Our small town relies on knowing everything, whether it be good or bad. Our folks in Highland Falls all knew there was no love lost between Victoria Tuckerman and Sam Watson. Sam loved the money that was given to him and his wife from Victoria, but word was spreading that the purse strings were tightening, at home, and at the library. Now we know that right before her vacation was to begin, that Sam was going to be severely reprimanded by his mother-in-law because of what happened with the Holtzman boy three years past. Victoria was livid about how this affected her grandson. The embarrassing truth was uncovered and neither Sam nor Victoria would want any of this brought out into the eyes of the public. So it would be concealed and buried. Perhaps Sam thought with Victoria gone, that was his answer to resolving his pending financial issues." She added one more thought. "Remember, the body was carefully covered with a brand new tarp, which usually indicates that there was a personal connection to the corpse."

"Okay, Mom, I do think you need a better job than a short order cook at the eatery. You are far better than Jessica Fletcher."

"Thanks, but I love being just where I am, in such a tranquil town." Zoey let that comment go.

"We will stay here as planned, but here on St. Maarten. I do not ever want to go to St. Barths again. I will bet that Marjorie feels the same."

"Tomorrow, I head to the beach and then, later, the casino with free drinks served all day."

I have to call Jonas tomorrow to see when he will meet with Miranda and the whistleblower. Gil Andrews is very anxious about this and I can't blame him. A courageous thing to do, as he could end up in some trouble too."

"Just not murder." Liz sighed to herself.

Beyond belief, both Liz and Zoey managed to have a decent night's sleep. Awakening around 7:30, both felt relieved that the truth about the murder would soon go public. In an hour, Zoey would call Jonas and find out what was next. They would all have to protect Marjorie and A.J. from Sam. Hopefully he was not back from his trip abroad. So far he was unaware of all that Miranda Prescott had discovered through Sam's business friend. Over breakfast, Liz tried to organize their thoughts to calm the waters that had been so volatile the last twenty-four hours.

An hour's difference from the island to the United States made Zoey wait until 9:30 to phone Jonas. When she turned her cell phone on, she saw two messages from Kim. She assumed Jonas had told her what was happening. First she called Jonas.

The receptionist at the Highland Falls station switched Zoey over to Jonas without delay. "How is that vacation going for you, by the way?"

"Can you believe what Miranda Prescott was able to do?"

"I guess I had better go back to school, along with all of my other colleagues."

"Come on, Jonas, let's not go there. Give her some her credit and also give the courage award to Gil Andrews who you will meet soon."

"I guess I will learn it all around 11 o'clock today. It appears that Victoria Tuckerman might be buried behind our library, her library." He sounded repulsed. "Good Lord, all she did was help that entire family."

"And, you do not know the rest of this."

His eyes opened wide, and his breath paused. "There is more?" With a suspicious look, he told Zoey, "You need to be in a different profession, crime solver maybe, instead of owner of an eatery."

"It just seems to fall into my lap." She was sure that Jonas needed to hear what happened the day before Victoria was to leave on her longtime voyage. Miranda Prescott didn't even know about this. "You'd better close your door and hold all calls as I have to fill you in. It is all about Sam Watson and how we never really knew him, all these years."

"My God, Zoey, he is pretty much accused of murder and you are going to add another layer to that?"

"Sorry, but you need to know and understand exactly what has happened to this family, especially A.J."

"Let's hear it."

"You need to know what has happened here in St. Maarten. Please no interruptions, gads it's like ten dollars a minute on my phone plan." Catching her second wind, she began. "Marjorie and A.J. are here in St. Barths at their condo. If you remember, they left Highland Falls over a week ago. No one knew where they were going. Sam is on a business venture abroad, so none of the Watsons have been at home. Mom and I went on a catamaran ride to St. Barths, and coincidentally, we saw them at a restaurant we were lunching at. Since I had just been informed about the cold case by Miranda the evening before, I felt that I had to tell Marjorie just what was happening to her family. But, right in the middle of this explanation, A.J. interrupted me, extremely upset. A.J. had thought for many weeks that his grandmother was in danger. He never believed that the postcards sent to his mother were sent by Victoria. Marjorie was in a bit of denial, not wanting to believe something had happened to her mother. Holidays came, the second postcard arrived and A.J. was given a new Audi. Happiness prevailed. As I filled in the Prescott details to Marjorie, A.J. broke into my conversation. That is when Marjorie was forced to tell us all about Sam and why A.J. was so distant from him for some years now.

It was just three ago when A.J. began to see just what his father really was. Mom and I knew something was not right with the father-son relationship for a while now. A.J. arrived home one weekend, supposedly staying with his friends in Newport. They were forced to come home, due to some family thing and it was after 10 p.m. when they dropped A.J. off. He heard some noise in the pool area, which was dimly lit for that hour. His dad was out of town, like his mother, so he thought it was a burglar. Sneaking up to look over the fence, he spotted his father and a teenage boy in the hot tub with him, nearly nude. The boy was Conner Holtzman."

Jonas had to interrupt. "Are you kidding me, the boy at A.J.'s school who just took his own life weeks ago?"

"It is all connected, Jonas. Poor A.J. never told Conner what he saw, as he was embarrassed and did not want to lose his friendship. A.J. assumed it was a one-time thing."

Now Jonas had to be honest. "We know that is not true, don't we?"

Zoey thought for a moment and then panicked a little. "Kim told you, didn't she?

"I know why you left as Sam's assistant. She just told me a while ago, worried about you and your relationship with

Sam. She feels he is dangerous. And, she is right on that count."

Zoey finished what had to be told. "It is important that you hear this. Miranda Prescott found out that the day before Victoria left on vacation, she or someone cancelled the trip." Adding to that, "Also, A.J. had just confided in his grandmother about what happened to him and what he saw. Victoria promised she would reprimand his father and straighten him out, once and for all before she left on her trip. She told A.J. not to worry anymore."

"This case against Sam is mounting with every one of your statements."

"I know that and so does Marjorie. Before she left for St. Barths, she saw her attorney. Due to what happened with A.J. and the hot tub episode she planned to file for divorce. She also had him hire an investigator to find her mother. I guess he had no luck, so you should not feel so bad either." Zoey laughed quietly, not to hurt any feelings. "If you need a DNA comparison for Victoria Tuckerman, as you saved your own sample, Marjorie will grant permission, to do it at her house. Sam is gone, and you'll deal with the housekeeper. You remember Millie." She gave Jonas a cell phone number for Marjorie.

Jonas Parsons tried to hide a smile before telling Zoey, "Well, when Sam Watson arrives home at Bradley Airport, I might consider being there, just to welcome him home."

"What happens next?"

"Let's not get too far ahead. I have to make sure what you have been told is all factual." He wanted Zoey to know he was supporting her. I believe you and I fear what Prescott has discovered will sink Sam Watson."

"So, if all is true what happens when Sam arrives home?"

"A warrant for his arrest from our county will be done. The State Police will accompany me and we will need support from the airport security department."

"Lots of strings to connect in this web."

"And paperwork that I will have to do. Kim will be really busy, no time for the eatery."

"We will be back by then, no worries." Zoey really wanted to be back in Highland Falls.

"Be careful, Zoey." Jonas told her in a sincere goodbye.

As the next three days seem to fly by, there were some delectable island meals, sunny days and a time to calm down before they flew home on Saturday. Zoey made two hasty calls to Will and Kim telling them to touch base with Jonas for the full account of what had happened. Zoey also kept in touch with Marjorie who surprisingly seemed to have a handle on what had happened. Zoey was sure her meds were close at hand to keep her composed. She and A.J. would head for home next week as she really wanted no contact with Sam. Her attorney arranged with a judge to serve him a restraining order keeping him away from their property.

Zoey told Marjorie she had spoken to Jonas and explained what would happen next. Jonas had already called her and she was able to fax permission for Jonas to retrieve that DNA sample of her mother. A.J. was very relieved that the truth he had to keep buried had finally been exposed.

However, he felt guilty blaming himself for what finally happened to his grandmother. Suddenly, the truth didn't feel right. Look at what happened, because of him. A.J. and Marjorie would have to be strong and rely on each other because this horrific happening was way far from over. Jonas was right, Sam Watson should be feared by everyone.

On Saturday, Liz and Zoey were thankful that their early flight back to Highland Falls was on time. Luck was on their side, calm flying, good weather, and even the baggage claim area was a quick walk through. They arrived home a little past dinner time, a bit weary. Dropping Liz off, Zoey was eager to see Will and her three feline friends. Will was at the door with a warm hug and lingering kiss. Cats were entangled between them both, seeking attention. The rest of the night was spent with lots of cuddling. Will cradled her within his warm arms, "I really missed you….again."

"Let's never be apart again. Time to head up to bed." Zoey yawned, "I will call Hannah in the morning. Boy, she will not believe just what happened on my restful vacation."

CHAPTER 35

When Zoey woke up, she felt a bit disoriented. Like, where was she? She felt Dewey and Spencer across her lower calves, both her feet tingly and half asleep from the fat cats on them. Then she knew where she was, a broad smile erupted. Will was already out of bed and she smelled coffee. She yelled down the stairway, “Are you down feeding my birds?”

“All done.” Will was already heading upstairs, Mika trailing behind, with a muffin and large cup of salted caramel coffee with cream. “Are you all right?”

“I am but right now, I feel spoiled.” Zoey bit into her buttered muffin. “Did you get these muffins at the Eatery?”

“I did and it is new one, made just for you.”

“Tastes like cherry and peach?” She looked dubious. “They taste like fresh cherries and peaches.”

“Can’t fool the cook, you are right.”

“I have some special girls there, don’t I? Mom has to have one of these.”

“I have extra and I can drop one off if you like.”

“That would be good, I will give her a call and let her know.” She told Will, “I can call Hannah and probably wake her up. But, she needs to hear what happened this past week. Soon she’ll see it on the internet, like last time.”

With another hug and kiss, Will left to bring Liz her breakfast.

Calling Hannah, Zoey had too much to tell her in one call. "Mom, I was asleep." Barely awake and no happy face she asked her, "And how was St. Maarten?"

"A lot happened there and it had a lot to do with our cold case here in town. Miranda Prescott has this case solved."

Waking up very slowly she exclaimed, "Mom, can't you just go on vacation?" Pausing with a yawn she asked her mother, "Oh my God, what happened?"

"Too much to absorb. I will text you right now. After you take it all in, call me later okay?" She requested Hannah to do as she asked, "Maybe by then, you'll be fully awake. What I have to tell you will certainly open your eyes. I am also shocked by all of this but I am okay, so don't worry."

Zoey went into detail as she texted her daughter, using her voice so she did not have to type one letter at a time. When Will got home they sat down by the fire to talk about all that had happened. Before Hannah called Zoey back, she heard from Jonas. It was confirmed, all that Gil Andrews thought was possible had happened. Unfortunately, Gil was not having a good time here in the states. The main issue of Sam Watson and a murder investigation was one reason and the other was his mother-in-law. Susan Rothens passed away just days ago and his wife completely fell apart. His stress level was extreme knowing he needed an attorney due to repercussions regarding this murder case. He was going to use his mother-in-law's attorney from Old Millbrook, Connecticut. He had been a good friend to both Caroline and her mother for many years. Gil would be lucky to have someone with him throughout this cold case murder incident. The questionable jewels would be a serious involvement. Jonas was praying Andrews would hold strong to the end. It was too far along the line to back out now. Andrews did a courageous thing knowing he might be in jeopardy, not only with the law but with Sam Watson. No one enjoyed tangling with Samuel Watson, as they rarely won. Thorough and signed affidavits would allow Andrews to return home soon.

Jonas tried to reassure Zoey, "Sam is due back to Highland Falls Tuesday, a late flight. We plan to be there with an arrest warrant." He finished with a telling statement, "The DNA sample matches what we kept on file for that woman's body buried behind the library. We now know that it was Victoria Tuckerman."

"Does Marjorie know this?" Zoey was concerned for her as well as A.J.

"I phoned her and she came home very late last night, a bit earlier than anticipated."

"How was she?"

Appalled, he asked Zoey, "What do you think?"

"Sam won't be allowed to go to see her, will he?"

"No, as she has a restraining order in place. It is a done deal."

"So, Sam will be arrested by you all and held for what 24 hours before he sees a judge?"

"That is about right. You realize that he may be released on bond?"

Zoey's eyes bulged out. "On a murder charge?"

"This is Sam Watson, he knows the governor."

Zoey was frightened now, for Marjorie, A.J., and herself. "They won't let him out, look at the evidence against him?"

"It depends on the judge, Zoey."

"Do we have to worry?" In panic mode she pleaded with Jonas. "What if he gets out on bail and he comes to the eatery?"

"Let's not get ahead of ourselves. No need to have an ulcer over this." He added some reassurance. "I would get bulletins on anything that might affect Sam Watson's contacts. Gil Andrews might be one person he will be upset with. Then there is Marjorie. I believe that you are way down on the list, except for all your annoying snooping abilities."

Mentally, she gave Jonas a really offensive look. "I am very intuitive, and not a snoop, Jonas." They both laughed as their phone call ended on a lighter note.

When Hannah called her mother, she was really concerned for her safety. "Mom, you simply have to butt out now, out of this case. You don't need Sam Watson on your ass."

"Jonas promised to protect me," she told her daughter. """If Sam somehow gets out on bail, he will not be aiming for me. Do you realize what has happened? Sam is accused of murder, illegal jewel sales and who know what else, chasing teenage boys….."

"Well, I doubt he will get bail with that long list of accusations tied around him pretty tightly."

"I can only hope you are right."

"Mom, he does have contacts with the higher ups, mainly due to Victoria Tuckerman's influence. He is accused of killing her. He'd better hope the judge he sees wasn't good friends with his mother-in law."

"Now, I feel better. You make solid sense of things. That is what you do." Zoey breathed a long, calm sigh of relief.

"When does Sam Watson arrive from London?"

"Tuesday, late and he will have a group ready to welcome him home."

"Where is Marjorie, now?"

"Just got home from St. Barths."

"Now, she should be worried." Hannah told her Mom as she was headed to the library. "Gotta' go, if you want a veterinarian in the family to take care of your family, no time to waste."

It was a busy Sunday after a trip away. There was laundry, mail, too much catch up work. Good thing, day off Mondays for tomorrow. And, Tuesday night Sam would be home, and in jail Zoey hoped. Wednesday, he would most likely go before a judge to see if he would be allowed bail. Imagine what that would cost. A million dollars? It was hard to fathom that bail would happen. He was certainly a flight risk, he traveled abroad all year long. He had so many contacts too, and it was beginning to look like some were not so worthy. Zoey was sure he would have to suspend his passport. She thought of speaking to Jonas, but Hannah was in the back of her mind, reminding her to butt out.

By the end of the day Marjorie called Zoey. She was rather quiet, probably jet lagged, arriving home late last night. She had a request. "Do you have time tomorrow to help me locate any of that material that Sam had locked away, pictures of those boys?"

"I can come by." Being candid, she replied, "Those images may be long gone."

In an incensed tone she said, "We will soon find out, won't we?"

Zoey thought, sorry Hannah, I am back in the middle once again.

CHAPTER 36

This was not due to be a great day off Monday. Zoey would go to see Marjorie and A.J. after lunch to snoop. Maybe Jonas was right. He would most likely not approve of this move. Will had thumbs down too. She never told Hannah. She would be in no danger, as Sam was not there. Why worry? But, she was. Her wish was that Sam had destroyed all that was there, if he was a smart man. She would not allow A.J. to be part of this, either. She already told Marjorie that but it appeared that she needed or wanted proof of what Sam really was, so he'd never be released from jail. Zoey thought the murder charge was quite enough. Marjorie did not think people would believe that Sam killed her mother. He could talk anyone into anything with his smooth and persuasive personality. He had done that to her for years.

Finally all organized after arriving home from her trip, Zoey wanted to tell her mother about seeing Marjorie later today. When she called, all she got was the answering machine. Right before Zoey left for the Watsons, Liz called her back.

"What don't you understand about Butt Out."

"I really had no choice here Mom."

"You always have the right to choose."

"Well, my morality said to help a friend."

"Did you ask Jonas about this?"

“No need to do that. This is Marjorie’s home.” Sounding confident, Zoey added, “The material I saw is most likely gone. But I have another card up my sleeve.”

Liz could not imagine what she had that would be connected to this years ago incident. “What on earth….”

“I took a photo of the picture he had with that young boy.”

“Zoey,” Liz gazed at her daughter in dismay. “Why did you do that? It was not your property.”

“I did it to protect myself, in case Sam ever tried to intimidate me. He does that, you know, a lot. Back then I had plans to leave the library and what if he wouldn’t let me? I had leverage.”

“You mean protection in the form of extortion?”

Zoey’s upper cheeks reddened. “You know Sam Watson and how he treats people. He was not ever going to coerce me. When I saw what Sam had been up to I was just sick. He was the director at Tuckerman Library. I had to put up with him so I could enjoy all of my patrons, the kids, the seniors, everyone. You don’t know how many times I had to look the other way when Claire checked our finances to make sure all was correct. Sam made me sign a few bills that I knew were not right. When I questioned him, he said, not your concern. You take care of library books, not the finances, understood? More than once, I saw bills that were inflated.”

Liz held back a huge sigh, disillusioned by what she just heard. “Okay, then.”

After the call ended, Zoey felt hurt about how she had spoken to her mother. But, it was all true. Now, she wondered why she had ever felt doubtful that Sam killed Victoria Tuckerman. The latest findings made her think that Sam must have been desperate to kill her. Both he and Marjorie relied on the rich old woman for everything, especially her precious library. The purse strings were tightening with more and more being allocated to the library. Modernization costs a lot of money. That meant that Watson personal expenses would have to be adjusted. Sam would never accept that. He was always first.

What had happened on the day before Victoria was due to leave on her extended voyage? Zoey tried to piece this altogether and she had to leave soon to handle Marjorie. When she got home she would organize her thoughts and figure out what happened on the day of that murder. Filling cat bowls with dry kibble, fresh water in their fountain, Zoey swallowed a large protein drink with a grilled PB sandwich for energy. She left for the Watsons before 1 p.m.

In all of the years Zoey had known Marjorie, friendly was not an adjective often used. Marjorie was always above the crowd, any crowd, and her aura was a bit overwhelming. You rarely saw this woman looking like anything but perfect. Very generous with her charitable events, people were in awe of her. Unlike Sam, she was a compassionate individual, often willing to help others not as well off as her. She inherited that from her mother, Victoria Tuckerman. When Zoey knocked on the front door, A.J. let her in with a welcoming smile. Shaking his head he told her, "Nice life we all have, right?"

"It can only get better."

"Not a betting man, but I think I would hold off on that one." He pointed to the sunroom, "Mom is out there. I have errands to run, as I head back to school soon."

"Are you doing okay?" She looked doubtful.

"Yeah, I am, as long as I don't see my father." He added, "I just hate him now. I really loved Gram, always able to count on her for everything."

Zoey hoped this snoop event would not take long. She told Marjorie that Sam's foreign business belongings were housed in his office above their four-car garage. "Don't be discouraged if there is nothing there."

Marjorie didn't look so perfect today. There was just no time for a salon visit and she appeared very uncaring about her looks. Still, she was a beautiful woman. Zoey's blondish pony tail hairdo and skinny jeans portrayed the total opposite of her newly earned friend. As they headed into the office, Zoey did see the large tall bureau that had a hidden space behind its many shelves. Anxious, Marjorie watched Zoey delve into the cabinet. However, the shelves were not movable. It appeared they had been strengthened since Zoey worked for Sam almost two years ago. "They won't budge." Zoey looked surprised.

Marjorie looked furious. "Break them open!"

"Are you sure?" Zoey was a bit startled at Marjorie's order.

"We have to see what is there, for my sake."

"Marjorie, we have no tools, we can't just smash this open." Zoey looked around for something that would aid her in forcing this piece of furniture open. “This is a really nice antique. We’ll ruin it.”

“Do you really think I give a shit? It belongs to Sam. Smash it open.”

Zoey hurriedly looked throughout the desk area and found a large, sturdy letter opener. She began to pry open the spaces beneath the shelves and one popped open. This scrape left visible scratches. Marjorie was right there trying to get a look at what was behind the shelf. Nothing.

Zoey managed to pry open another area and again, there was nothing there, certainly not any incriminating evidence of teenage boys with Sam. “I’m sorry Marjorie, how much more should we ruin? I knew he would get rid of this stuff, just to protect himself.”

“So, it would be my son’s words against his own father as to what he saw.”

Zoey thought, no it would not be that as I have a photo that illegally took almost two years ago. What should I do, she was in limbo. “No, we will never put A.J. through that.”

In a manic tone, Marjorie erupted, “Sam always wins, he always wins.”

“Not this time.” Zoey thought of the discussion she just had with her own mother. All along, Zoey thought she would be protecting herself with this photo, and now this was going to help A.J. and Marjorie Watson. Who would have thought that? “Marjorie, don’t ask why, but I have an image that can help. I took a photo of Sam and that boy.”

Startled, Marjorie couldn’t even speak. Then she did. “May I see it?”

Against everyone's intentions, Zoey opened her purse and retrieved her iPhone. As she opened it, she showed Marjorie the picture of Sam and the teenage boy. Marjorie's eyes began to water, "It's Conner Holtzman, isn't it?"

Zoey never recognized the face of this boy. Or maybe, at the time, she was just in denial. She did want to forget that whole episode of this discovery while Sam was away. Looking at it with Marjorie, she did see that it was Conner.

"That is why A.J. came home from school wanting to see his grandmother." Marjorie was piecing it altogether. "Victoria just found out about Conner and Sam from A.J. She told her grandson that she was finally going to straighten out Sam. If that occurred, Sam would never allow that to come out about him. Sam used this poor boy, and Conner most likely killed himself because he was gay. A.J. must have felt responsible, as he was never there for Conner. That is when A.J. became frantic about my mother. He must have thought that Sam killed his grandmother to silence her from the truth about Sam was really like."

All Zoey wanted to do was help. It seems like everything was worsening. Did she really not understand what 'Butt Out' means?

CHAPTER 37

Back downstairs in the garage, Marjorie asked Zoey to please stay for a few minutes until she settled down. "I don't want A.J. to worry about me as he heads back to school either tonight or tomorrow morning."

"I can stay for a while." She suggested that A.J. leave for school later today. "A.J. should settle back to school tonight. It's only a matter of time before all of this is either on the internet or in local papers. Focusing on his studies and being away from Highland Falls might help him."

"What about that Prescott woman?" A bit disgruntled, she asked Zoey what would happen next. "Will there really be a second segment on this case? I couldn't stand it." Tears formed again, streaking down her cheeks. "This is about my mother. Can we stop her?"

"I doubt anyone can stop the show." She tried to reason with Marjorie. "People are interested in these types of mysterious cases. Her ratings will soar, if all that she has learned is true."

"Please tell me that none of what Sam did years ago will surface. It would be a real tragedy for A.J."

"I agree but it may be connected to motive. A.J. feels that is why his grandmother was murdered, because his grandmother was about to expose the truth." Zoey carefully continued with her thoughts. "To my knowledge, Prescott knows nothing about any of this. The motive appears to be connected to stolen jewels, all about the money and Sam's greed."

“What is happening to my perfect life?” Marjorie poured herself an ample glass of pink Moscato wine, sprinkled with a small amount of ice. “Would you like some?”

Zoey thought about her mother’s comments about perfect people and their perfect lives. Certainly money does not buy happiness, at least within the Watson family. “I am all set, Marjorie. I really need to head home.” She buttoned her jacket and headed for the door. “It is early work Tuesday tomorrow. First day back after being away. I am still in transition mode, or that is what my therapist would say.”

“So, what happens now when Sam gets home tomorrow night?”

“From what Jonas told me, he along with the State Police will be at Bradley Airport to greet him. I believe there are lengthy affidavits supporting an arrest warrant.”

“Will he be locked up?” Marjorie was edging close to panic mode.

Zoey had to be careful. “Why don’t you call Jonas? He has pertinent facts about when all of this occurs. I don’t want to give you the wrong info.” Zoey gave Marjorie a meaningful hug as she left.

Marjorie just stayed in the open doorway silently weeping, waiting for A.J. to come home.

When will this be over? Zoey got home and had no idea what they would have for dinner. She decided to whip up a creamy pasta and veggie dish with fresh rolls and big tossed salad. Will would wonder where the meat was, but tonight would be a healthy filling dinner. She missed her garden greens while she was on vacation. They just did not taste the same as here in the states. Gads, most fresh veggies were shipped there from wherever and spent more time on boats than in the kitchen. Will would want to be filled in about the visit at the Watsons. Before he got home, Liz called Zoey to see how the visit went.

"Mom, it went as expected. There was nothing left behind those shelves." Adding to that, "And Marjorie was quite disappointed."

"Zoey," In a very reflective tone, she asked her, "There is no way Sam suspected you knew about these images of him with that boy, or is there?"

"No, there is no way." Zoey explained. "When I went into that bureau for Sam, the shelf just came apart. That is when the images fell out. I was very careful after what I saw to replace the images and the shelf exactly how they were." She concluded with, "Sam never knew what I saw."

"You had better hope that's how it happened. If he suspects you knew about all of that, you would be next on his hit list."

"Really, Mom. Stop." She was a bit ruffled. "Victoria Tuckerman is dead and it looks like Sam did it. I am not next and he is going to prison for a long time, thanks to Miranda Prescott and Gil Andrews."

"Kim called to say Jonas would not be home for dinner, as he had a lot to do with paperwork regarding Sam Watson. Sam is due in from London tomorrow, Tuesday evening, around 9 p.m. Since warrants are issued in the county you live in, we are part of Branburry County, and that is where they will cart him off to jail."

"Aren't you a basket of information tonight?"

"Thank your sister for that. She is worried about you, you know."

Zoey looked at the clock that was well after 4 o'clock and dinner was not started. "I will call her now, but just for a minute. I need to make dinner. I have to be up bright and early tomorrow, along with you, kitchen lady."

"See you early tomorrow, sweetie"

When Zoey called Kim, they discussed what would happen tomorrow and Kim was worried about Jonas as well as her sister. "He had better not get out on bail." Kim said in a huffy tone.

Zoey had a hidden smile telling Kim, "I guess it all depends on the judge. Bail will be a lot of money. Unfortunately, Sam killed the person who supplied him with all of that cash."

Will and Zoey had a really good dinner, despite the lack of meat on Will's plate. They sat by the fire with dessert, just some vanilla bean gelato that was the smoothest way to end the evening.

"So, Marjorie really needed to dig up dirt on Sam and found zippo, correct?" Will sat close to Zoey, trying to provide some comfort for all of her effort today helping a friend.

Zoey was afraid to tell Will that she really had no other choice but to show Marjorie the picture she had taken of Sam and that boy's photo, hidden away from the world.

"You really did that?" He was a bit heated when he heard that. "Zoey, you do not want to get in the way of Sam Watson. This is not good."

"I did it to protect myself from him. Now it will protect A.J. and Marjorie. What if something happens and he skirts free of this murder?" Zoey was troubled with this possible scenario. "We all agreed that this event that happened years ago has a bearing on the motive for killing Victoria."

"You all?" Will looked dubious.

"Marjorie, A.J., and me."

"What are you now, members of The Murder Club?"

Exhaling a big sigh, Zoey got up off of the couch to make a cup of tea before bed. "We have this proof of what Sam was and what Victoria thought of him because of that event. A.J. was crushed by this, and Victoria loved her grandson, to the depths. When she confronted Sam the day before her voyage, it must have gotten out of control."

"Maybe you should work on the cold case show, instead of Miranda Prescott."

"Will, we all needed to know what happened with that body buried behind the library. And, now we do know. Sam must have paid someone else to send those postcards. That proves he planned this whole thing."

Will came over to the counter and gave her a long expressive hug and kiss. "I love you and I want no harm to come to you. Understand?"

“I do know that.” And she returned a loving kiss.

Zoey had a rough night’s sleep but rising early, she was overeager to go to the eatery. Nothing would appear in any paper or online regarding Sam. It was too early. So, Zoey, Liz, and her girls would have a nice Tuesday for catching up, and no Sam Watson talk. At least for today, so she thought.

CHAPTER 38

Another snow event was predicted for Wednesday so the Eatery was full of residents eager to get out ahead of the storm. So many friends were glad to see Liz and Zoey back on the job. Claire Harris was in around 10 a.m. asking for two of her favorite egg pies.

"I don't plan to go out for a few days with this snow coming. They say at least 8 to 10 inches." Claire sounded a bit down and out. "Oh, gosh. I need some audio books to listen to Zoey. How about a good murder mystery?"

Whoa, thought Zoey, taken aback, just a bit. "Let's go see what we have, Claire."

Zoey knew that she owed it to Claire to tell her what had happened. However, it would be in strict confidence until Sam Watson was arrested at the airport later on tonight. She trusted Claire and she needed to know the truth.

"I see two mysteries I would like." She picked up a Miranda James audio book, *Cat Me if You Can*, and a *Murder She Wrote* title too. "That should keep me busy for a few snowy days."

Zoey thought, we have a real murder mystery that will occupy you as well, Claire. "Come sit down, Claire. What I have to tell you must be kept strictly confidential."

Claire nodded, a bit perplexed. She stared seriously at Zoey.

"I have some sad news regarding our cold case, the unclaimed body at Tuckerman Library."

"Really? Oh, dear, you discovered who this woman was." Saddened, Claire lowered her head.

How am I going to tell her this? "Claire, a business associate of Sam Watson has surfaced. Gil Andrews is from London and has handled jewel and antiquity sales from Sam for a few years now. He discovered that some of the jewels sold were owned by Sam's mother-in-law. The cold case episode caught his attention and for many weeks now he suspected Sam had something to do with this. To resolve this he contacted Miranda Prescott. There's a lot to explain but the buried body behind the library was Victoria Tuckerman."

To say Claire was shocked was being kind. Her whole body seemed to collapse and she had to sit down. "Are they sure about this?"

"Quite sure as they did a DNA match. If you recall, they kept samples from the body prior to her cremation."

"You need to tell me the rest." She wiped a few tears away with some tissue she saw on Zoey's desk. "Do they know who did this?"

Zoey was surprised she did not figure out the rest of this mystery, since Sam was the main clue.

"There has been a warrant issued for the arrest of Sam Watson. He arrives home from London tonight. Both Jonas and the State Police will be at the airport to greet him."

"Oh my. Does Marjorie know about this?" Sounding distressed she told Zoey, "I believe she and A.J. are still away, where I do not know."

Zoey would only tell Claire most of what had occurred. "No, she and A.J. are back. They went to their timeshare in the Caribbean. A.J. had a tough time because of his friend at school. Conner Holtzman committed suicide weeks ago and A.J. came home suddenly to be with his mother. He had a really difficult few weeks."

"So, going away helped them." As she shook her head she added, "And now they have to face this."

"Claire, you need to understand that their marriage did not portray a strong bond. Before they left, Marjorie filed for divorce. None of us need to know details of that issue. She is fully aware of the details on her mother's murder."

"But, Sam Watson?"

"It looks like he had been selling her jewels illegally for quite a while. Something happened the day before she was due to leave on her extended voyage. During the investigation, it was discovered that Victoria cancelled her trip. She never left Highland Falls."

"Oh dear." Sighing, she was becoming angry now. "Tuckerman Library meant the world to her. She has dedicated her entire life to this institution. How cruel Sam was if he did this to her, at her namesake."

"I agree, but Miranda Prescott was very thorough when speaking to me about the evidence she had compiled. In my mind, there is no doubt that it was Sam who killed his mother-in-law."

"Rather frightening." Claire handed back one of the audio books to her. "I think I will only take one of these mystery books. Perhaps you have a Danielle Steel? I need an easy read tonight."

Claire zippered her winter jacket and gave Zoey a hug goodbye. "I guess I will read about this in the news very soon." Distressed, she asked Zoey, "What will the library do now?"

"I will help all I can to get through this misfortune. We now have a really cordial and well- educated librarian. Working together, it will be fine. It has to be for the sake of Victoria Tuckerman."

It was not long after Claire left when Caitland popped in the back swap are to see Zoey. "So, was St. Maarten just the best, or what?"

A bit of a lie, Zoey replied, "Just the most beautiful island and such friendly people there to help you enjoy your stay."

She looked over, unsure how to tell Zoey about the stranger who had visited the eatery while they were away. "We had a stranger stop by coffee while you were gone last week."

Not sure why this was a big deal, as many out of town tourists enjoyed Sips and Swap. "And why do you remember this stranger?"

"Well, for one thing he was British with a really nice accent. He just ordered vanilla bean coffee but when I took his order he seemed focused on what Jonas had mentioned about our murder mystery."

Zoey stood at attention when she heard that. "What exactly did he say?"

"Not much. When I took his order, he asked me what is happening, did you have a murder here?"

"Anything else?"

"I just told him, well, it happened a while ago." She tried to remember exactly what she said. "I asked him if he was from around here and he seemed ruffled by that. Sounding a bit dismissive, he told me "Please just get my coffee, I am running late for a meeting." And he was gone.

"When did this happen?"

"Maybe Tuesday or Wednesday?"

"What did he look like?"

"Just average, maybe in his fifties, greyish brown hair, nice looking. Dressed to the nines. He had on a nice suit and tie with some bright flower motif on it."

Oh my God, it must have been Gil Andrews going to meet Jonas for the meeting. "Well, we certainly have a lot of tourists stopping by, even in the winter season."

"I just thought you might want to know. It just felt strange to me when he wanted to know about our murder case. We are just a small town. Why would he care?"

Zoey knew exactly why he cared. She would have to ask Jonas about that fancy tie to see if Gil Andrews, the one person helping to solve this murder case, had stopped at her eatery.

"Thanks Caitland, something for me to wonder about." She smiled, heading back to the kitchen area.

Zoey called Jonas at work, looking at the clock, it was nearly lunch time. "Jonas Parsons here."

"Hi Jonas, I wanted to wish you luck tonight at the airport, and I have a question."

"Go ahead." He told her in the midst of a hectic morning.

“Do you recall if Gil Andrews wore a fancy tie when he came to be interviewed by you?”

Zoey, you are a strange one, he thought. “Yes, I do, a bright golden flower in the middle.”

“Well, we were lucky to have served him that day. He stopped at the eatery and heard you mention the murder case. Caitland said a British guy was here, enjoying our vanilla bean coffee, before seeing you and the State Police. How is that for a coincidence and I missed it?”

CHAPTER 39

Before Sam Watson headed for Heathrow Airport, he had an important call to make. He also had to pick up two new shirts from his favorite store on German Street. They had custom made Sam's dress shirts for years. Extremely pricey but a perfect fabric and fit. Gil Andrews used the same place for his ties and suits so he recommended the store to Sam. While waiting for the sales person to bag his items, Sam decided to call Colin to see if the third parcel he requested him to mail was done.

"I mailed your parcel off a week ago. I can't help it if the mail is slow."

"Colin, you are so overpaid for just mailing items back to the states for me."

"I do what you tell me to do." Colin thought what a strange request, postcards with one sentence on them from his mother-in-law. Don't ask don't tell and the five hundred dollars for ten minutes of work was worth it.

"I am late for my flight out. When I arrive home, that parcel should have arrived."

"Have a safe flight, Sam."

Sam headed for the airport, smiling that he would have some new clothes when he got home. There was a lot on his plate for the next month. No time to visit his timeshare in St. Barths. The library was demanding a lot of his time and then there were A.J. and Marjorie. Just no time for himself. Sam was planning exactly what to do as Victoria never did return from her trip. He would choose the private detective and pay him well to complete an investigation that would fit in well with Sam's scenario. Perhaps after she traveled extensively and planned to head home, she just vanished somewhere in the United Kingdom. It happens. Some older woman wandering around at night. Gads anything could have happened. That is why it was significant that the third postcard arrived in Highland Falls before he got home.

After he worked his way through customs, which was annoying, he boarded the plane and sat down, already weary of traveling. He decided to phone Marjorie to warn her he was headed home this evening, a bit later than planned. To his disbelief, the phone rang with a message saying this number is no longer in service. He thought that a bit strange. Marjorie relied on her cell phone, never going anywhere without it. He thought perhaps she bought a newer one with more sparkly icons to use. Oh, well, he would see her later this evening and was not too thrilled about that.

Back in the United States, the weather in Highland Falls was deteriorating as daylight came to an end. Snow was scheduled to arrive earlier than Wednesday morning as originally predicted. It would start sometime before midnight. Kim decided to call her sister as she was worried that Jonas would be caught in the midst of a blizzard, greeting Sam Watson at the airport. Around dinner time she phoned her. "Zoey, I am really concerned about Jonas."

Trying to encourage her sister, Zoey was upfront. "The weather isn't the obstacle here, Kim. Jonas and the State Police are focused on Sam Watson, not a few snowflakes. It won't start until midnight. From what Jonas said, flight lands just before 9 p.m. and they locate him as soon as possible, when he deplanes, before baggage claim. Security Police from Bradley will be there too for support." She finished with, "So, this will be fairly quick. Off to the county facility in Branburry where he will stay the night before seeing a judge in the morning."

"I won't be able to go to sleep tonight until Jonas gets home, probably well after midnight."

"Kim, he will be fine. It's not like Sam is an armed and dangerous suspect. He will be extremely surprised tonight. He has no clue as to what he did not get away with. And still, I want to know who he paid to send postcards from a dead woman. It's revolting."

"It was not that Andrews man who sent the cards for Sam?"

"No, they asked him that during the interview with Jonas."

"So, there is another person involved with this."

"It certainly appears that way."

"When will this end? Highland Falls has taken a serious hit."

"We will be fine." She told her about Claire stopping by. "I promised Claire that I would help her out. The new librarian will be a bit distracted due to this murder especially with Sam Watson as head of the library board."

"Who will be the head honcho, with Sam out of the picture?"

"Not sure about that. But when I spoke with the new girl at Tuckerman, Moritza mentioned something strange. She asked Sam if she could meet Victoria Tuckerman one day. He told her she should not hold her breath on that request."

"Wow, why didn't you notice that?"

"Well, at that time, the former librarian had just resigned, due to the murder at Tuckerman. I was headed for knee surgery and my ex-husband was moving into our old home."

"Okay then, I get it. You were busy."

Zoey smiled to herself. "Soon, this will pass, like a kidney stone. Some pain and then gone. When Sam appears in court, it is highly doubtful that he will be granted bail. It would be at least a million dollars and the evidence against him is strong."

"So we, and I do mean you, will be safe with him locked up before his trial?"

"No doubt about it." Zoey slowly held her breath in with that last comment.

CHAPTER 40

Will arrived home from work around 6 o'clock. "Well, has Jonas headed to the airport yet?"

"I think he may have just left from the station. Takes a while on that drive to Windsor Locks and there are forms to be done at Bradley, before Sam arrives."

"I suppose Kim is ready to fall apart, over anxious?"

"She just called me. I settled her down assuring her that soon Sam will be in custody and of no harm to any of us."

"Are we sure about that?"

"No, but Kim doesn't need to know that. And, really, what bail bondsman would help Sam?"

"Are you serious? Sam will lawyer up before he ends up in his cell for the night. He has to go in front of a judge tomorrow morning. So, we are all safe for tonight."

"Enough talk." She took Will in her arms and planted a heavy duty kiss right on him "Let's have dinner and head up to bed early. I need a good night's sleep."

"And maybe before sleep a nice massage would help."

"Yes, sir, it certainly would. Do you know a masseuse?"

"I work pro bono."

An early bedtime occurred.

No matter how hard Zoey tried, sleep was very intermittent. All three cats were restless too, trying to find a comfy spot near Zoey or Will. By 4:30, Zoey got up and had her first cup of coffee. There were no messages on either phone so all must have gone according to plan. Kim would not hesitate to call her sister with any bulletins regarding Sam, had the evening gone badly. Zoey had an English muffin with her coffee and chuckled slightly wondering if they had English muffins in London. Gil Andrews was on her mind and she was sure that Gil was feeling rather anxious about Sam's arrival back in the states. It was far too early to call Kim or Jonas so Zoey checked the internet for news and weather. Looking outside, snow was falling but very sporadically. Several inches were due to fall by day's end. Nothing urgent appeared on the headlines for news and as she checked the weather, the forecast was the same as yesterday.

Zoey used the guest bathroom to take her morning shower so she would not wake Will. Extra time would be needed on the drive over to get Liz and heading to the eatery. Zoey was sure that by mid-day the news would hit the fan about Sam Watson's role in the unsolved murder case in Highland Falls. Residents would be stunned. It would be a busy day at Sips and Swap. By 6 a.m. Will was up and dressed, asking Zoey how she slept.

"Not as good as you, I guess." She asked Will, "Is school on for you today because of the snow?"

"No, I got a text really early saying we are cancelled. Do you need help at the eatery?"

"Because you love to cook, or are you interested in all of the town gossip that will erupt today among the residents?"

"Maybe a little of both."

"I am leaving in a few minutes to pick up Mom, but I have to call Kim first."

Kim was up and had been for a while. "I can't believe you didn't call me last night."

"I figured that you needed your sleep if Jonas got home late."

"He did, but the arrest went as planned at the airport. The State Police had to use handcuffs as Sam want a little nuts for a short time. As the commotion continued and Sam noticed people looking at him so reprehensibly, he settled down. He continued with a lot of verbal abuse to Jonas and the others, saying this was ridiculous, how dare they, how stupid could they be and there were just too many expletives after that."

"So, he is at the Branburry holding area until he sees a judge?"

"That should happen at 11 a.m., unless the storm delays court. Jonas says that shouldn't happen."

"So, what else did Jonas tell you?" Zoey wanted all of the gossip.

"No surprise that Sam was very irate, but he was acting as if he were really innocent. What a smooth operator he is." Kim thought for a moment. "Who said he would lawyer up right away?"

Zoey knew. "I think Will said it. Did he?"

"Right on, girl. He made the call in the cruiser before they arrived at the jail in Branburry."

"I am sure they took his phone away after he was processed there. They take all personal belongings."

"Well, now we wait for court this morning." Very sure of herself, Kim added, "Jonas thinks he will get bail. I do not."

"He certainly has a lot of cash, just from the last jewel sales, so enough money is of little concern."

"He still needs a place to go. Didn't you say that Marjorie has a restraining order against him, so he can't go to their residence?"

"Correct, but Sam has influential friends and will spin this story to the best of his ability. Sam will persuade some important people who can help him that he has been framed. Don't forget the postcards sent, supposedly from Victoria. That actually is persuasive to most people, until these cards are examined, to prove it was not her handwriting. He will be the victim, not Victoria Tuckerman who he killed and buried behind our library."

Arriving at her mother's house, Zoey was glad the snow remained light on their way to the eatery. She filled Liz in with all of the details from Sam's arrest at the airport the evening before.

"Is Kim okay?"

"She is now, but I think she had a rough night waiting for Jonas to arrive home."

"So, the murderer is in jail?"

"For now."

Doubtfully, Liz shook her head. "No way he gets bail." Some doubt lingered. "What does Jonas say to that theory?"

Zoey hesitated for a moment. "Well, he already has a lawyer. Good thing they seized his phone. Otherwise he would have been calling his influential friends for help all night long. Jonas thinks he will be out on bail."

"When does he go to court?"

"I believe Kim said at 11 this morning. His lawyer will also be there."

"Do you think anyone knows about all of this?"

"We will soon find that out, won't we?" And they pulled in to park in back of Sips and Swap.

Caitland and Selena were already busy preparing for the morning rush. The coffee had the best fragrance as you come through the door. Zoey had to tell the girls what happened in case anyone else stopped by with the news. She owed them the fresh gossip.

"How was the snow, driving?" Selena asked Liz.

"Not bad at all. I think our Doppler Radar has this storm way out of proportion, again."

Zoey told the girls to come sit for a minute before they opened. "All right, you two have the first headline news of the day. Last night Sam Watson arrived from his London trip to be arrested by the State Police and Jonas Parsons for the murdered woman buried behind the Tuckerman Library."

Both Selena and Caitland were shocked into silence. Staring at Zoey, they had to ask, "Who is this poor old woman he killed and why?"

Barely able to mouth out the words, Zoey blurted out, "It was Victoria Tuckerman."

"Oh my loving God." Selena looked taken aback by the result of this cold case file.

"And, Caitland, the British guy who stopped in at the eatery while I was away produced the final clue to solving this murder."

"Holy shit," Caitland realized who this man was, now. "And I talked to the guy. Now I know why he wanted to know about the murder here in Highland Falls."

"It seems that all of the rare jewel sales he handled for Sam Watson had a bad odor on the ownership tag." She added, "When Gil Andrews started to doubt who owned these gems, he did some research of both the Watsons and Tuckerman family. He and his wife saw the segment by Miranda Prescott. That is when he contacted her about the murder. He began thinking that Sam had killed his mother-in-law. He was also troubled about repercussions on those jewel sales. Sam lied and swore to Andrews that he owned all of these jewels. Because the profit was so suitable for all involved, he was in denial for some time. As the investigation escalated, Andrews wanted no part in any of this."

"Why was Andrews here in our town?"

"That was the day he was interviewed by Jonas, the State Police, and Miranda Prescott. And I missed it!"

“Wow, all of this happened here while you were away?”

“Well, long story. While we were in St. Maarten we took a boat trip to St. Barths. Marjorie and A.J. were there at their timeshare. Because I was in constant contact with Miranda Prescott as this case intensified, I was there to help get through this dreadful period. It sounds like the Watson marriage had been crumbling for quite some time. Before she left for her timeshare stay, Marjorie hired an investigator to find her missing mother. She also filed for divorce and slapped a restraining order against Sam Watson. Pretty good timing there, I would say.”

Both girls were stunned to say the least and it was time to open Sips and Swap. “When we have more time, I can fill you in with details. This news will be in tomorrow’s morning paper. I will guess it hits the internet today, right after Sam goes to court at 11 a.m.”

Selena looked troubled. In a frightened voice she asked Zoey, “What if he gets out on bail and comes here?”

“He won’t get out on bail.” She hugged both girls. “We have Jonas to keep us updated on all that happens this morning.” Warning all of them, Zoey said, “For sure, someone has already heard about this.”

Even though the old lady buried behind the town library was not considered popular, Liz, Zoey, Selena, and Caitland all replied, “Poor Victoria Tuckerman, she did not deserve this.”

CHAPTER 41

The eatery was buzzing with customers despite the light snow falling. Will came by early to see Zoey hoping she had more details about the case.

She handed Will a raspberry and peach muffin and said, “This is all you get, no news until after the court appearance.”

“Have you spoken to Marjorie?”

“No, I just have not had time.”

“She left you a message, not urgent. She sounded okay.”

“I am still catching up here from being away.” A bit stressed she told Will, “I will call right now.”

Marjorie was relieved to hear from Zoey. “I am holding my own. A.J. insisted on coming home to be with me today.” Then, Zoey heard Marjorie starting to fall apart again. “I just thought you’d like to know that a third postcard arrived this morning from my mother. Well, not my mother!” All at once, anger then replaced the tears. “How could Sam possibly think he could fool us all? How cruel he is.”

“I agree, Marjorie. It’s important that you save all of those cards. It is evidence and proof of a co-conspirator. Sam must have paid someone pretty well to mail out these cards to you. The prosecutor will need these cards. And Marjorie, try to remain calm today. I am glad A.J. is coming home for you. I will touch base with you later.”

Everyone was on pins and needles all morning, eager for the court appearance to see if Sam could convince the judge that he should go free until his trial. Then, it happened. Gil Andrews came into the eatery. Zoey was not in the swap area so she got to see him too, for the first time. He was definitely a sharp dressed older man. He did not look like a Highland Falls resident. A bit too fancy pants.

As he sat down at a side table, the room was suddenly quiet, and Zoey walked over to introduce herself. "You must be Gil Andrews." She offered her hand to him, "I am Zoey Mitchell, owner of this Sips and Swap and you may know already that I was the former Librarian at Tuckerman."

He smiled faintly and shook her hand. He had the most appealing accent. "I do recognize you, from the first segment on the cold case murder here in Highland Falls."

It was very close to 11 a.m. and court would soon be on the block. "I understand we need to thank you for coming forward in helping us solve this case."

"To be honest, it was not my intention as I try to avoid any type of legal involvements." Shaking his head back and forth, very uneasy, he added, "I simply had no choice."

"I have to tell you that Jonas Parsons is my brother-in-law and he thinks what you did was a sign of courage." Zoey looked at Gil thinking just how charming and cordial he was.

"The more I dealt with Sam these past months, I kept feeling like something was very wrong. He has been extremely edgy and bad-tempered. It was hard for me to understand why. He had such a good life, with such an attractive spouse and money never a problem."

“How long did it take you to realize that all of this wealth and such a good life was due to Victoria Tuckerman?”

He sighed, head down and replied honestly. “It was just simply greed. We had a good business arrangement, profitable for us both. For the longest time, I believed Sam that the jewels he brought me for re-sale were his. It wasn’t until I researched both the Tuckerman and Watson families that the proof was in the many images that appeared in various articles throughout the years.”

Zoey tried her best to dislike this man because of the greed shared by both Sam and Gil Andrews, but she could not. “I would say that by now, you do know the real Sam Watson.” Looking at her watch she told Gil, “Sam is currently doing his best, lawyer at his side, to persuade the judge that he is innocent.”

Gill looked uneasy, wondering how the judge would rule on bail or no bail. “What will this town do if Sam is allowed out on bail? People will be terrified.”

Zoey had to agree with Gil. “We should all hear this decision very soon. I highly doubt if bail will be allowed. The prosecutor has a strong case. But, if he does somehow get out on bail for like a million dollars, he would be seriously monitored.”

“Do you mean confined to his residence here in town?”

“Yes, exactly, and he would have to wear an ankle restraint that would not allow him off of the property.”

“Well, that is a bit of relief for residents.” He added, “And soon, my wife and I will be able to return to London.”

“Sam will have a problem though, with his residence. His wife has filed for divorce and has a restraining order against him. Not allowed on the Watson estate, he will have to find another residence to stay at, and I am sure it is limited to Highland Falls.”

Zoey’s phone rang and as she answered, she saw it was from Jonas. “At least I called one thing right.” Very sure of himself, Jonas told Zoey, “After 1.2 million dollars is paid, Sam Watson will be allowed out on bail, until his trial starts.”

It was only a matter of a few minutes when the news people burst into Sips and Swap with the court news that Sam would soon be allowed out on bail until his trial would commence. Zoey was flabbergasted at the news and saying anxiety would now be part of her daily life was being kind. Her stomach was already in knots. Where was Jonas? After the news reached him about Sam, Gil Andrews hastily said it was time for him to head back to his hotel where Caroline was packing their clothes ahead of their flight the next morning. Before he left, he handed Zoey a piece of paper with some information she hoped Jonas could use. It was the name of another friend of Sam. Gil just remembered this fellow who did odd jobs for Sam while he was in London. His name was Colin Earley. He was a decent young man but somehow got involved with some low life people now and again. Perhaps he was the one who mailed all of these postcards for Sam, supposedly from Victoria Tuckerman in London.

Zoey wasted no time passing this on to Jonas, as he entered the eatery. “The last of the clues for you. More evidence.”

“Was I right or was I right?”

“Okay Jonas, but it is hard for me to believe it actually happened. Where will he stay?”

“He will be at his lawyer’s for now and find a place, I guess. Certainly not with Marjorie. She hired her own private security people for the time being.”

“Good for her. Sam is such a snake.” She told Jonas she had spoken to Marjorie earlier and that a third postcard from her mother had arrived in the morning.”

“Well, maybe this Colin person can help us with that issue. It is illegal you know, mailing cards from a dead person.”

That sounded so heartless. “What people do for money.”

“Sam had to turn in his passport and is limited to where he can and cannot go. Back to court to set his trial date next week.”

“And we should not be worried or concerned? Who was this judge?”

“I know him and he is well respected. Perhaps Thomas Roncari is afraid of Sam and all Sam’s connections. The prosecutor did a bang-up job with evidence but Sam’s lawyer, Kevin Grayson, was very persuasive saying Sam was innocent, was an outstanding citizen, blah blah…and it worked.”

So many residents stopped by at the eatery hoping to find out all about the murder. People were shocked and saddened to learn that it was Victoria Tuckerman who had been killed and buried behind the library that she and her family had founded many years ago. Surprisingly, as Zoey and her staff listened to the many voices discussing the issues, not many were surprised that Sam Watson was allowed out on bail. People mentioned how many connections Sam had made throughout the years with wealthy and influential people here in the states and abroad. Not many seemed frightened by Sam either. Unlike Zoey.

Later in the day, the eatery closed for the day and Zoey headed home to Will and her three loving companions, all eager to see her. "Jonas stopped by. What a nightmare." He gave Zoey a warm hug hello. "Are you going to be okay?"

"No other choice, Will. It is what it is. Sam is guilty and soon, he will finally pay." She added, "But, this is far from over. Sam is just beginning to plan what will work best for just himself."

CHAPTER 42

Days ago, Zoey made a promise to Marjorie to help with funeral arrangements for her mother. After much discussion, A.J., Marjorie, and Zoey decided that having a small private service honoring Victoria was the only way to go. In lieu of flowers, donations to the Tuckerman Library would be appreciated. Holding this service on an intimate basis would keep the media and press at a distance. Marjorie said her phone never stopped ringing. Her housekeeper, Millie, answered calls and left messages for the Watson family. They were piling up as Marjorie had no strength to wade through pages of condolences. Zoey offered to help her with this but she refused, saying eventually she would get to it. The small service would be on the following Monday, at St. James Church, where Marjorie attended service while she was in Highland Falls. Father Berwick was a good friend to the Watsons and respected the family's wish to hold a private service. He promised to keep the church service as brief as possible. However, he told Marjorie he had to welcome any people wanting to attend the service, as it followed his beliefs. So, that meant a ton of media and press would be there. What would be limited is anyone stopping by the Watson home, after the service.

It was only days before the funeral would happen and people in town had not seen Sam Watson at all. He was still living with his lawyer, Kevin Grayson, who had handled other legal issues for Sam in the past. He was scheduled for his court appearance on Monday, the day before Victoria Tuckerman's funeral. Of course, he would not be welcome or attend the service. It might be what he was planning, in order to profess his love for Marjorie. His goal was to proclaim innocence in any form or manner. Marjorie had contacted the State Police stating her opposition to Sam being anywhere near the funeral service. She also had private security on standby.

As days passed by at the eatery, Miranda Prescott made a trip to Highland Falls, touching base with Jonas. She was invited to the funeral and would be at the courthouse on Monday. Booking a room at the local B and B for the two days, she stopped for lunch on Friday to tell Zoey of her plans. She needed more information for the second segment of her cold case show, so she would meet Jonas after lunch. He and the State Police would have a brief part in the second segment. Zoey would not appear on this episode. Miranda had already interviewed Gil Andrews so he would be able to return to London. Both Gil and Caroline were still overwrought over the death of Caroline's mother. Strange how she was the one to start this investigation into high gear. That is when Gil Andrews started to pay attention. They were flying out tomorrow morning finally heading home to London.

Before leaving Sips and Swap, Zoey called Gil Andrews to wish him good luck and a safe flight home. "I want to thank you again for helping us to resolve this cold case. It was Caroline's mom that really began all of this. How is Caroline doing?"

"Better, but it will take loads of time to see her smile once again. One star in this sky is that her mother will be mentioned in the second segment of Prescott's show. It is only right. Caroline was pleased with that, Susan Rothens, a hero. We will google and record the show."

"I have inside info on the release date for that show. I may be able to get a DVD copy for you too."

"That would be great." And they said goodbye. Zoey still wanted to know what would happen with Gil and his role with these jewels, apparently not owned by Sam. She sensed that he really wasn't up for this discussion. Maybe in weeks to follow, she would contact him to see what occurred.

Zoey checked on A.J. and Marjorie every day. Although they were on guard with A.J. going into protective mode, this long lasting slice of their life would all straighten out early next week. The numerous condolence calls to the Watson family had slowed down. Sam's brother left messages but Marjorie passed these on to her attorney. Sam had called his younger brother several times, hoping for his sister-in-law's legal help. She passed on this saying she was just not qualified to handle such a case. Zoey thought, smart move. Sam only called Marjorie one time leaving a pleading, loving message. Of course he claimed he was innocent and someone was framing him. He would hire investigators to prove just how right he was. He begged her to reconsider the restraining order, asking when he could return home. Never, Marjorie thought. A.J. refused to speak to him or return his call.

Marjorie had close contact with the District Attorney producing all of the information needed to prove that Sam killed Victoria Tuckerman. The postcards were handed over. A.J. was interviewed with full disclosure on the event that happened three years ago. This event angered Victoria as her grandson meant the world to her. That is when she and Sam confronted each other, the day before she would leave on her extended vacation. It was clear Sam was threatened by this soon to be exposed issue and that was

Sam's motive. Zoey did produce the images that Sam had so carefully hidden, of the teenage boys he intimidated for his own pleasure. Everything they all provided for the trial said GUILTY.

On Sunday, Zoey had the whole family over for dinner. Even Hannah came home for an overnight, excited for the court appearance the next day. Lucky for Day Off Mondays. The only one to head for the courthouse would be Jonas. Zoey, Kim, and Liz had no desire to see Sam. A special dinner of tender pot roast, mashed potatoes, thanks to Liz, and even some spätzle as Will loved the German noodles that went well with the roast. Oatmeal rolls trickled with some rosemary and crispy coleslaw would complete the meal. Of course the court case discussion was also on the menu.

Zoey asked Jonas, "When will the trial begin?"

"Most likely within 60 days. I am sure Sam's attorney needs an ample amount of time to get all the details he needs."

"There is so much evidence against him. Sam has no idea what we know about the confrontation he had with Victoria."

"There is no proof of that. It is exactly what Sam's attorney will say, over and over again." He added a bit more, "That is what is known as DOUBT."

CHAPTER 43

How this all happened. Sam's life would only improve if he planned correctly. He was not happy. He had never lost control on any issue in his entire life. He had, for years, been able to control Victoria. That ended on the day she confronted him about what happened with that Holtzman boy. He couldn't let Victoria shame him. It would never happen. She had been the bitch in his life for years, controlling purse strings, the library, Marjorie. It ended that day before she left on vacation. She was old, dying soon anyway. He had to get rid of her.

It was easy. First he cancelled her trip. On the way to the airport, they side tracked. He was a smooth operator, asking her for please, just one more chance to be the perfect family man. Leaving early for the airport, he headed out to a quiet spot along the bird sanctuary area. That is when he pulled over and strangled her, fast and quick. She had no strength against him. Sam had a storage spot outside of Highland Falls and that is where he left her, covered with a brand new tarp he had in his bin. Later that night, saying he had a business meeting, he buried her behind the Tuckerman Library. He thought that was quite the best place for her. Before he buried her, Sam removed all jewelry and her dentures, placing the dentures in a small plastic bag. On his way home, he tossed them deep into the ocean where the tide would take them far away. Quite a night. It was weeks later when the construction crew screwed up his design plan for the handicap ramp at the library. That is when the body was discovered. Not a good day for Sam.

He never admitted killing her to his lawyer, claiming innocence as he had been framed. Right before Sam went to bed, his cell phone rang. There was no caller ID on it, saying UNKNOWN. Strange, he thought. He took the call. “Sam Watson here.”

A bit distressed, the man was speaking too quickly. “Sam, it’s Colin.”

What the hell, why was Colin calling him? “Colin, I am in the middle of a court case tomorrow.”

“I know, you are all over the internet.” Angrily he blurted out at Sam, “What have you done, involving me in this murder?”

“What has happened with you?”

“What the hell, Sam. The authorities came by about my mailing out cards from a dead woman?”

Sam felt like he was beginning to disintegrate over this phone call. “You denied this, right?”

“Yes, I absolutely rejected their accusations.”

“Well, that was smart of you considering how much I paid you to do this.”

Colin Earley had the record button on for his own protection. “They told me I would have to have my handwriting analyzed.”

“Refuse this Colin.” Sam added some advice. “Perhaps you should disappear for a while.”

Now, Colin was beyond overanxious. “Sam you are such a loser, and what have you done? Did you really kill your mother-in-law?” A short silence, then, the call ended.

Sam was now in alarm mode. He couldn't think straight. No one was helping him with this. Where were all of his trusted friends? Even his lawyer was experiencing doubt. Kevin Grayson just asked too many personal questions. Sam needed to make a better plan. And before tomorrow morning.

Sleep never came on that last night before he was due in court. Sam had a locked valise that his attorney allowed him to retrieve from his private storage area as soon as they left the courthouse in Branburry. When Grayson asked why, Sam told his attorney if he wanted to be paid, the valise had some very important financial documents that were pertinent to these issues. Sam now frantic about that last call from Colin, knew how detrimental it would be to his court case. In just a few hours, Sam would initiate the only scheme that would work to set him free.

There were just two associates that Sam needed to call who would help him plan this escape. His passport has been suspended, but Sam had others that would work with a few minor changes in his appearance. There was no time to waste as it was already 3 o'clock in the morning. His first call would be to Raymond, his Uber friend, or that is what Sam called him. Travel agent was a better description. The second call went to his immigrant friend, Antonio, who was keen on technical problems. What to do about his ankle bracelet. Antonio would be paid well, via his Uber friend, after Sam was on his way. Antonio told him exactly what to do with that monitor device wrapped around his left ankle. Because he was allowed fifteen minutes with this off, due to bathing or personal issues, Sam needed to slightly change the timer. Antonio told him just what to do.

His valise locked, bags packed, Sam was ready to leave Kevin Grayson's home in Highland Falls by 4 a.m. Every minute counted and as he crept downstairs toward the back door, he practically held his breath just to listen for any sounds. The alarm shut off, Sam was out the back door hastily walking to the street where Raymond was waiting for him, auto running. No questions were asked, as Sam handed Raymond a hefty envelope for the ride and also payment for Antonio. A nod from Raymond was all that was needed. "Who is on the boat today?"

"Your favorite, Marco. We are all sad to hear about what has happened."

"Thank you for that Raymond. I have been framed. For now, I have to go." He handed him an envelope overstuffed with large dollar bills.

"Understand, Mr. Watson."

Soon, they arrived at the marina dock located on long Island Sound miles away from Highland Falls. Payments handed over to everyone, Sam was soon on his way to freedom. Removing and crushing the ankle bracelet, and from the side of the boat, he hurled it far into the sea. That was when Sam began to breathe at a normal pace. The first time in days.

CHAPTER 44

Monday morning arrived in Highland Falls with phones ringing in many places. Where was Sam Watson? Calls began a little after 6 a.m. Jonas called Zoey after he spoke to Marjorie warning her that Sam was missing. Kevin Grayson awoke about 6 o'clock to find Sam gone. No sign of the monitor and he could not comprehend how he escaped with the monitor as it would have alarmed the authorities. He meant Jonas.

"Hey, the alarm system works. How Sam figured out how to outfox it is news to me. Nothing went off on my end."

Zoey just knew something was going to occur. It was clear that Sam was guilty and his only way out was to vanish. He has a ton of money and many acquaintances here and abroad. Who knows where he went? "Honestly, Jonas, tell me you are not surprised at this." In an angry voice, still yawning, she added, "They never should have allowed bail. How stupid are they?"

"Hey, they took his license, his passport, and enclosed his ankle with a monitor. Not many people disappear with that monitor secured on their leg."

"Marjorie must be frantic."

"She is, but her security people are there guarding the house." Jonas laughed at all this drama sequence. "Do you really think he would go there? He preferred going elsewhere while he was married to Marjorie." He began to rant, telling Zoey, "He wants to disappear, forever I guess. No limitations on a murder charge though. It's not like he can return in two years and say, Hey there, I am back.

“Okay, then. I got it.” She asked the Marshall, “Are they looking for him?”

“State Police landed a while ago, checking everywhere. Airport, trains, etc. They will not find him. He is long gone.”

“Well, that is good for all of us.”

“Until he decides on a revenge plot and returns, like he disappeared. Unnoticed.”

“Thanks for that theory, Jonas. Makes me feel not apprehensive at all.”

By then Will was coming out from the bathroom, after showering for work, and said, “Who are you talking to?”

“It’s Jonas.” She told him good luck and goodbye for now and ended the call. “Sam is gone.”

“Whattttt?” Will just stood still gazing at Zoey.

Almost shrieking it out, Zoey glared at Will. “I told Jonas, NO BAIL!”

“It is not up to Jonas, you have to stop with the criticism. It is really bothering him, how all of this has happened on his watch.”

“I didn’t mean him, I meant them.”

“Well,” he reminded Zoey, “Marjorie is right, Sam never loses.”

Zoey just shook her head. “I guess by now, I should accept that.”

All that morning, Zoey was on the phone with a list of people. Miranda Prescott called and now had to edit her entire segment due to Sam's disappearing act. At least by vanishing and doing it with a flair, he showed the world just how guilty he is. That might bring some closure to the Watson family. Tomorrow, they would have the service for Victoria. Marjorie had been given permission to bury her ashes on the back lawn of the Tuckerman Library. Marjorie accepted what had happened and how it totally collapsed her once perfect life. Her son was now the most important facet in her world and that would never change. She realized that Sam was gone and hoped that meant forever. There was no way he would return as it would mean arrest and a prison sentence for him.

By midafternoon, there was no news on the disappearance of Sam Watson. He simply vanished. Liz and Kim spent most of the day with Zoey, knowing how she felt, usually in fear of Sam and what he was capable of. Hannah called as she noticed the news online about Sam. She was glad Zoey had company for the day, knowing it would be difficult to handle.

A.J. stopped by to see them, later in the day. "Zoey, you have been such a comfort to my mother and we are glad you'll be with us tomorrow at the service. After church, we only have a handful of friends stopping by." He looked at Kim and Liz. "You are all welcome to join us."

"Everything will calm down now, A.J." Zoey gave him a hug on his way out the door.

In a somber tone, he said, "We need calm." And, he drove off in his Audi convertible.

When Will arrived home he gave Zoey the usual warm hug and kiss. “One good thing. At least we are back to where we were and where we should be.” Zoey agreed, returning the hug, with three lovable cats rubbing against their legs.

The phone rang, Zoey thought, do not answer. But it was Marjorie, on speaker.

“Zoey, it is not over.” In a tense voice, Zoey was afraid of what she was going to say.

“I do not know how, but I just received a text from Sam, unknown number. All it said was:

You all thought you won. You did not. I always win, and you will eventually accept that. Sam.”

Staring at one another and thinking, there were just no words left in our world for this scenario.

THE END

Made in the USA
Middletown, DE
07 October 2022